A Kind of Life

A Kind of Life

Dawn Annandale

Cutting
Edge
Press

For JVK, with my eternal gratitude and much love.

A Cutting Edge Press Paperback Original

Published in 2013 by Cutting Edge Press

www.cuttingedgepress.co.uk

Printed and bound in Great Britain by CPI Group (UK) Ltd, Croydon, CR0 4YY

PB ISBN: 978-1-908122-48-3
E-PUB ISBN: 978-1-908122-49-0

"Every Saint has a past and every sinner has a future."
Oscar Wilde

Chapter One

'Jesus Christ! Fuck! Fuck! Fuck!'

Laura sobbed, relinquishing control as innate mechanisms took over her body. Until this moment it had all seemed like a game, unreal, something she could walk away from. But now, as she felt the warm fluid dripping from within her, cascading down her legs and making a bloody puddle on the tatty lino of the kitchen floor, she knew one hundred per cent this was very, very real. It wasn't a board game she could say she was fed up with and put back in the cupboard; her waters had broken and she was going to have a baby, whether she liked it or not.

Sighing loudly, resigned to what was inevitable, Laura's mother did her best to soothe her distraught daughter. The small suitcase which had lain under Laura's bed packed and ready for the past five weeks was retrieved, car keys were eventually found and the short journey to the hospital was made. Regular contractions were stabbing at Laura, mocking her stupidity, the agonizing pain serving as retribution for the dim and distant memories of pleasure.

Massive shaking sobs reverberated through her entire being – her tears a concoction of self-pity, pain and fear. Her mother held her hand more tightly now, squeezing and making soothing encouraging noises. The older woman wiped away her own tears of anguish for the youth her daughter had now lost and the awesome responsibility she was on the brink of gaining. The journey to the hospital and onto the maternity ward passed in a blur. Once there, Laura was dazed with the copious amounts of gas and air she was inhaling each time a contraction attacked her fragile young body. Voices floated around her consciousness as she gripped the plastic mask over her mouth and greedily swallowed the cold air which gave her the relief she craved.

'Come on my love, come on, soon be over, there now, there now...'

More voices cooing and crooning, familiar and warm. The midwife, Amy Spalding, prised the tube from Laura's tightly clenched fingers. For Laura, being here, in this hospital, was unreal, a fantasy world induced by the drugs entering her system but this hazy make-believe existence was her world right now and it was where she wanted to stay.

It was the only place the pain couldn't reach her. Not just the pain of childbirth but the pain that was her life and she willingly embraced the semi-conscious state where she felt comfortable, secure and safe – floating into oblivion. But, as Laura tried to lose herself, the midwife penetrated her cocoon with firm instructions.

'I need you to push now, on the count of three, listen to me Laura, one... two... three... I can see baby's head, that's my girl, well done lovie.'

Lost in her dream world where she barely registered the soothing kind words, Laura heard the voice again.

'This is the last one, my love, one last big effort for me and baby will be born.'

Laura obliged with that grunting groaning noise unique to childbirth as she was told to bear down on a pain so excruciating it was almost other-worldly. She screamed in agony as her child was born and the pain miraculously vanished.

Laura's baby had entered the world – an unwanted burden to a family already on the brink of collapse. Laura's mother watched the midwife gently clear the baby's mouth of mucus and give an experienced speedy initial check of the now mewling bloody bundle. Laura's mother's tears were mistaken for those of happiness but they were not – they were tears of fear for the life ahead for this pathetic being. As a midwife of many years' experience, Amy knew not to expect too much from the new mother as she dealt with the cord and the placenta, trying to contain the mess as best she could. Wrapping the tiny infant in a soft cotton blanket, Amy handed what she now knew to be a baby girl to the mother who was but a child herself. The girl was still crying, softly now, tears of sadness masquerading as those of love and overwhelming joy for the infant but which, in reality, combined a lament for herself, for the life to which she was now resigned. She had feelings of a kind of love and joy but these were swamped with helplessness as she thought of the strains it would place on her and her already dysfunctional family unit.

Amy watched the awkwardness of the young mother, this girl, trying to find a comfortable position as she held her new daughter – the grandmother looking on whose tears were recognized by Amy as tears of deep sorrow.

Laura was fourteen years old and the beautiful baby girl was the result of a Saturday night in what passed for normal in her life. Pissed out of her head, generally accompanied by a handful of pills or weed, or, when it was offered, very occasionally, a line of speed, followed by a stoned and less than memorable fuck by whoever she happened to be going out with that week. Laura wasn't choosy and besides, it was nice, being fucked, kissed and cuddled. Sometimes, if she was lucky, the boy would take her to the pictures or buy her some chips before he fucked her. A few times they had found somewhere to sleep for the night and she loved it when she woke up in the morning and the bloke wanted another fuck and gave her a cuddle.

Her mother didn't bother to tell her when to come home or not to drink or have sex as she was too preoccupied with her own love life. Her daughter was a pain in the arse and she was glad of the peace if she stayed out all night. Laura had no idea who the baby's father was; she told her mum it was some bloke who had taken advantage of her and she hadn't wanted him to shag her at all but she was scared. Laura's mother, Deb, had her own problems and just accepted Laura's lies, knowing that they were just that, because the truth brought home the inadequacies she felt as a mother. She knew there was more to life than the rundown estate in an impoverished part of North London but lacked the confidence and courage to change her life and that of her children. She took perverse comfort in the familiarity of her squalid surroundings though the guilt of her selfishness overwhelmed her at times. Too scared of the unknown to change her life, to make things better for her and the kids. Sometimes she hated herself.

Deb had only been fifteen herself when Laura had been born and amazingly had managed to keep the baby and bring her up herself in an era when most illegitimate babies were spirited away and adopted. She knew that Laura was a ticket to benefit and a council flat of her own, away from the chaos and squalor of her own mother's home, so, against the odds, she had clung to her child and the cycle had repeated itself.

'Only a miracle can break the cycle,' Deb thought, as she looked at the tiny, helpless, beautiful baby.

Amy went through the motions and plastered a huge smile across her face. The Whittington Hospital was not exactly on a par with the place she used to work. The majority of her patients there were too posh to push. Now she was getting used to the diverse reactions from parents and grandparents as she delivered yet another unwanted and unplanned child. The social problems of the locals were horrendous – unemployment, poor housing and neglect were the everyday worries her patients constantly battled against and generally resigned themselves to, coping as best as they could. Amy saw it all – the faces of the Asian mothers when they produced a girl, the heavily pregnant women who were admitted on a Sunday morning after a drunken Saturday night beating, the babies born with a drug dependency. She was on first name terms with most of the social workers and police around here. But what could she do on her own? For the first few years she had felt angry and determined to change the world but now she was merely resigned to deliver the babies as swiftly and painlessly as possible. She told the impoverished mothers that they could be sterilized while they were there, to at least ensure that there were no more mouths to feed, no more kids to try to accommodate in already overcrowded homes, and, wisely, some took her up on the offer. She was fighting ignorance and poverty, and was losing.

'There now, isn't she a lamb? What a little beauty, all that gorgeous curly black hair. What are you going to call her?' Amy did her best and smiled, telling herself that this one would be OK.

* * *

And so Renee Mary Lovell was born, on the 24 January 1965, the day that Winston Churchill died. Born into a world of poverty and hate, prejudice and ignorance and that was just at home. Renee and Mary were Laura's grandmothers' names and Deb had thought it a nice touch that her daughter had chosen to remember the old dears this way. Laura didn't really care what the baby was called, just so long as it was quiet and could be cared for with the minimum of effort. Ree, as she became known, left the Whittington five days later, in the arms of her petrified teenage mother who in turn was supported by Deb and Deb's current boyfriend, Malcolm.

Home was only a few miles from the hospital which Laura was very grateful for as she had painful stitches from the birth and the upholstery in Malcolm's ancient Zephyr was definitely past its prime. Baby Ree, as Laura was already calling her, was dressed in a white hand-knitted outfit that had been part of a bagful of clothes a woman from social services had brought round. Laura had washed everything and packed the case for her confinement, still playing a game, never understanding the reality of becoming a mother and the responsibility of having a child to care for. She walked along the corridor, shuffling only slightly now as her stitches were slowly healing. The fresh air hit her as she stepped into the pale January sunshine for the first time in nearly a week. With all the impact of a lightning strike, Laura realized that the infant she carried in her arms was hers, it was coming home with her, back to the flat, for ever, not just a few days. She, Laura, was now a mother and this baby would need looking after twenty-four hours a day. She almost cried, but on seeing the grim look on her mother's face knew there was no point in shedding tears. Nothing would be accomplished and her mother would probably only say something like 'I told you so.'

The estate was covered in graffiti, strewn with rubbish, upturned dustbins, gangs of kids, rusty discarded shopping trolleys and the general flotsam and jetsam of life. It was all Laura had ever known and the flat on the tenth floor was the only place she had ever lived. She shared a bedroom with her sister Tracey who was twelve and her brother Dean had the tiny boxroom. Dean was eight and his dad must have been

Black, Mediterranean or a Gypsy because he had the swarthy skin colouring of a half-caste, but Laura couldn't remember the bloke's face let alone his name. Deb and the kids currently shared their space with Malcolm but before then it had been Stuart and before that Mark and before that some other nameless, faceless waster. Malcolm was a market trader, selling dented tin cans of food and boxes of broken biscuits. The labels often came off the tins and Malcolm brought these home. The kitchen cupboards were full of them but no one knew what they contained until they were opened. Tins were always being opened, found to be unsuitable and stuck in the fridge for another day. Deb had worked out that the tins with baked beans in them had a weird squiggle on so, when all else failed, it was beans on toast for tea.

A neighbour, Deirdre, had given Laura a cot which had belonged to her daughter. It was very old but had washed up well and the mattress was new. The blankets and sheets were from a jumble sale but they must have been donated by someone with more money than sense as they were practically brand new – no stains, holes or smells. The rest of the stuff had been given by the woman from social services, including the bag of clothes in which Laura had found the tiny knitted suit. Some of the clothes had light yellowish stains on them where they had not been washed properly but after a soak in Glowhite they nearly all looked as good as new.

Malcolm's old banger finally made the short journey across some of London's most decrepit areas and Laura held her baby daughter tightly as she entered the block of dilapidated flats.

'Welcome home, baby girl,' she whispered.

Laura put the baby in the cot, sat on her bed and stared at the silent creature wondering how the hell it had all come this far. She liked the warmth and the comfort of the sex but she hadn't bargained on ending up like those other stupid cows in her class – saddled with a kid. Everyone said she had done it on purpose, just so the council would have to give her a flat of her own but she hadn't, she really hadn't. She didn't even realize that she was pregnant for months and when she did she had tried drinking vodka to wash down a few pills she had found in the bathroom cupboard. Eventually Deb cottoned on and asked her outright, smacking her in the face and screaming at her when Laura admitted she was 'up the effing duff'.

'Fucking fucking stupid fucking little whore! Is this what you want you fucking stupid bitch? A life like mine? Can't you see what you've done? You stupid, stupid girl!'

That was the only time Deb bothered to get uptight about the pregnancy. What was done was done; it was too late for an abortion so she cried just that one time then resigned herself to another mouth to feed, another lifetime of misery. Laura left school and ate the cheap rubbishy food that she found in the flat, growing fatter and more lethargic as Deb blotted out another shit part of her life with yet one more cheap bottle of cider, ignoring the other two children as they moaned about having to share the already cramped flat with 'a fucking screaming bastard kid'. And so the cycle continued and would always continue for the numerous other inhabitants of the impoverished estate for whom there was seemingly no escape. The problem seemed to lie in the fact that the young girls who found themselves becoming mothers had no idea that there was an alternative, a different life to live. They had no aspirations or ambition. Their only wish was to have a council flat of their own, a Friday night out at the bingo and a bloke who didn't fuck off the minute a kid was on the way. A dismal and mindless existence unless the smallest glimpse of another life had been tasted, illuminating a different route even if it only included the wish to be married to the father of the child.

As the months passed, Ree knew not to bother screaming for attention because invariably no one came, or, if they did, it was to shove a bottle in her mouth and prop her up in front of the telly. Sometimes she was plonked in the pushchair and taken to the park but she knew she was just there as a fashion accessory for Laura to go with her miniskirt and white boots. 'Shut up and sit still,' being the only words of comfort she heard.

As her first few years passed and Ree walked, then talked, she knew when not to do either. She learnt to sit still and fade into the background. The social worker found Ree a place at a nursery where she dreaded home time. Nursery was wonderful – if she tripped, a lovely cuddly lady would pick her up and kiss her better. No one ever told her to shut the fuck up like they did at home; no one ever slapped her or shouted at her. The cuddly lady gave Ree breakfast and biscuits and milk and lunch and apples. Laura gave her nothing, no emotion of any kind – her baby didn't exist apart from being an encumbrance, something to be dropped off at nursery and collected again at night after she had finished her shift at Tesco. Laura was different from many of her friends in that she did have a job but the main reason for this was her hatred of being cooped up in the flat all day with the brat, her mother and whomever her mother happened to be shagging that week.

When Ree was four, Laura met Adam Jackson and announced that she was leaving home to move in with him. Adam worked at Tesco too but Laura had known him at school – he was a few years older than her, and a friend of her cousin, James. Adam was a bully and made Laura feel grateful every day for the fact that he was prepared to take on her and her 'fucking kid'. Laura would have done anything to leave the cramped conditions of her mum's flat and after weeks of looking for something they could afford to rent, they found a two-bedroom flat near Walthamstow which was barely habitable. Adam told Laura she should stop working and stay home with the kid and besides he had a bad back and was going to go on the sick so they could get loads of money from various benefits. He also wanted Laura to have another baby so that they might qualify for a council flat or even a house. Laura did as she was told as she felt that being with Adam was as good as her life was ever going to get – finally she would be free of her mother, the endless and ever-changing string of men Laura bumped into in the hallway and her brother and sister who were either in trouble with the police or running with the gangs on the estate.

Ree didn't like Adam at all. He shouted at her and sometimes when he was really angry, he slapped or even punched her mum and called her mum bad names. She coped by becoming invisible, never being any trouble and staying firmly out of sight unless it was absolutely necessary to interact with her step-father. She made her bed, cleared up after herself and tried to cause the minimum of fuss and disruption to family life. Laura and Adam got married, had two more children and finally got their wish and moved to a three bed-roomed council house nearby. Ree, who was eight years old by now, was allocated the smallest bedroom but didn't care because she was away from her horrible brothers and had some privacy when not at school. She loved school. It was her escape from the brutality of home where her brothers were treated like gods by their domineering father and their timid subservient mother jumped at their every wish and command. Home was where Ree slept in her tiny room, staying there as long as possible to listen to cassettes or read. She wrote endless stories, filling exercise books with her fantasies, all with the aim of occupying the time between coming home from school and going to bed, anything to be away from the rest of her family. She joined every club, took part in every after-school activity and played sport to delay having to go back to her family. She was clever, read constantly and devoured knowledge, amazing the teachers at her school who never saw her parents at a sports day or a parents' meeting. Amazing them too because they knew that the child could easily have fallen by the wayside like so many of her peers, one of the far too many children who gave up for lack of encouragement, let alone a smidgen of love.

At eleven, the year James Callaghan became prime minister, Ree moved to the huge comprehensive school a few hundred yards from her primary school. She was in the highest streams for all subjects and found a few friends, no one particularly close but girls to hang around with at breaktime and sit with in the canteen at lunchtime. Her brothers didn't bother her and her parents were too wrapped up in their own lives to waste time or effort on her. Adam went out and attended to his 'business' as he called it but was really small time wheeling and dealing while Laura cleaned the house fearful that a speck of even the tiniest dirt would be visible. Adam's temper had not improved and he ruled his family with an iron fist, flying into a rage at the flimsiest excuse. His bullying had only ever increased with time and all too often, whenever a day had gone badly for him, or a deal had fallen through, the family would suffer. Ree knew that as long as she stayed out of his way then everything would be as good as it was ever going to be. She habitually woke herself up at six, went to the newsagent's and finished her paper-round in record time before grabbing a piece of bread and butter as she left the house for school. She was always quiet, respectful to her mother and Adam, never late or untidy and always did exactly as she was told.

Adam watched Ree early one Sunday morning as she came back from her paper-round. She was thirteen now, quite tall and slim. That morning she had chosen to wear a pair of denim shorts and a cotton top with thin straps over the shoulders – the bright summer morning had started exceptionally warm so she had dressed accordingly, never thinking as she did so that she was showing off a shapely, very attractive body which her step-father admired as he stood with his back to the kitchen sink. Ree was startled as she walked into the kitchen, carefully hanging her newspaper bag away in the cupboard in the hall. He was never usually out of bed until long after she had gone to school and, on a Sunday, noise before 10 a.m. was an offence certain to cause Adam's temper to boil over. Her hands were filthy from the newsprint and all she wanted to do was scrub them clean. Saying a very quiet hello to Adam who barely acknowledged her but continued to watch her closely, she walked to the small cloakroom off the hallway to wash away the black smudges. Feeling intimidated and anxious, she lingered in the tiny room, hoping that Adam would be gone when she opened the door, but he was right outside and immediately reached out, putting his hand over her breast, threatening her with his eyes. She took a step back and felt the bile build up in her throat as Adam opened his dressing gown, exposing his erect penis.

'Hold it. You know you want to,' he sneered,

Ree retched and he punched her shoulder hard.

'Fucking stuck up bitch, I'll have you, don't you fucking worry.'

He turned away and Ree heard the thud of his footsteps on the stairs as she locked herself in the toilet and wept.

After this, she found every reason imaginable to stay out of Adam's way. When she turned fourteen in the January, she took a job as a waitress in the Wimpy bar in town working every Saturday and some nights after school if she could. Still, her step-father would drop in and shout at her, demanding coffee or a sandwich and would try to touch her as she walked past him. Such public attention was almost unbearable but, she reasoned, it was better than being on her own with him. She took to pushing a chair against the door of her bedroom every night and lay there in fear as she heard him trying the handle. Whether her mother realized what was happening Ree never knew. All she did know was that before something terrible happened she would have to get away.

Adam seemed to realize that Ree was not going to give in easily and relished the fear he instilled in the young girl. The power his strength and size commanded terrified her and this gave him a deep satisfaction. She was frightened and scared of a man who enjoyed the thrill of the chase, a man who was empowered by her fear and who smirked each time his hand brushed her breast or bottom. She knew that it was just a matter of time before he got her on his own, and what might happen then frightened her to the core. He was so obviously determined to have her.

⋆ ⋆ ⋆

Summer lingered that year and very slowly turned to an extremely mild autumn which was balanced by the bitterness of an exceptionally harsh winter. In early January, Ree continued the ritual of her morning paper-round welcoming the opportunity to leave the house despite the freezing cold or the driving rain as it provided her with an escape from Adam and his perverted behaviour. She would leave the danger of the house (never her home, never a place she belonged) in the winter blackness of 6 a.m. and return when the sun was still very low in the sky or occasionally not yet having made an appearance. As Ree pushed open the gate at 7.15 on 14 January, the clouds obscuring the weak sun obliterated any chance of daylight. Adam was waiting for her in the garden as she shut the gate behind her and lifted the luminous orange newspaper bag from her shoulder. He grabbed her arm and covered her mouth with his clammy soft hand, pushing her into the tiny shed in the corner of the garden.

'Don't make a sound or I'll fucking hurt you.'

Ree knew it was useless protesting and after he had raped her he laughed.

'I told you I'd get what I wanted. That I'd have you, bitch.'

She knew that this day had been a long time coming and that she would never, ever let it happen again.

Running into the house she soon stood under the shower washing him off and out of her body – scrubbing away her shame, rinsing the blood away from between her legs. She was red raw by the time she timidly opened the bathroom door. She listened to Adam whistling and saying goodbye to Laura, then heard her brothers leaving for school shortly before Laura went off to her cleaning job. She quickly dressed and packed her holdall.

She was alone, alone in the place that was supposed to be her sanctuary, her security, her home. Dressed in jeans, trainers and anorak, she grabbed her holdall, picked up her Post Office savings book and walked to the newsagent's to collect her wages. Telling Mr Patel that she would no longer be able to do the paper-round resulted in little more than his muttering about finding a replacement. He failed to register the fact that this was the girl who had always been so reliable, never letting him down and who could always be counted on to cover extra rounds. Neither did he notice that she was carrying a holdall and wasn't in school uniform at 10 a.m. on a Monday morning.

Ree walked and walked, thinking about what had happened to her and what was going to become of her.

'Couldn't get any fucking worse,' she said to herself as she got onto a double-decker bus heading for Marble Arch. A million other thoughts flew through her head as the bus took her past Piccadilly Circus, up to the top of Regent Street and then swung left into Oxford Street. She climbed down the steps and, as she placed her feet firmly on the ground, took in a lungful of the polluted cold exciting West-End London air. For the first time in her life she smiled from her very soul.

Ree had wandered up and down Oxford Street many times, passing uncountable hours, to be away from the house and from the people who called themselves her family. She had been over this moment in her head so frequently that she knew exactly what to do, where to go, what to say. When she calmly walked into the post office in Hanover Square and asked the young Asian girl behind the counter if she could withdraw fifty pounds the clerk didn't look twice at her, just asked her to sign a slip of paper and then handed over the money. Inwardly, Ree's heart was racing, wondering if she had been missed yet.

'Silly cow,' she muttered to herself. 'Get a fucking grip.'

It was only 11.30 in the morning, of course she hadn't been missed. She bought some clothes which would make her look older than her almost fifteen years; trendy jeans, boots, leg warmers and a new jacket, taking care not to spend too much of her precious savings. Then, armed with a new fashionable oversized bag, she went into the toilet of Marks & Spencer where she sorted through her new clothes and discarded anything too childish or immature from the stuff she had packed that morning. The make-up counter of Boots saw the young runaway enlist the help of a typically over made-up sales girl to select a new look and try it out with an instant make-over which, combined with the clothes, made Ree look like a nineteen-year-old. She left the store and strode confidently to a hairdressing salon she had spotted on one of her previous trips when she had dreamt and planned her escape. The final transformation was staggering and she hardly recognized her own face in the mirror. The sad, tatty, straggly girl who, earlier that morning, had looked resignedly back at her, had been replaced by an attractive, determined young woman in the space of just a few hours.

'If life was like the movies,' she whispered, ' I'd now go on to get a great job, live in a fantastic flat and have an adventure before Prince Charming swept me off my feet.'

'If only,' she sighed. 'But it ain't. I'm not Dorothy, this ain't Kansas. Still, it ain't Walthamstow neither!'

Chapter Two

Gavin pulled the sleeping bag over his head and hoped his breath would give him some heat. It was really too cold to sleep ; he only ever dropped off for a few minutes at a time. The bitter January wind and rain seemed to penetrate every item of clothing he wore, and crept through the layers of cardboard that formed his bed. The intense cold made his head throb and the discomfort he felt even in his fit young body was at times unbearable. He had at least eaten that night – sandwiches donated from one of those chains of trendy shops and a cup of tomato soup from the back of a car down at Victoria Passage. Some of the scum-bags he bedded down with called them 'wanky fucking middle-class do-gooders with bad consciences' but Gavin thought they were pretty decent people to stand there night after night dishing out hot food to people who smelt of vomit, sweat, piss and shit. But the warmth of a couple of hours ago had long gone and he could only huddle down into the mangy nylon sleeping bag and wait for the morning. The cold made his nose run and he sniffed and wiped it constantly. Since finding himself sleeping rough in London he never really slept, just closed his eyes and prayed for the morning to come quickly, with, on a good day, a smidgen of sunshine and warmth thrown in.

Gavin was sixteen years old and had run away from the nightly beatings dished out by his drunken father. Ever since he could remember his life and that of his mother had been a living nightmare, a product of his father's love of alcohol. Sometimes the old man could actually be a nice person, begging forgiveness, promising never to drink again, promising that this time it would be different – always promises, promises. His mother would look happy and kid herself that her husband had finally seen the light and they would all start again and end up in the pub having a social drink with the lads. Gavin's mother's purse would be emptied yet again and another bruise would decorate her body. For years Gavin had begged his mother to leave her husband, urging her to walk away from the house, to start again, but she couldn't because she loved Frank and that was that.

'He'll stop drinking, he wasn't always like this. He really does care for us in his own way,' she would say pathetically.

He could picture her, his battered, bruised, broken mother, face glistening with tears, saying those words, every time Frank had hit her, every time he had hit Gavin. The last time was the worst ever and Gavin had asked his mother once more to leave the monster created by drink but she had sat at the kitchen table with her head in her hands and whispered 'No love, I can't, I just can't. He needs me.' Gavin went to his room, packed his bag and walked out of the flat, tears cascading from his eyes, but refusing to look back. How could she choose that bastard over her own son, even over herself?

He had no idea what to do or where to go – his departure had not been planned. It was four o'clock in the morning and raining. He had very little money and so walked several bitingly cold miles to the main road out of Grimsby, thinking about his future. This was an 'A' road but single carriageway so he decided to hitch a lift to wherever the first car that stopped was going, purely to feel warm again because he really didn't care where he ended up as anywhere would be a vast improvement on the place he'd just left. After about forty minutes he was climbing into the cab of a huge lorry which had mercifully pulled over for him. The lorry, full of fish, was headed for Billingsgate, the home of the fish market in London, so that's where Gavin decided to go too. He had never been to London before nor had he ever been particularly interested in going there but, feeling like a fish out of water, it seemed appropriate to be going to a fish market though the idea of travelling to the capital city was a mixture of excitement and fear. The warmth of the cab and the cup of coffee he was offered by the lorry driver lifted his spirits. Sid had been driving to and from Grimsby for nearly thirty years and cast his eyes over the young angry lad he had picked up. How many times over the years had he found these guys (they were mostly guys) at the side of the road, full of adventure and expectation? He had lost count. This one didn´t talk much but seemed polite enough. Said he was eighteen but Sid knew he was only about fifteen or sixteen because he had kids of his own and wasn´t stupid. The boy had no idea where he was going or how he was going to get by but had just told Sid that he had had enough and wanted a new start in another town. Fair enough, Sid thought as he shared the scalding sweet coffee from his flask. He pulled the lorry into the services and invited Gavin to join him for breakfast. Mindful of his lack of funds Gavin declined, as Sid guessed he probably would.

'Seems a shame to waste all these vouchers I´ve got, they give me chits from work for food, got loads of them. Come on, I´ll never use them before they go out of date.'

'Oh well, OK, thanks Sid.'

Helping Gavin out with a ride and a meal made Sid feel better about himself and he felt protective of the young runaway. He was always turning up here with some young kid.

At first his fellow truckers hinted that he might be a pervert but now they just thought that he was a bit soft in the head. He had been a young runaway himself and this was the least he could do to repay some of the kindness he had been shown all those years ago. With full stomachs the two of them climbed back into the cab and settled into the remainder of their journey. Gavin told Sid a little of his life and Sid listened. He tried not to interfere too much. He casually mentioned a few places he knew of where Gavin might find a cheap or even a free bed for the night and some food. Gavin absorbed all the information and stored it away, hoping that he would quickly find work and lodgings and not need to rely on handouts. Quite how he was going to manage this he had yet to figure out. The journey, as promised, ended at Billingsgate and from the overpowering smell in the air Gavin was left in absolutely no doubt as to what was sold there. Thanking Sid profusely for his kindness he alighted from the warmth and relative safety of the cab and wondered which way to head, not just at that moment but with his life in general.

Three weeks had passed since then and now he wandered around London during the day and sought the company of fellow dossers at night. He had soon found the hostels mentioned by Sid where he could have a wash and get some clean clothes, and had discovered the time and place of the soup kitchens. Finding work had not been so easy. With nowhere to live and unable to provide an address, he had quickly discovered that no one was going to give a homeless boy a job. Gavin was forced to swallow his pride along with endless mugs of soup and out-of-date sandwiches. All he could think about was how he could end this life, this existence for that's all he decided it was, an existence. He passed his days and nights with some of the most tormented people he could ever have imagined – ex-soldiers, ex-prisoners, ex-everything if he believed half the stories and what motivation would any of these people have to lie? Surely not pride or the desire to impress. Even to his young and relatively inexperienced ears the tales of his fellow homeless brought a lump to his throat and filled his eyes with tears. The old man who had been wandering the streets for years after a fatal car accident had wiped out his family. The ex-soldiers who had come out of the army with no family or home to go to. With no support system and only the images in their heads which tormented their sleeping hours and reminded them of tours of duty in Northern Ireland with long-term pals. The youngsters who had run away from children's homes and various local authority institutions choosing a life on the streets which they found preferable to the abuse they suffered while in care. Virtually all of these poor pitiful souls drank whatever they could or injected or smoked whatever was available just to pass the time, to forget whatever it was they were running from or what had put them there in the first place. Life's most vulnerable, discarded people in a pit of despair, ostracized and misunderstood.

'I'm not like them,' Gavin would say to himself as he stood under a lukewarm shower in a hostel, scraping the grime from underneath his fingernails, trying to scrub the smell of defeat from his body.

'I am so fucking not like them,' he repeated to himself as he queued for his clean clothes.

The hostel was understaffed and the few people who worked there seemed to be trying to fix the problems of millions with the resources fit for a handful. But they did their best and Gavin admired their faith in human nature. The town he was from was a close community and never had he experienced the agony faced by the people he now called his acquaintances and in some cases friends.

He was young and healthy and had only been living rough for a few weeks but had already seen at first hand the cruelty of the mental problems of some of those poor tortured souls living with him in the cardboard kingdoms – the heavy drinking, the fighting, even the death of one old man who didn't wake up one morning, frozen in his cardboard coffin. Gavin stayed inside at the hostel for as much of the day as he could, anything to stay warm. He volunteered for any chores, glad of something to occupy his time and avoid having to wander the streets aimlessly.

He soon became familiar with the drawn pinched faces of his homeless peers. As he queued for lukewarm soup at Waterloo a boy of roughly the same age as him nodded a greeting of recognition.

'All right mate,' he said. 'Fucking freezing ain't it?'

They moaned about the cold as they shuffled slowly forwards, damp and stiff through to the bone by the time they reached the front of the queue. Huddling in their small groups the men, and women, exchanged gossip and details of hostels, cheap lodgings and free food. The soup vans left and Gavin and the homeless Londoner exchanged names and brief backgrounds. Trevor was sixteen and had been sleeping rough for three months, but said it felt like three years. The boys bedded down for the night, pulling their dirty sleeping bags tightly around them, grateful for the thick layers of cardboard and the fire blazing in the middle of the circle of sad and lonely individuals.

A headache was attacking Gavin at the base of his neck and throbbing quietly. He was cold, hungry and tired again. The pale winter sun was barely visible and he took no comfort in its feeble rays. Pushing the now damp, frost-covered cardboard away from him he stood tall and stretched as he did so. Gathering the driest pieces of cardboard, he pulled them apart and threw them on the embers of the fire, hoping to inject a little heat back into his weary body. Flames shot up, devouring the cardboard, and he threw on some broken slats from pallets someone had already smashed into useable pieces. The heat permeated his body at last and invigorated him into life. The men around him waking to heat for a change were grateful to him for his efforts.

Trevor and Gavin collected their few belongings and decided to head towards a Salvation Army hostel nearby for a meal and hopefully a shower. Approaching the junction just before the hostel a lad maybe a year or two older than the boys spotted Trevor and called his name.

'Oi Trev, result mate!'

'Yeah ? I never thought you'd do it.'

'Beats living like you poor bastards. I got a bedsit now, how about it? Just do it a few times, get yourself out of this shit, it's a way. Let me know if you change your mind.'

The boy, Ryan, wandered off.

'That lad, what's he talking about?' asked Gavin.

Trevor looked almost surprised that Gavin needed to ask.

'Selling his arse. It's meant to be good money, don't know if I'm that desperate yet.'

Horrified, Gavin looked at Trevor in disbelief.

'You mean you would actually do it, go wi' a bloke, for money?'

'I'm not saying that I would, definitely like, but fucking hell, mate, he's got a gaff now, he ain't dirty, and he ain't hungry. It's a start. Even if you just do it enough to get sorted then find a job, 'cos when you got somewhere to live you can. Three bloody months I been doing this, and I'm so fucked off with it. Yes, mate, I have thought about it. There's always plenty wants to pay good money for a shag with a kid of our age, so why not? It's got to be better than living in filth the way we do most of the time.'

Stunned into silence, Gavin followed Trevor into the hostel where they queued for tepid showers, clean clothes and food. The boys passed the day playing cards and pool, grateful for the warmth the hostel afforded them. The shelter was full that night and so the boys went their separate ways, knowing that they stood a better chance of finding a bed elsewhere if they were alone. Agreeing to meet up in a few days, they walked off into the night, each one wrapped up in their own private misery.

* * *

A week later Gavin sat on an upturned empty wooden crate warming himself against a fire, eating a supper of shepherd's pie dished out by ladies from the Simon Organization to whom he would be eternally grateful. A familiar voice called his name and Gavin turned to see a grinning Trevor walking towards him.

'Gav, thought that was you. All right mate, how you been? You got anywhere to kip tonight? Come back with me if you want, it ain't much but I got a room same place as Ryan. You ain't havin' my bed but you can kip on the couch if you want. 'Ave a clean up too.'

Gavin looked at him, knowing instantly what he had done to achieve his own little palace.

'Look mate, yeah, I did it, OK? Couldn't cope with this shit any more. Was brickin' it the first time but it's not that bad. Most of the geezers are OK – just want a wank or a blow-job really. Some are just happy to pay to watch me play with meself which I do a lot anyway so why not get paid, eh? Get a few drinks and a hot meal sometimes too. I got a start on the buildings next week, and I won't do it no more, but I had to get out – all this shit was killin' me.'

Finishing his food, Gavin followed Trevor back to his bedsit. The room was one of many in a large Victorian semi in Islington. It was sparsely furnished, just a bed, a settee, an old sideboard with a two-ring cooker and a fridge in the corner of the room. An old mahogany wardrobe stood against another wall with a matching chest of drawers beside it. The carpet was fairly old and a bit threadbare but it didn't matter, the room was clean, dry and even warm thanks to the plug-in electric heater fixed into the space where a fireplace stood. It was the Hilton compared to cardboard boxes and a pavement.

Trevor gave Gavin a fifty pence piece which was slotted into the pay box next to the boiler in the shared bathroom. As he sank back into the hot water, he thought hard, very hard, about the mess that was his life and the options open to him. Trevor's decision to become a male prostitute, to sell himself to the rich city boys, or whoever wanted him, didn't sit very well at all with Gavin but this hot bath, the comfortable, if basic, room were testament to the few hours' work to which Trevor had turned out of need. The experience was undoubtedly horrendous but was it a path worth taking? Climbing out of the bath, Gavin stared at himself in the small mirror above the basin, not recognizing the face that stared back at him.

After a few beers Gavin snuggled under the blanket Trevor gave him and fell into the first untroubled sleep he had had since leaving Grimsby all those weeks ago.

The smell of frying bacon hit the boys long before they could see the café. Trevor had promised a big breakfast to set Gavin up for the day and Gavin felt strange knowing where the money to pay for the food had come from. Hungry and despising himself for his weakness he followed Trevor into the café. Shutting out morality and ignoring temptation for an hour the lads ate huge amounts of good food and drank copious amounts of sweet tea. Trevor paid for their breakfast and, finally satisfied, the boys left the café and returned to the room. Gavin had already been told he could stay as long as he liked but he knew that he couldn't sponge off Trevor for ever and was determined to find his own way, set himself up and help himself. Trevor offered to introduce Gavin to the man who arranged things, the pimp, the fixer.

'Look, mate, I don't know. I've not done anything with a bloke before. Sure I checked out what the guys were packing in the showers after a match and there was the one time when a gang of us got pissed and wanked off together while watching some porno vid but that's it,' said Gavin to his friend.

'Like I told you, mate, it's no big deal really and it's good easy money. I've done it a few times and when I start my new job I'm going to get me a bird. Messing about with the geezers ain't turned me into no poof!'

Feeling sick with himself Gavin asked Trevor to make the call, just to get himself a few quid together, he didn't need much, just a start, enough for a cheap room like this and then he could find a job, a proper job, and turn his life around. After all, he thought, Trevor had done it, so there was no reason why he shouldn't do exactly the same. Was there?

Trevor went out and made the call.

The boys waited anxiously outside a shabby pub in Hanover Street. Trevor had only met the pimp, Johnny, twice before and was very wary of the man. Johnny had a reputation for being cruel and hard, ruthless with his demands. But it was money, Gavin kept telling himself, it was a means to an end, a way of earning enough to take himself off the streets and into some form of normality, a world he had only ever dreamt about since coming to London.

Johnny sauntered over, spitting on the pavement as he approached them. He lit a cigarette and inhaled deeply as he sized Gavin up.

'Trev, all right are ya? So, Gavin, how do you feel about some queer sortin' you out? Sure you got the stomach for it? You've got the looks and I'm guessing it's not a sock you've got stuffed down the front of your jeans, eh?'

He inclined his head towards the pub and the boys followed him into the bar. He told them to sit while he got them something to drink. A few minutes later as the boys nervously sipped their Coke and Johnny swirled a brandy around a large glass, the pimp asked Gavin when he wanted to start work. Gavin gulped and the reality of what he was about to do hit him. They made arrangements for him to go to a flat behind Oxford Street that evening and Johnny told him how much money he could expect to receive. Doing a few sums in his head, Gavin reckoned that if he went with a guy just three or four times he would be free of his life on the streets, maybe get a start on the buildings like Trevor had done and at least be able to rent a room for a month to get him on his feet. As he daydreamed of his future, Johnny's voice brought him back to reality.

'So, got that address have you? Don't be fucking late and once the punter has gone I'll be there to pay you. Oh, and Trev, sort him out with some poppers.'

Johnny flung two ten pound notes on the table as he stood up and put his jacket on.

'Well done, Trev, that's for you.'

He threw another note down. 'Here Gav, get a fucking hair cut out of that, you look like a bloody bird and that's no good for my punters.'

Laughing at his own sick joke Johnny turned and left the

boys with their thoughts.

An old-fashioned barbershop was a short walk away and as Gavin sat in the chair having a cape wrapped around him, his emotions were nearly at boiling point. He felt fresh anger at his father, sadness for his mother and scared for himself.

'Hello, anyone in? Wake up, mate, you're miles away.'

The voice of the barber brought Gavin back to the present and the man asked him what he would like him to do. Twenty minutes later he was brushing the hair from his neck and concentrating on the practical issues immediately facing him. He had a few hours before he was expected at the flat so after returning to Trevor's bedsit he sorted out the clean clothes he and Trevor had collected from the launderette then had a bath and washed his newly cropped hair.

Two hours later he was ready, or as ready as he would ever be. He tried to remain focused on the thought that he was earning money and it was just like any other job. He began the long walk to Oxford Street and wondered if, when the crunch came, he would actually be able to go ahead with the act of having sex with a man. Besides the mucking about he'd described to Trevor he had very little sexual experience. He'd only had a couple of girlfriends and had slept with just one of them a couple of times. Now, here he was, preparing himself to meet with a man, not entirely sure what was expected of him. All sorts of things flew through his head. He calmed himself – Trevor had done it and said it was easy money.

Pushing the buzzer on the outer door, Gavin thought he caught a glimpse of Johnny in the pub directly opposite the entrance to the flat. A tinny voice spoke to him through the intercom, inviting him up to the flat. Each step Gavin took was more difficult than the previous one – a step into the unknown but which could be the first one towards the answer to his financial problems although at the cost of losing his self-respect and any dignity he had left. Reaching the top of the stairs, the door to the flat was open very slightly and the same voice called out to come on in. Hesitating for only the briefest of moments Gavin grasped the handle and walked inside.

'Close the door behind you, mate.' Gavin did as he was asked.

'My name's Steve. What should I call you young man? Johnny said you were a bit of a looker. He wasn't wrong, was he?'

Steve was in his mid-thirties and was wearing a polo shirt and jeans which promised a muscular physique underneath.

'I'm Gav.' Gavin hoped that his nervousness didn't show.

'Fancy a drink, mate, or shall we just get friendly?'

Steve put his arm around Gavin's shoulders and gently led him to the bedroom.

Naked, Gavin thought that it wasn't too bad and even surprised himself by becoming aroused. Steve moved closer.

Later, much later, Gavin, face down on the bed, felt Steve penetrate him. 'No,' he thought. 'No', but said nothing. He forced himself to relax – it's what Steve was paying him for.

Afterwards, Steve kissed Gavin on the forehead and left the flat.

Gavin dressed. He was shaking. He wanted to cry. He almost thought that a beating from his brutal father had been easier to deal with. Sure it hurt but only for a short time and, in the early days, when it was over they both acted as if it had never happened. Gavin knew how he'd got himself into this particular mess, he only had himself to blame but he was sure that he'd never forget and vowed he'd never ever do it again.

Johnny arrived, gave Gavin his money and told him to go home. As he left Johnny slipped him an extra twenty pounds.

'Steve liked you, Gavin, and wants to see you again

– give me a call and I'll sort something out.'

Trevor wasn't in when Gavin got back to the bedsit. He had a bath and looked in the mirror not liking what he saw.

He wrote a note to his friend.

'Thanks for letting me stay, Trev. See you around.' He left all the money Johnny had given him – it felt dirty.

Pulling the door closed behind him he started the walk back to the hostel hoping that they had a bed for the night.

* * *

Keith, the manager of the dilapidated building, suited his impoverished surroundings. He blended in. He was constantly tired, endlessly defending his guests, as he preferred to call them, to social workers, the police and any number of other authorities, while trying to perform miracles on the meagre budget he was allocated. Witnessing vulnerability and hopelessness every day, Keith kept trying to help those who came to him and prayed for those who didn't. He saw hope in Gavin and hoped that it wasn't too late to save him. Save him from selling his body on Tottenham Court Road, save him from heroin and pills, save him from despair. Gavin didn't even smoke as far as Keith could tell and, until recently, he came in every day – queued for a bed and was always one of the first up and in the showers. Keith badgered everyone he knew to give work to the few that he thought would make the best of the opportunity and, with this in mind, he approached Gavin one morning.

'Gavin, all right mate, can I've a word, son?'

Gavin liked Keith very much because he really did seem to care about all the old dossers who smelt like shit and looked worse. He treated everyone with respect, never prying into anyone's past but always ready to listen if one of the homeless men felt the need to talk.

'It ain't my business, son, and I don't wanna know, so why you are here and how you ended up here is your business and fuck all to do with anyone else unless you want it to be. I can help you, but you've got to really want to be helped and be ready to do it yourself. I don't want to know how old you really are 'cos I 'ave a feeling you ain't eighteen like you told me you was. But, if ever you want to go back to where you came from or let anyone know where you are or just that you are OK, let me know and I'll sort it. All right, son. It's a fuckin' hard life, ain't it?'

Gavin followed Keith into his office and Keith hoped that he had guessed Gavin right.

'Right, son, this life ain't for you and before you end up a loony tunes like most of that lot out there I may have a job for you. Now don't get excited 'cos it's fuck all really but well, it's a beginning and we all gotta start somewhere, ain't we? A young one like you, that's all you need really, a start and the rest is up to you. A mate of mine, fat Greek bloke, Telly we call him, like the bloke who plays the detective on TV, he's got a café down London Bridge and he needs a general dogsbody to wash up, serve the customers and, if you're really lucky, he might even let you fry eggs sometimes! Pay is shit but you get a share of the tips and the best bit is there is a bedsit above the café which is yours with the job. So, you get all the food you can eat, crap wages and a little place of your very own. What do you reckon, mate?'

The relief Gavin felt at that moment lifted his whole body and spirit as if he had won a million pounds on the football pools. Brushing aside the boy's thanks and seeing the water forming in his eyes, Keith busied himself with shuffling papers around on his desk, not speaking for a few moments in case his voice betrayed his emotions.

'Right, as you are now vacating these palatial surroundings, for good, I bloody hope, I can give you some vouchers to get you started. So take them, get some clean clothes from the stores and fuck off and never darken my door again.'

Keith grinned at Gavin and went through the small amount of paperwork involved. He handed him an envelope with vouchers he could exchange for shoes, toiletries and a few basic items like bedding for his new home. The address of the café and Telly's name and a note of the wages were also there. As he would have to work a week in hand a small allowance was given to him and after signing for everything he retrieved his rucksack before picking out some clothes in reasonable condition from the stores. He shook Keith's hand and walked out of the hostel feeling the thrill that comes at the start of an exciting journey.

'I'm never coming back here Keith, mate. Not as a customer at any rate!'

Chapter Three

Ree stood on the pavement outside the hairdresser's and reality sunk its claws into her once again. Nowhere to sleep, no job, and a few quid in the bank which would soon be gone, so now what? A man bumped into her, winking as he eyed her up and down. 'Sorry darling, my fault.' The bloke grinned at her as he walked away.

Ree knew she wasn't ugly but now, with a little help from her new clothes, trendy new hairstyle and light make-up, she was stunning. The little girl was now a woman and from now on she would have to make herself and everyone else believe she really was eighteen when she was in fact still ten days away from her fifteenth birthday.

She bought an *Evening Standard*, found a cheap café, ordered a big meal and, as she drank several mugs of builder's tea, she examined every 'to let' advertised. There were masses of them and as she sifted through she realized that time was flying by and she would have to go back to the post office for more money. She would need a deposit and the first month's rent which she could cover from her savings but that wouldn't leave very much at all. Gulping down her tea she paid her bill and went to a post office in Tottenham Court Road. She asked for two pounds in ten pence pieces, finally found a pay phone which wasn't vandalized and knee deep in urine, opened the paper to the adverts she had circled and, armed with pen and paper, began her search for a new home. She had a great deal of self-confidence which was amazing considering the start she had had in life. It was as if she had been building up to this day, the one when she would escape the bullying and the intimidation, the abuse and the neglect. After an hour and about fifteen phone calls Ree had run out of money but had a list of six bedsits and flats to look at that evening.

She walked down to the Northern line to emerge a short while later at Waterloo and quickly find the address she was looking for. The door was swinging open and looking at the debris left on the floor it was obvious the place had been used as a squat by junkies. Judging by the people she passed on the stairs she guessed some of the other bedsits were still operating that way. Leaving quickly she moved onto the next place on her list in a small road behind Southwark Street, a wide main road a few minutes from London Bridge Station, which in her optimistic way she thought would be handy for the tube and work, wherever and whatever that might turn out to be. She decided to walk the short distance from the Elephant. The woman on the phone had told her to ring the bell for flat C and she would show her the vacant rooms. Despite being about half an hour early she took a chance and pushed the bell at the main door and after being buzzed in without any word through the intercom, tapped on the door of the flat on the first floor. The door, fixed to a chain, opened a couple of inches and a partially obscured face peered around.

'Oh, hello, you must be Ree? You're early, won't be a tick, love.'

The door shut and after a couple of minutes the woman reappeared wearing the most amazing over-the-top outfit Ree had ever seen. Leopard print coat, matching high heels and so much make-up the woman must have had shares in Boots.

'I'm Pixie, love, nickname obviously as I'm so fucking tall.' She grinned as she pointed out another door on the landing.

'I'm here on the first floor and so is the flat I'm letting. I own the house. Downstairs is two flats and there's another two on the second floor – there's a basement too but that's just used for storage. Go on in,' she said, unlocking the door.

Ree stepped into what, to her, was paradise. She was standing in a small lounge; a couple of easy chairs and a coffee table were the only furniture. The floorboards had been sanded and covered with rugs, not new but clean. The walls were pale pink and the chairs were green, huge and welcoming. Ree could already imagine herself curled up in one of them. Pixie opened a door to what Ree thought was a cupboard but which was in fact a tiny bathroom. A shower, a toilet and a basin, scrubbed immaculately clean. The kitchen was minute too, sink, fridge and cooker, a few cupboards, the whole room about six by five but perfect. The bedroom had a double bed, a wardrobe, chest of drawers and a bedside cabinet. The bed was made up with what looked like clean bedding and the whole flat smelt of bleach and cheap air freshener.

'So, I want a month's deposit, and a month up front. A day late with the rent and we'll fall out and believe me, love, you don't want to fall out with Pixie! Any damage and you pay for it. No fucking noise, I can't abide noise. Keep yourself to yourself and we'll get on fine. Now do you want it and if you do when do you want to move in?'

Ree handed over the money and asked if it was OK if she stayed tonight. Pixie looked at her quizzically.

'I don't want no trouble here. No one looking for you is there? 'Cos you ain't very old are ya and what about yer stuff?'

Ree told her new landlady that she couldn't be arsed travelling back to her parents' house that night but that everything was fine and she would bring her things at the weekend. The pale pink scarf wrapped loosely around Pixie's neck unfurled itself leaving her throat exposed. Ree had been suspicious the minute Pixie had opened the door but now she realized for definite that Pixie was actually a man. Pixie readjusted her scarf and invited Ree into her flat.

'Takes all sorts, love, wouldn't be right if we was all the same.'

Ree just laughed and agreed with Pixie.

Now she had paid for her flat, Pixie seemed to soften and Ree found herself confessing to not yet having a job saying that she planned to sort something out first thing in the morning. Pixie just seemed to take it all in as she ushered Ree inside, made a cup of tea and told her where things were locally. Although this was a different part of London to where Ree was from she had a vague idea of the layout of the area but happily listened to Pixie tell her where to find the launderette and which cupboard the spare sheets were in. Pixie's flat was as outrageous as she was – all garish colours, soft lighting and luxurious throws and at least twice the size of the one that Ree was to make her home.

Eventually she feigned tiredness, left Pixie and dumped her bag in her new lounge. She hung her clothes away and opened cupboards and drawers. It was all very basic but there were a few mugs in the cupboards along with other essential kitchen utensils. She found an ancient iron in one cupboard and some thin towels in another. Taking her purse, she went to the shop on the opposite corner of the road and bought some bananas, a pint of milk, a loaf of bread and a block of butter. Ree hated the cheap margarine her mother bought and decided that from now on she would live her life the way she wanted to. If she wanted butter she would bloody well have it! That night, she relaxed in her new home despite knowing that the following day was going to be a bloody hard slog.

She knew that Adam would have made up some story as to why she hadn't come home and no one would ever look for her. With sadness and regret for a life she had never lived, she felt lonely and desperately miserable as she realized her mother would probably not even miss her. Falling asleep, she was determined that the next fifteen years of her life were going to be very different from the first.

Chapter Four

The smell and sound of the café hit Gavin long before he could see it. As he walked along the road counting the numbers down, Adam Ant chanted louder and louder, droning on about Ant Music. And there it was. The café had a simple sign painted on the glass, 'Telly's Café' – an inconspicuous white building tucked in between a betting shop and a hairdresser's, identical to a thousand other greasy spoons in the capital. Gavin walked over to the fat guy behind the counter and asked for Telly.

'I am Telly. Who the fuck wants to know?'

Gavin explained who he was and that Keith had sent him.

'Fuckin' brilliant. I'm struggling here with dolly fuckin'-daydream over there. Dozy cow ain't got a clue.'

Telly laughed then smiled affectionately at a strikingly beautiful girl who was dishing up beans on toast.

'Keith said you'd done this before. Well, son, come on, let's dump your stuff and you can start right away.'

'Shit,' thought Gavin, 'bloody Keith. Oh well, I suppose I'd better be a quick learner.'

Telly led Gavin through the café, up a set of stairs and unlocked a door opposite an open storeroom which led to a very plain, whitewashed bedsit. It held a single bed covered in a faded candlewick bedspread. A wardrobe, an armchair and a bedside cabinet threatened to fill the small space not occupied by the bed. Back on the landing, Telly opened a door to the left of the bedsit revealing a small bathroom. Gavin was pleased to see that the bath taps had a shower attachment – imagining having a shower in the morning and a soak after work. Also on the landing was a small recess with a sink, a wall-mounted water boiler, a small hob and a tatty fridge under the work surface. Everything was clean and Telly pointed to a radio in the kitchen area.

'Last wanker left that here, it's yours now. Right, lose the bag, here's the key and come downstairs soon as.'

Telly left Gavin who could not believe his luck. The room was sparse but he was already imagining a portable TV in one corner and savouring the feeling of safety, of peace.

He locked the door behind him and came down the stairs. Telly threw him an apron and told him to scrub his hands with the thick green goo next to the sink. 'Dolly daydream' was Nikki, Telly's daughter, seventeen years old and the apple of his eye. A beautiful girl kept under strict scrutiny by her widowed father. Gavin answered Telly's questions carefully, telling him he was eighteen, that the northern town he was from was dead and he wanted to see a bit of London for himself. Telly seemed satisfied and barked orders at his new helper, rapidly at first but more slowly as the day wore on. Telly did most of the cooking, Nikki making sandwiches occasionally. Gavin had washed plates, scraped away leftovers, hauled the rubbish out of the kitchen to the bins around the back of the café, cleared tables and generally done what he was told. Five o'clock came and the closed sign went up on the door. The tables were bleached, the floor was hosed down and the last of the grease was scrubbed from the kitchen surfaces.

'Well done, son, you worked bloody hard. Tonight you come to my house and I'll cook you a proper meal. Real

Greek food fit for a man, not this unhealthy English crap you all eat so much of.'

They pulled the shutter down and Telly showed Gavin how to open the part that gave access to the café door.

'You've got to make sure that the shutter door's lock catches when you go in and when you leave, mate, or my insurance will be fucked. Turn the caff light off at the switch on your landing – I'm not made of money. Now, tonight I'm feeding you but you'll get your own stuff in future, right? No midnight feasts made from food for paying customers!'

Nikki gave Gavin their home address and jokingly told him to make sure he had a bath because he stank of chips, fat and cigarette smoke.

'See you at seven,' she said with a smile.

An hour later Gavin soaked away the day with some bubble-bath he had found in his bathroom. As he washed his hair then used a nail brush on his hands he couldn't get over his good fortune, smiling to himself as he savoured the hot water, thinking about dinner later. 'What a difference a day makes,' he grinned to himself as he lay back in the bubbles.

It was about a ten-minute walk to Telly's home. Gavin was early so walked around the block a couple of times enjoying the sound of the bunch of keys jangling in his pocket. He had trudged all over London in the three weeks he had slept rough. There wasn't much else to do and to keep warm it was the most sensible. Standing at the door of the semi-detached house with its outside lights and mini conifers in pots either side of the front door, he admired the floodlit front garden with its neat borders and precise hedges. Telly didn't strike him as a gardener but his sixteen years of life's experiences and three weeks' worth of rough sleeping had taught him not to judge a book by its cover.

He pushed the bell and heard the *Starsky & Hutch* theme

tune reverberate through the house. Trying hard not to laugh, he fought to compose himself as Nikki came to the door, clean and fresh from her day at the café.

'A word of advice, my dad thinks he's the best cook in the world so eat everything he gives you or you'll never get on and at no time ever insult anything to do with Greece! And please don't say you like the doorbell or I'll never persuade him to get rid of the bloody thing!'

Telly truly was a great cook, dish after dish was produced and Gavin managed somehow to plough through the mountains of traditional Greek fare placed before him. His host had him in stitches with tales of life in Greece before his parents brought him to live in London as a ten-year-old boy. He felt like all his birthdays and Christmases had arrived at once. He left Telly's home feeling truly happy and content for the first time in his life.

Chapter Five

For a few seconds Ree had no idea where she was then the events of the previous day clicked into her memory and she absorbed the peace around her. Not that it was particularly quiet – she could hear traffic, thumping footsteps on stairs, doors banging, muffled shouts, but none of that mattered, she was free. She pushed the bedclothes back and looked at her watch. It was gone eight which amazed her; she was normally up at six for her paper-round – she never had the luxury of a lie-in before. 'Sod it,' she thought to herself as she stretched and made her way to the bathroom, 'better get a move on.' She took her time washing her hair and doing her make-up, dressing smartly as she intended to spend the day searching for a job. God knows what the hell she was going to do and who the hell was going to give a full-time job to a fourteen-year-old girl? She shook her head and reminded herself that from now on she was eighteen and of course she could get a job, she bloody well had to. Two cups of tea and a banana sandwich later, Ree locked her door and pulled the main door to the house closed behind her. She stood out on the street not having a clue where to go or what to do. Turning left, she headed towards London Bridge Station. She thought about likely jobs she could apply for. Losing her confidence she walked into a café and asked for a cup of tea and a bun, not really wanting either. A young boy of about seventeen brought

Ree her tea and gave her an appreciative smile which lifted her spirits no end. After picking at the bun she finished her tea and paid, smiled at the boy and left the café, this time striding confidently towards the station.

She soon discovered that the only work she was likely to get was waitressing or behind a bar, and that was only temporary or cash-in-hand as she had no tax details or national insurance number to offer an employer. All the employment agencies asked her the same questions: 'Can you type? Can you take shorthand? Can you work a telex? Can you work a switchboard?' Knowing that there was no way she could pretend, she told the truth and was informed that there were no jobs for people without experience. She spent the whole day trudging in and out of shops, employment agencies and offices. On the journey home she realized that her options were extremely limited. Leaving the station, she neared the café where she'd had her bun and cup of tea that morning. A voice said, 'Hello luv.' And, startled for a moment, she thought that maybe Adam had found her. She turned quickly to see the boy who had served her that morning pulling metal shutters over the front of the shop. Recognition of the friendly harmless face made her relax and she smiled at him, saying 'Hello' as she walked past.

'Not bad at all,' she thought to herself as she put her key in the street door of her new home.

'Not bad at all,' thought Gavin as he slammed the shutter down and padlocked it before putting his key in the door of his new home.

As Ree got inside a man came scurrying past her, nearly knocking her over in the process, closely followed by Pixie's shouts.

'Fucking twat! What did you think I fucking was, you bloody moron!'

She came thudding down the stairs, muttering obscenities and stopped abruptly when she saw Ree standing there.

'Oh, hello darling, all right? Any joy wiv yer job 'untin'? Sorry about that. Most of my punters are fine. I think his mates must 'ave bin 'avin a laugh wiv 'im. Come in for a cuppa?'

Not quite sure if she had understood correctly, she followed Pixie into her lounge and took in the leopard print negligee, the hairdo which must have been a wig, the long bright red finger nails and the stiletto heels. Pixie had said 'punters'. Did that mean?... Was she a...?

Pixie was laughing at her new tenant who was completely speechless as realization dawned on her.

'Does it bother you, luv? I am what I am, everyone knows me round 'ere and I sort of thought you might have worked out how I make some pin-money. I can see now you 'aven't got a fucking clue 'ave ya!'

The mist cleared and the truth finally hit Ree like a ton of bricks – her landlady, was a transvestite AND a prostitute! Trying to keep a grip on herself and her reactions, she answered Pixie's questions about her day.

'There's so many bleeding jobs out there, come on love, tell yer auntie Pixie, how old are you really? I didn't come off the last banana boat y'know.'

Ree hesitated then, fighting back the tears, she confessed.

'I'm nearly fifteen, please don't make me go back, I can get a job waitressing or something, I'll pay the rent, I won't let you down, I promise.'

Pixie hauled herself up and flopped down next to Ree, thrusting a tissue into her hand.

'Start at the beginning, love. Next punter 'ain't due for an hour or so.' So Ree told her everything and sobbed. Pixie held her tight. Ree could not remember the last time anyone had ever given her a cuddle.

'I've got a spare telly in the other room. You can take that with you. Now, go and have a nice hot shower and you'll feel better in the morning. We'll have a chat tomorrow and see what we can fix up for you. And no love, I ain't gonna tell no one. Bastard like that needs fuckin' shootin. Go on, sod off!'

Ree did as she was told, had her shower, watched TV, ate some toast and went to bed grateful for her strange new friend.

* * *

Gavin was falling into bed at about the same time, totally exhausted. He didn't mind the hard work at all, Nikki was funny and sweet, Telly was bloody hilarious and hugely likeable. His day started at six thirty when the alarm woke him from a deep sleep. Ten minutes in the bathroom then he dressed, shut the door to his room behind him, flicked the lights on downstairs and unlocked the shutters. Telly and Nikki would appear as he was pushing the shutters away for the day, yawning and stretching together, turning the fryer and the urn on and taking the chairs from the tables. As soon as the lights went on in the café the first customers would be queuing up, waiting for seven o'clock and opening time. The same faces appeared at the same time each morning and Gavin soon remembered who had a bacon sandwich, a full English, chips with everything and endless cups of tea.

Telly was hilarious, asking people what they wanted and when someone hesitated or started their response with 'umm', Telly would say, 'Umm's not on the fucking menu and neither is tofu, make yer fucking mind up!' Despite the insults the customers were loyal and the café thrived. Gavin sliced endless loaves of bread, made countless cups of tea and coffee, became friends with the regulars and discussed the football, the weather and the government of the day as if he were born to it. He ate well, worked hard and was happy. The days rolled into weeks and suddenly it was Easter. Telly was conscious that Gavin never mentioned his family and obviously also knew through Keith that Gavin had lived rough. He made a generous invitation to Gavin and asked him to spend some of the holiday with him and Nikki. Gavin was touched but had already decided how he would spend the time. Keith never had enough volunteers so Gavin decided that he would spend his time off at the hostel, serving food, cleaning up, the same thing he did every other day of the year. Only it would serve as a reminder of just how fortunate he had been.

After spending the few days at the hostel Gavin offered help on a more regular basis and soon became involved on the support side of the rough end of society. He became aware of just how many hostels, shelters and detox centres there were in the small part of London he was familiar with and the amazing efforts of the dedicated people who did their utmost to bring relief to the lives of people whom society had thrown on the scrap heap. He volunteered at a detox centre for addicts of both drugs and alcohol and marvelled at the dedication of the staff who supported the men and women who had often been users for years. Finding real fulfilment in his life at last, he settled into a routine of working at the café, volunteering at the hostel and spending evenings with Telly and his family or with friends from the café watching a game of football in the pub.

Chapter Six

All the self-confidence of the previous morning had left Ree as she showered then dressed. Yesterday, she had felt truly alive, ready to take on the world – today, she was just another runaway. Knowing that self-pity was the most useless of emotions, she brushed her hair, put on some make-up, grabbed her handbag and knocked on Pixie's door. Pixie yelled out from somewhere within, 'It's open!' and Ree nervously wandered in, wondering what Pixie had in store for her. And there she was, all six gorgeous feet of her, in her high-heeled boots and that amazing leopard print coat, dark pink lipstick and blue and gold eye shadow.

'Come on, love, first things first, breakfast. Can't think on an empty stomach now can we?'

Pixie said hello to so many people as they walked up the road. She was obviously a totally accepted fixture of the place and no one batted an eyelid upon seeing this vision at 9 a.m. on this crisp and bright January morning.

'Pixie my love, all right sweetheart? Lovely to see you. Full English and what about your beautiful little friend here? Same for you, darling?'

Telly greeted Pixie with a kiss and a hug as they entered his café. Nikki said hello and Pixie patted her cheek and told her how beautiful she was growing, just like her lovely mama had been. Telly's wife had died fifteen years ago and Nikki had no recollection of her mother but knew she had inherited her good looks. Auntie Pixie was one of her favourite of her father's rather eclectic group of friends.

'Hello again,' said the young man as he placed mugs of tea in front of Ree and Pixie, a huge smile plastered across his face as he recognized the pretty girl from the previous day. Ree blushed and smiled back, pleased he had remembered her.

Pixie would have preferred Ree to have worked in the local Wimpy bar wiping tables and serving frothy coffee rather than enter the murky world she herself occupied but there was a chance that someone from her former life would spot her and then who knows where that would lead. Would Adam make her come home? Would she be brave enough to tell someone what Adam had done to her? Would her mother even believe her? Would she end up in care, in a foster home or a children's home at the mercy of some social worker? No, Pixie decided, Ree would have to stay indoors and maid for her. She had had a succession of maids during her working career and some had been OK and some had been a bloody disaster.

Pixie, or Alan Edmund Dixon as she was also known on the rare occasions she chose to face the world as a man, was a transvestite who had always loved the feel of the soft silks and satins his mother had worn, the high heels and the make-up. The rich smells of the lotions and creams, the bath oils and the touch of the silk stockings and luxurious underwear in his mother's closet formed some of his most fond memories.

Alan was born in 1930, into a middle-class home. His parents were comfortably off and Alan was adored. As he grew into a teenager it became obvious which way his sexual tendencies lay. His mother understood and loved her baby regardless. His father, on the other hand, disowned him. Alan had reluctantly worked in the city as a messenger in a bank, wearing a suit during the day and a dress at home in the evenings and at some very private clubs at weekends when he was able to be Pixie. The double life he led caused him much stress and anxiety but despite this, he only truly felt alive when he was Pixie. When Alan was twenty-two and Pixie slightly younger, his father had died and his mother, who had continued her relationship with her son discreetly, was free to lavish the love upon him that her husband had denied. When she died some years later, Alan, an only child, had inherited the family home behind Southwark Street and a small amount of money. After dividing the house into flats Alan decided to take the plunge and leave his job at the bank so that he could be Pixie more or less full-time. He gradually became more open about his way of life and began to go out dressed as a woman. Having grown up in the area and been at school with most of the local hoods and 'faces' when he was known as Dixie it was good to be back. There was the odd bit of teasing at first but now Pixie was 'one of the boys' and was accepted as she was. Telly, Nikki and the customers of the café welcomed Pixie without a second thought and, naturally, any friend of Pixie's was a friend of theirs.

Insisting that Ree finish every last morsel on her plate, Pixie shouted across to Telly to get two more mugs of tea. The café was packed, every table was occupied, but no one gave Rcc's rather odd companion a second glance. Ree felt comfortable and safe, a feeling which was alien to her but incredibly welcome.

'Lovie, I could do with a maid, and no, I don't mean someone to make the bloody beds or wash the floors neither! Someone to look after the gents when they arrive at the flat, take my bookings for me and the money. Make them a coffee, look after my clothes and all that sort of stuff. It'll keep you away from prying eyes and you'll be safe. Forget about the rent and I'll give you a wage too. What do you think?'

Ree knew that every time she left the flat she risked the chance of bumping into someone she knew from her previous life and although she had never come across anyone like Pixie before, somehow the warmth that she and her friends exuded reassured her and made her feel completely safe. Though the job being offered was hardly conventional it solved so many problems that she readily accepted and the two of them said their goodbyes to Gavin, Nikki and Telly before the short stroll back to the house. Pixie had a punter at noon and so had time to take Ree through her new duties as a maid.

Within a few weeks Ree had it all off pat. She kept a diary of appointments, had notes of what each regular punter liked Pixie to wear and laid the outfits out for her. She took the money and banked it, did the laundry and chatted to clients keeping them happy if Pixie was running late. She became part of Pixie's world and loved it.

* * *

Weeks went by and Pixie and Ree shared the Easter break with a couple of the 'girls' and a few punters who had become very good friends over the years. Ree now lived in a strange world, full of misfits and oddities or at least that was how she knew that most of society would view them but they were good kind people and she was happy. Occasionally they would go up west shopping, and then wander through Soho finishing with a dinner in Chinatown. Weeks and months had passed when Ree was rudely woken by Pixie holding a cake ablaze with candles doing her best to sing happy birthday.

'Pixie, what on earth are you doing? Have you been

sniffing the hairspray again? It's not my birthday until January!'

'I know luv but you know your Pixie – she loves a party and it's been six months since you came here, which is sort of a birthday and as good an excuse to have some cake as any I can think of. Now indulge an old gal eh?

First, they had breakfast at the café where by now Ree was a regular, one of the family, then a shopping trip in Oxford Street, a matinee performance of *Evita* followed by a party in the flat that night with all of her new friends. It occurred to Gavin that Telly and Pixie were maybe indulging in a spot of matchmaking so he rather shyly asked Pixie if it was OK to ask Ree to go to the pictures with him. Pixie was delighted, as of course was Ree.

* * *

Ree and Gavin had always stopped for a chat since their first meeting six months before and often shared a cup of coffee at the café but now their relationship moved to a different level and they became an item. The pair had so much in common, both desperately unhappy as children and being forced to leave the only homes they had known through no fault of their own. Over time they shared their experiences, each revealing to the other some of the circumstances and the events that had caused them to run away. They understood one another's deep feelings of insecurity and shared the desire to create a solid and safe haven for their own families when the time came.

Chapter Seven

Two years passed by. Ronald Reagan was elected US President; Peter Sutcliffe 'The Yorkshire Ripper' was arrested. Gavin was working even harder at the café as Nikki was now married and expecting her first baby, much to Telly's delight. Ree and Pixie lived very quietly and business was good. Pixie had a particular friend, Colin, a punter who had become much more to her than just a paying client. Married, with three kids, he was a policeman, an inspector who had a reputation for being fair and turning a blind eye to the petty crooks as long as no one took the piss. Colin knew he was taking a huge risk every time he went to Pixie's, but what had started as a sexual need had developed into something much deeper. He loved her.

He knew that he was sexually attracted to men dressed as women and could even pinpoint when it had started – the result of a boyhood trip to the pantomime, followed that night by his first wet dream featuring the dame from the performance. He had fought with his urges but his sexual fantasies were constantly fuelled by thoughts of what it would be like to be intimate with a 'woman' who hid a special prize beneath her glamorous dress.

After marriage, children and promotion Colin pushed all these feelings to the back of his mind, blocking them out for fear of ruining his career and, by extension, the lives of those he loved.

Then he had met Pixie at a jazz club in Dover Street. She was there with a party of friends and the attraction was colossal, mutual and instantaneous. Encouraged by the drink he had consumed he struck up conversation with this extraordinary creature – the epitome of all his fantasies. Pixie, never ashamed of how she made money, invited Colin to visit her the following day, delighted to be able to mix business and what promised to be real pleasure. The following day all the suppression of a lifetime washed away and Colin's visits to Pixie's house on what used to be his beat when he joined the Met became more and more frequent. What started as an easy way to explore his sexuality and fantasies drifted into something deeper. The feelings they had for each other were profound – Colin totally and utterly loved his unconventional 'woman' and wanted to spend the rest of his life with her. Until the time was right, however, they agreed that they would have to be the souls of discretion – if their relationship were to be discovered then he knew that his family would disown him and he would lose his job. He didn't know which he would regret more.

* * *

Jimmy sat in the window of the pub, taking small sips from his glass, making his drink last as long as possible. Three old men sat in one corner of the Tanners Arms playing dominoes, barely making a sound, muttering to each other so quietly that he couldn't hear their conversation. He turned the tatty beer mat over and over in his hand, wondering what to do with his life, how to make some serious money. The beer was warm now and he hated warm beer but he didn't have the money for a refill. Jimmy had a long skinny face with high cheek bones which made it look almost pointed. The rest of his body was equally bony and angular – his cheap clothes seemed to accentuate the lack of flesh rather than hide it. He was one of those petty crooks that Colin really couldn't abide and their professional paths had crossed many times in the past. Jimmy was a guy who always pushed his luck, always overstepped the mark and would stitch anyone up if there was money to be made. He had been in and out of prison all his adult life, graduating to Brixton from a stint in borstal when he was sixteen. Most recently he had been involved in selling pills to kids and Colin had seen to it that Jimmy was put away for two years for the offence. He had only been out of Pentonville for three weeks but being on the wrong side of the law was the only life Jimmy had ever known so he sat and pondered his future, nursing his beer, wondering who would give him a job. His money had run out and he badly needed a plan. He was particularly good at debt collection, possessing an ingrained evil streak. He was not popular but someone would usually throw him some work. As he pondered who to approach first he lifted his pint to drain the dregs and saw a familiar figure emerge from the doorway opposite.

Detective Inspector Colin Arnold lit a cigarette as he stood on the tiled steps of Pixie's house before walking to his car which was parked some twenty yards away.

'Well, well, well,' thought Jimmy, 'what's he up to?'

Being South London born and bred, Jimmy knew everyone on his 'manor' – every face, tart, dealer, nark, bent copper, grass and muscle. He knew Pixie of course, knew what she was, what she did for a living and where she lived.

'What would that fat fuck Colin want with that bleedin' bender Pixie?' Jimmy muttered under his breath.

He waited until Colin had driven away before emerging into the weak May sunshine from the gloom of the pub.

'What's going on?' he wondered. Smiling spitefully he

decided to do some digging – it might turn out that he had stumbled on something that would be useful, something that might be worth a few bob.

Obviously, just seeing Colin the Cunt, as Jimmy called him, come out of a house where a known transvestite prostitute lived and worked didn't prove anything but he was determined that if there was anything going on between Pixie and the policeman then he, James Sidney Watson, would turn it to his own financial benefit. He spruced himself up as best he could and visited a couple of dealers who owed him favours, mainly for not giving their names when he appeared in court. It wasn't because he was into honour amongst thieves or any of that bullshit, he was just more scared of the dealers and the kind of retribution they might come up with so preferred to take some extra time in the nick. Jimmy knew that he was not at all liked in the area – the ones that didn't need him to do some dirty work tended to give him a wide berth, more tolerated him as someone to use for whatever scummy job needed to be done. Within a couple of days Jimmy was driving for one of the dealers, known as Happy Harry, a supplier of uppers, downers and even ecstasy. His job was to drop off and pick up brown envelopes in his ancient battered Ford Escort, so inconspicuous that no one would ever waste a second glance on it or remember its driver. When he had time to spare, Jimmy sat in the pub opposite Pixie's house and kept a look out for Colin. His 'discreet enquiries' had led him to some very interesting rumours which tallied with a person like Pixie being a part of Colin's life. Jimmy was sure he had hit the jackpot. Colin the Cunt would not exactly relish his wife, let alone his bosses, knowing about his sordid sexual preferences, he thought, so now he just needed to back-up his suspicions with proof – enough to make the perverts cough up some serious money.

Evil thoughts of pure hatred spun through Jimmy's twisted mind as he formulated ideas then dismissed them as too fantastical. He knew that he couldn't just write a letter or ring Colin at work saying 'Hello, I know you're fucking a tranny brass,' he needed proper evidence. He bought a camera and took shots of Colin arriving at the house and of him leaving but he really needed one of his two targets together. He went back to Harry's and made his list of drop-offs and pick-ups, thinking hard all the time. Keeping out of the limelight, he made enough money to tick by and stayed away from trouble, biding his time, gathering information. He did his homework and discovered who lived where in the house and learnt as much about their business as he could. He knew that a couple of queers lived in one of the ground floor flats; the other flat on that floor was sometimes used by a tart who needed somewhere quieter than a back alley or a punter's car. Pixie and Ree were on the middle floor. The small flat on the top floor was empty at the moment. Gavin from the café was redecorating the place at weekends and occasionally in the evening but never before six o'clock. Apparently he was knocking off the bird that maided for Pixie – she was often in the café or the pub with him. They were tarting the place up so they could move in; someone had said they were engaged. A tasty blonde woman lived in the other top flat; she did something in the city and worked long hours. Could Colin the Cunt be visiting her? Jimmy took in all of this information and waited patiently until the time was right. He needed to get into Pixie's flat and find something, anything, that would prove that Colin was indeed visiting Pixie and not dipping his wick in the woman in the attic. He didn't think it would be enough to just place Colin at Pixie's flat either – that could be passed off as a policeman visiting his informant. No, there had to be something more and the only thing he could come up with was getting an intimate photo of them together. Night after night Jimmy sat in the pub, nursing his pint as evil conspiratorial thoughts swam about his head.

* * *

Jimmy rocked back in his chair casually reading the paper and slowly drinking the large mug of tea Gavin had placed before him some ten minutes ago. Gavin knew by now 'who was who' and Telly had warned him that Jimmy was not someone to socialize with.

'Be polite, like you do with all of them, but that skinny bastard is bad news so stay clear,' Telly had worriedly warned Gavin the first time Jimmy had come into the café.

Jimmy watched a gorgeous young girl come into the café – it was that Ree and she was over Gavin like a rash. She hugged Telly and was quickly making herself at home at the small corner table with a cup of tea. He had no way of striking up a conversation with her to glean any gossip while she was in the café as Jimmy felt sure both she and her boyfriend would have been warned off him. He was also pretty sure that, given the nature of her job, she would be unlikely to gossip about her mistress – unless there was a huge amount of cash involved. Jimmy continued to keep a note of the visits Colin made to Pixie's house and how long he spent there. He was in no rush, he thought, but one of these days he'd get the bastard.

* * *

It didn't take him long to figure out the routine of each of the residents of the house Jimmy reckoned he could get in, have a good look around Pixie's flat and get out again within about ten minutes. He was amazed at his own audacity but was also completely blinded by his hate for Colin and the desire to extract what he considered fair revenge. He took his time and waited for the opportunity to present itself while still running errands for Harry and watching the house, trying to contain his excitement and temper it with sensibility. He needed to be absolutely certain that the house was empty and then hope that no one would come home for whatever stupid reason, denying him the chance to get the dirt on Colin.

⋆ ⋆ ⋆

Jimmy sat in the pub, drinking, reading his paper, always waiting for the right time. He managed to sit and watch and wait nearly every day and was sure that as long as he kept his cool, his patience would be rewarded. The majority of the regular drinkers in the pub knew Jimmy, knew him for the thug he was and steered clear of him trying not to provoke any kind of confrontation as he was trouble, always had been, right from the off. No one bothered him as he watched and saw the front door open as Ree and Pixie emerged, all dressed up in their finery. 'What a fucking sight,' Jimmy thought to himself as he couldn't help but gawp at Pixie in the highheeled boots and bright red coat. The girl was as gorgeous as ever and looked so bloody normal. Jimmy didn't think she was on the game or had any history of it but he knew she'd make a fortune if she gave it a go. That was it, every occupant was out. 'Do it now!' he told himself. 'Before you lose your bottle.'

As Pixie and Ree climbed into a black cab and disappeared into the traffic, Jimmy's excitement at the opportunity and fear of discovery nearly made him pass out. He waited, they had definitely gone, hadn't forgotten anything, weren't coming back in hurry. He put his coat on, pulled the collar up, wound a scarf around his neck and over half his face then left the pub. He turned left but stayed on the same side of the road and walked about fifty yards until he came to a set of traffic lights where he crossed over. He walked at a normal pace back down the road towards the pub and held in his hand within his coat pocket a set of lock-picking tools – lock picking being one of the many skills he had learnt in prison. Coming to the main door of Pixie's house, he made a show of ringing one of the bells and was in the communal hallway within moments. If anyone had been watching they would have thought that he'd been buzzed in. He let the outer door shut behind him. Beads of sweat formed on his upper lip despite the cold and his certainty that every resident had left the building. Taking the stairs two at a time, he was soon outside what he was sure was Pixie's flat. Swiftly opening the door with his collection of tools, he stood in the middle of a room decorated in what he considered the worst possible taste. Chastising himself for almost forgetting what he was there for he opened a couple of doors and found Pixie's bedroom. The room was overwhelmingly cerise pink with a zebra print throw over the bed. Lava lamps projected their weird colours and shapes on the walls while he looked for signs that Colin came here for more than a chat with Pixie. The wall opposite the bed was formed of a bank of mirrored wardrobes with a gap above full of boxes, blankets and some dusty wigs that looked like strange dead animals. He opened one of the wardrobes and began to search inside although, he thought, even if he found a full police inspector's uniform inside, he'd need something more. He felt a fool and was angry with Colin all over again for making him feel this way. Could he maybe hide in the trannie's own flat? In the bedroom? Could he see for himself what they got up to? Could he take a photograph of them together? Maybe just a picture of the tart and one of her punters? 'Fucking lunatic!' he said to himself. In his mind it had all seemed so easy and there would be love letters signed 'Colin the Cunt' strewn about waiting to find their way into a blackmailer's pocket. He realized that this was going to be tricky – tricky but worth it. As he looked again at the top of the wardrobe he thought about how he could get some photographs of Pixie hard at work, preferably with the most irregular Inspector Colin Arnold.

The last of the wardrobes was piled with boxes on top of each other. Pixie's clothes hung on a rail at head height and above that was storage space. He could see a couple of spare blankets and two large suitcases. He could easily get in behind them; there was plenty of room. He took his coat off and climbed up and hid, concealing himself behind the suitcases. He practiced opening and shutting the wardrobe doors from the inside and they glided easily. But he'd need something a bit more technically advanced – it really would not be possible to hide, take pictures and then hide until he was alone again. He decided to get out of the flat fast and think hard – he had plenty of time for that. 'This had better be fucking worth it,' Jimmy thought to himself as he climbed down from the top shelf of the wardrobe taking great care not to disturb any of the clothes and boxes. He grabbed his coat, shut the wardrobe doors, closed the bedroom door carefully and left the flat, nearly falling down the stairs in his haste. With his head down as he paused in the small doorway he waited until there were no pedestrians passing. He wrapped the scarf around his face again and walked briskly up the road after shutting the outer door behind him. All the practical and logistical problems flew through Jimmy's head over the next couple of weeks. Was there a pattern to Colin's visits; what if they had a row and Colin didn't come? What if they just stayed chatting in the living room?

He continued to courier for Happy Harry and thought constantly about Colin and Pixie, watching the house, following Colin and always plotting, waiting, thinking and observing.

⋆ ⋆ ⋆

The first time Jimmy noticed that Colin stayed the whole night at Pixie's house and hopefully in Pixie's bed, he made a note of the time and the date. The second time it happened Jimmy realized it was two weeks later on the same night of the week, a Wednesday. The problem was that the tart downstairs, Pixie and the bank clerk were all in so Colin could have spent the night with any of the three. The third time Jimmy could hardly contain himself – the only people in the house were Pixie and the perverts. Yes, a pattern existed – for some reason Colin could get away with staying over-night twice a month, on a Wednesday, and it had to be that he was visiting Pixie and not the couple from downstairs. 'I've got him! I've fucking got the cunt,' Jimmy whispered to himself as he watched Colin emerge from the house on the fourth Thursday morning. He had to be sure though, had to know why Colin could get away with leaving his family home every other Wednesday.

Jimmy had cautiously followed Colin home on several occasions and now needed to see if Rita, Colin's wife, had her own fortnightly plans. He watched as she walked down the drive of her house and put an overnight bag in the boot of her car. As she drove off he followed her, taking great care to keep a couple of cars between them. Rita headed for the

North Circular and took the Watford junction driving cautiously and observing the speed limit at all times. Jimmy hoped she wasn't heading for Scotland but soon found himself following her to a housing estate where she parked on the driveway of a bungalow which looked identical to every other bungalow in the road, the only difference being the quantity and actions of the garden gnomes of each immaculate front garden. A woman, who could only have been Rita's mother, stood at the open door and embraced her daughter warmly as they entered the bungalow together, Rita carrying her small tartan bag.

'Aww, she goes to see her old mum. Fucking lovely,' Jimmy gloated.

* * *

Nikki gave birth to a huge, healthy baby boy on 29 July. A day more significant to Telly than the Royal Wedding. A lavish baptism was held soon afterwards. The baby, named after both his grandfathers, was the most perfectly behaved angel all day as he was fussed over and petted by Telly's mother and sisters who were competing against Nikki's mother-in-law and her sisters for a chance to hold the baby. Pixie was 'godmother' to baby Telly which raised more than a few eyebrows but Telly senior was a loyal friend to Pixie and had no prejudices or judgements. His old schoolfriend Keith, who still ran the shelter, stood proudly in the church as he too became a godparent. Keith and Gavin had now become great friends; Gavin never forgetting that this man had had faith in him and had given him a chance to climb out of the gutter, literally. He still helped out at the shelter regularly and Ree often accompanied him, helping in any way she could.

Nikki would not be coming back to work at the café now that she was a mother; both Telly and Nikki's husband Andreas were very traditional and looked forward to many more children. Keith found a young lad to replace Nikki and the storeroom opposite Gavin's bedsit was turned into another bedroom. Mark claimed to be sixteen but he slipped up a couple of times and it soon became obvious he was probably only fourteen or fifteen at a stretch. Gavin and Mark quickly became friends over the weeks, Gavin never failing to be amazed at the number of homeless kids in London and appalled at the terrible lives they had led. Circumstances had fortunately brought Mark to Keith who, with Telly's help, was able to give another young runaway the chance to start again. Gavin felt that he had gained a younger brother in Mark and Mark idolized Gavin.

* * *

Pixie took her wig off and carefully placed it on the bald polystyrene head on her vast dressing-table. She looked at herself critically in the mirror examining the crow's feet and the lines around her mouth. She was now fifty-two and was tired – tired of the punters and tired of hiding away when all she really wanted to do was live openly with Colin without people thinking them some kind of freak show. Colin was due for retirement soon and they didn't want anything to rock the boat now, they had been so careful for so long. She had taken a backseat while Colin's older kids had finished university and now were married and had families of their own. Another year and she would be away from this life. They loved to talk about where they would go eventually – maybe the Costa del Sol, or a quiet tropical island on the other side of the world. Pixie snapped back into reality and reached for the pot of baby lotion and the cotton wool. She wiped away the theatrical make-up and peeled off the false eyelashes. She pinged off the false nails and wiped Pixie away. Alan Dixon came out of the shower ten minutes later, dressed in a suit and tie and, collecting everything he needed, he left the house.

* * *

Jimmy was getting a pint at the bar and failed to see the neat-looking middle-aged man hop into a taxi and disappear with all the other faceless nameless millions who entered the city every day.

* * *

Half an hour later the receptionist called Alan's name.

'Mr Dixon, excuse me, Mr Dixon, Mr Wells is ready for you now.'

Alan smiled to himself, as he realized the girl was talking to him. It was only ever at these annual meetings anyone ever called him Mister anything! He stood, dropped the magazine he had been reading back onto the coffee table and walked into the office of his solicitor and old schoolfriend Martin Wells. The two men shook hands warmly and exchanged pleasantries. Alan took the seat indicated and the young receptionist came in with a tray of tea and biscuits. Leaving them alone, she closed the door behind her.

'OK, well Martin I need to make a few changes to my will and could you then start looking for a place for somewhere for Colin and me to retire to; Marbella I believe is the place to be'. Alan had absolute trust in Martin's judgement and

Martin was the only person Alan had ever confided in over his relationship with Colin.

With business over the pair wandered over to an Italian restaurant where no one gave them a second glance.

Chapter Eight

Gavin was being paid more than just pocket money now as he had taken over most of the day-to-day running of the café. Telly loved to spend time with his grandson and knew that his business was in good hands with 'the lads'. Gavin had never had any particular ambitions when he was growing up, had never given any thought to what he would do when he left school and was very happy running a café. He got on well with his customers taking plenty of good-humoured ribbing about being a bloody northerner. Telly paid for him to take driving lessons and, when he had passed his test on the first attempt, threw him the keys to the van – his new duties would now include shopping at the wholesalers. A shrewd Greek businessman, Telly declared his ulterior motive!

⋆ ⋆ ⋆

Ree saw Gavin nearly every day – Telly adored the girl and thought she was good for his manager though he was constantly warning Gavin to behave himself and treat Ree with the respect due to a beautiful young woman. Gavin had coaxed Ree's painful story from her and had told her about the beatings he had endured and the drunken abuse from his father. The pair of them were far too old for their years in many ways and had seen too much. Often a youngster would come into the café, both boys and girls, trying to make a mug of hot sweet tea last an hour. Gavin could spot a runaway at fifty yards and, with Telly's blessing, would place a huge breakfast in front of the child and assure the face behind the hugely surprised eyes that it was a no strings attached 'welcome to London' gift. He would always try to persuade them to visit Keith where he knew that at least a slither of safety and sanctuary would be offered; the alternatives were often too awful to contemplate.

* * *

Pixie talked to Ree about her dreams of a life in the sun, away from the daily grind that was London. She had never directly mentioned Colin in these discussions but Ree was aware that Colin was a regular visitor and was very special to Pixie.

'One more year, love, one more year and Aunty Pixie will jack it all in, sell up and sail over the horizon with her true love.'

'You and Gav were made for each other. You can go and help him with the caff and live happily ever after like love's young dream. I want plenty of notice of the wedding though, got to find something really special in my role as mother of the bride!'

Ree rolled her eyes and clicked her tongue at Pixie's nonsense, happy that her boss actually cared enough about her to speak to her this way.

* * *

It was Tuesday morning and they were wandering around the nearby street market, oblivious to the few sideways glances from those to whom Pixie was a novelty. The regulars at the market and the stallholders were accustomed to her and never gave a second thought to her being 'different'. Ree laughed until her belly ached as Pixie described her dream wedding outfit – she had been unaware that leopard prints came in tangerine orange.

* * *

Meanwhile, Jimmy prepared to shatter their world.

The week before had seen him in the backroom of a camera shop on the Tottenham Court Road. Steve, the owner, knew all about the latest gear and how to use it – and was adept at improving on the most recent designs.

Jimmy knew about some candid shots Steve had circulated of women getting changed at the local swimming pool and explained that he wanted to do something similar.

'Well mate, I used a camera designed for guys wanting pictures of wildlife,' Steve said. 'It's got a motion sensor, is very quiet and, with the right film, will capture and focus on everything.

'You can borrow it for a reasonable fee but if I don't get it back in one piece then you'll owe me more money than you've ever earned either honestly or dishonestly. I'll even develop the film for you too, mate – if the pics are as tasty as the ones I took then we could do some business together!'

* * *

On Wednesday morning, certain that no one was in, Jimmy used his lock picks to get into the main entrance to Pixie's house and then, a few moments later, into her flat. Quietly closing the door behind him, he put his gloves on and placed the bulky camera under the rubbish on top of the wardrobe.

He hoped that the angle would capture anything that happened in the room and was sure that even the light coming from Pixie's lava lamps would be sufficient to capture the action.

Chapter Nine

Thankful that it was finally five thirty again, Gavin flipped the sign on the door to closed and breathed a huge sigh of relief. A car alarm had woken him the previous night and sleep had evaded him after that, tossing and turning until 6 a.m. when he finally hauled his tired body from his bed.

'Time gentlemen please, finish your bloody tea and piss off, go home to your beautiful wives and don't darken my door until tomorrow, come on, bugger off!'

As they laughed and joked with the last few stragglers, finally bolting the door after them, Gavin and Mark finished clearing the remaining plates and mugs from the tables, stacked the chairs and washed the floor.

A tapping at the door brought Gavin round from his daydreams and he saw a youth of about Mark's age waving at him through the glass. Mark waved in recognition and unlocked the door beckoning the boy inside.

'Gav, this is my mate Gary. We're going out later, up Catford Dogs.'

This was the first of Mark's friends Gavin had met and he was pleased to see his adopted brother getting on with a normal life, making friends and enjoying himself.

The laundry was collected up, the dishwasher turned on for the last time, rubbish bagged and finally the working day was over. Gavin told Mark to use the bathroom first as he was not due to see Ree until much later and he could see that Mark was itching to get going. He made himself a sandwich and flopped down on his bed, kicking his shoes off and flicking the TV on. A young *Blue Peter* presenter was giving instructions on how to make 'your very own Tracy Island' out of sticky backed plastic, cornflake packets, skill and a huge dose of imagination. Mildly amused but not really paying much attention, Gavin ate the sandwich then drifted off to sleep.

* * *

A banging on his door woke him sharply.

'See ya Gav, got me keys this time so I won't be fetching you out of bed in the wee small hours!' Groggily, Gavin muttered an acknowledgement and slowly came out of his deep sleep. It was almost seven o'clock, *Blue Peter* and the news were over a long time ago! He rubbed his eyes and shook himself as he stood up, took off his dirty clothes, grabbed his dressing gown and headed for the bathroom. Concerned that he would fall asleep in the bath he opted for a shower – the rivulets of hot water woke him up and he stood under them, savouring the heat, scrubbing the sweat and smells of the day from his hair and body.

The phone was ringing as he stepped from the shower, so, wrapping his towel around his waist, he dashed to the hallway and picked it up, correctly guessing that it would be Ree. They agreed to meet at Pixie's at 8 p.m. once Ree had finished work. Together they would cook some supper then watch TV and maybe go to the pub across the road for a quick drink. Gavin replaced the handset then wandered back to the bathroom where he shaved, cleaned his teeth and got dressed. As he did so he thought about his life and how happy he was now, compared to this time three years ago – it was a long way from sleeping rough with cold, rain, loneliness and social misfits his only companions. Now he had a job he enjoyed, a gorgeous girlfriend, a warm secure place to live and good friends. Life was pretty wonderful, all things considered.

* * *

Colin ate his cornflakes while Rita talked at him. She rambled on about their children, a proposed visit to the garden centre, gossip about the neighbours, friends at the golf club, the ongoing saga of her mother's health. He mumbled responses from time to time and she seemed satisfied. Her car needed a service and did he know that the garage now offered a full valet service? She would make the necessary arrangements. She fancied a curry tonight, did he? Could he let her know what time he was likely to be home, she might go to the cinema with her sister if he was not at home that night in time for supper so be sure to ring. Colin, a typical man, read his *Sun* back to front, catching up with the football results and having a look at what was on the TV that night. A quick flick to the front page and he was done. Colin hated cornflakes and would have loved a bacon sandwich, dripping in HP sauce and melted butter, but Rita wouldn't hear of it and insisted that he cut down on calories. In reality she couldn't be bothered with the mess of a dirty frying pan and Colin wasn't fooled. He went along with everything, from the sham that was breakfast to the more serious sham that was their marriage. The pair of them played the game, biding their time until eventually one of them cracked and reached a point of no return. Hopefully this would not be until their youngest daughter had finished university, and Colin could retire. Rita and Colin hadn't shared a bed for years. Rita long suspected that her husband was seeing someone on the side and, as long as no one knew for sure and it didn't interfere with everyone else's perception of them as a couple, she didn't really care. He was generous with the housekeeping and had never made too many demands of her in bed which suited her just fine. She had tried to be a decent wife and mother but their marriage had been necessitated through a split condom and an irate father, not love. Life was by no means perfect, just adequate as far as Rita was concerned. It was better than many of her friends' marriages and at least she wasn't short of money and had her daughters. She was content, for the time being.

Hearing the letterbox slam, she collected the three letters from the mat in the porch, a recent addition of which she was very proud. Slightly snobbish, she made sure none of the neighbours saw her in her dressing gown as she scooped the mail up and returned to the kitchen. Placing the mail on the table in front of Colin she said: 'All for you. Do you want toast?'

Checking his watch, Colin muttered a quick 'No thanks,' shoved the mail in his inside pocket, grabbed his car keys, kissed Rita's habitually proffered cheek and left the house. He had a late start to the day as he was giving evidence in court and it was great to have had a bit of a lie-in. Hopefully he would be finished at a reasonable time and he could visit Pixie. With that thought in his head, he drove to Woolwich magistrates' court, showed his badge to the ancient security guard and drove into the reserved parking bay. Finding himself with a good twenty minutes to spare, he pulled out his notebook and dislodged the mail from the same pocket. He opened a gas bill, a circular from his football team's supporters' club and the third, which made him retch. It was so amateurish it was nearly funny, only he knew it was deadly serious. The letters had been cut from a newspaper; Colin wondered how long it must have taken the bastard to do it. Whoever it was had been watching too many films, read too many bad detective novels. But the photos were clear enough – all three of them. One with him in Pixie's bedroom fully dressed but exchanging a kiss and the other two of them curled up together, naked, leaving absolutely nothing to the imagination. The clumsy letter informed Colin that unless the sum of twenty thousand pounds was left in a designated place of which he would be notified, Colin's sexual activities would be brought to the attention of his superiors and his wife and children. A surge of disbelief then rage hit Colin like a smack in the kidneys and he felt overwhelmed with hatred for the perpetrator of this vile attack on his life. A tap on his car window brought him round. It was the old security guard, Alfie.

'Come on Sir, you'd better get a shift on, you know what this judge is like, a right old bugger.'

Colin swiftly folded the letter around the photographs and shoved it back into his inside pocket. He slowly climbed out of the car and, forcing a smile at the old boy, offered him a cigarette. Lighting one for himself, he smoked it hard and quickly as he made his way to the court, trying to compose himself while feeling like his world had fallen down and had been smashed into a million pieces.

* * *

Pixie's face was a mess, multicoloured and wet, the mascara mingled with the blue and gold of her eye shadow in hideous streaks over her face. Tears and more tears ran down her cheeks as Colin tried to comfort her. He had come straight to

Pixie's after his stint in the witness box, desperate to finish giving evidence and talk to Pixie about what the hell they were going to do. What the fuck could they do? How the hell had this been possible? Who hated them enough to do this? The only person Pixie had ever actually told about Colin was Martin Wells and Pixie would bet her life that this rich solicitor whom she had known all his life was nothing to do with the blackmail. Telly had an idea about Pixie and Colin's relationship as did Gavin and Nikki and Ree definitely knew that Colin visited often but nothing had ever been said about Colin being a policeman.

'I'm being totally honest here Pix, if this gets out I could be left penniless. No pension, no job – Rita will get the fucking lot and my kids will disown me. What fucking good will I be to you if I'm penniless?'

'I couldn't give a fuck about the money, I've got enough for both of us love – there's only so much fucking lipstick and nail varnish a girl can buy you know! And, don't forget I own the house. One more year, that's all we need until you retire and your Louise finishes university. One more fucking poxy year.'

The most consistent plan had been to buy a place in Spain and just disappear when Colin retired and Colin's youngest had finished her studies. He was currently still subsidizing her despite the decent grant and he wanted her to graduate without a huge drama or anything that would affect her chances of getting a first, which was where she was headed. He would then sign the unencumbered house over to Rita, leave her a few quid in the bank and end his days in a whirl of fun and debauchery with Pixie, the love of his life who would be free to be who and what she wanted to be. And no one was going to ruin that for them of that they were both absolutely determined. So, as far as they could see they didn't have many options. They could pay the blackmailer off and risk them coming back for more or they could sit tight and do nothing, hoping that whoever it was lost their nerve and did nothing.

'I could fucking kill the bastard Pix, fucking kill them.'

Colin left Pixie's house with a face like thunder; Jimmy watched him from the pub.

Chapter Ten

Ree had no idea what was wrong but whatever the matter was with Pixie it was something more important than a broken finger nail or a dodgy punter. Pixie told Ree to cancel her clients for that evening. It was obvious she had been crying because her eyes made her look like a panda. Her face was blotchy and swollen, she wasn't wearing a wig and just sat staring at the TV, chain smoking. Every so often she pulled a fresh tissue from the box on the mirrored glass coffee table in front of her. She told Ree that she was fine, a tiff with a friend, nothing else.

'Go see a film with Gavin love, do something nice together eh?'

Not needing to be told twice, Ree took the hint and phoned the café. She told Gavin she needed to make herself scarce and did he fancy going out? She whispered down the phone that she thought Colin and Pixie might have had a tiff – she had let him in. It was nearly five thirty so Ree arranged to meet within the hour. She would help with the trip to the wholesalers and then they would go to the Odeon on Leicester Square – her treat. Ree hadn't been to the cinema for ages and as much as she was sad for Pixie and whatever it was that had upset her, she was happy to have a night out with her boyfriend – she might even stay with him tonight after the film as they were now almost officially engaged. Ree took a quick shower, changed into a clean pair of jeans and new cotton blouse, grabbed her handbag, called out goodbye to Pixie and strolled off to the café to find her date.

As Ree arrived at the café Mark was mopping the floor while Gavin nipped across the road to the bank and dropped the day's takings in the night safe. He reappeared and Ree wouldn't let him anywhere near her – he stank of sweat, grease and cigarettes. The boys went to their respective rooms and fought over who would get to use the bathroom first, a fight Gavin won as he needed to get the wholesaler errand done with as soon as possible and then spend the rest of the evening gazing into Ree's beautiful face. She flipped the closed sign on the door and noticed Jimmy – the horrible weasel of a man – strolling up the road. He turned and grinned at her as he saw her through the glass – the bloke was a creep, Telly was right.

Kicking off her boots, Ree went to Gavin's room and lay back on the bed to wait. The original lumpy single bed had long since been replaced by a double divan and Gavin had made an effort to make the small room as homely as possible. Ree could hear Gavin singing in the bathroom as he showered and shaved in readiness for their night out and she indulged in her favourite daydream – marriage, kids, a house in the country with roses around the door. Realistically, they would have to be near the café for Gavin and work, but they could still have a place around here maybe, with a small garden, a cat and maybe a dog too.

'Oi, dreaming about John Travolta again are you? Or some other bloke with a hairy chest and big medallion and loads of money? Don't suppose you were thinking about me, were you?'

Gavin threw his wet towel at Ree and she chucked it back at him. Lovingly Ree watched Gavin as he picked out a shirt and climbed into a pair of jeans. This man's body and soul were hers. She had never felt happier, safer or more content in her entire life. An hour later they were sitting on the top of a bus bound for Leicester Square, arms entwined, looking forward to the night out and a future together.

* * *

The Tanners Arms was warm and stuffy, thick with smoke and stale air. A crowd of noisy youngsters were next to the juke box, dancing and messing around, high on life and pints of snakebite laced with blackcurrant. Gus, the landlord, knew that most of them were a year or two shy of eighteen but as long as they behaved themselves he saw no harm in their fun. Jimmy sat at his usual table, alone, swirling a brandy around the bloated glass, watching the front door of the house opposite as he held a book in front of him, pretending to read. The happiness of the kids across the other side of the room annoyed him; somehow they made him feel even more isolated and alone. He watched Ree leave the house and stop to pull the door shut behind her and give it a push to check it was closed properly. Pixie was now alone. The punters had come and gone and the maid looked as though she was out for the night. After checking that Ree was definitely at the café and hadn't just gone out for milk or another quick errand, Jimmy went to one of the many telephone boxes outside London Bridge Station. Pixie, he knew, would be alone as she didn't see punters without her maid in the flat. He finally found a phone box that worked and dialled Pixie's number who picked the phone up immediately, answering without her usual perky tone.

'I guess your lover has told you about a letter he got. Tell him that I want the money by next Friday – twenty grand in used untraceable notes. I'll let you know where and when. Don't fuck me about or you'll both regret it.'

Feeling like Mr Big himself, Jimmy took the handkerchief away from his mouth and replaced the receiver, grinning from ear to ear. Pixie nearly passed out with shock and fear but had the sense to write down what had been said so she could show Colin. Trembling, she poured herself a very generous measure of Smirnoff and sobbed for the hundredth time that day, as she imagined all her dreams fading into the distance.

* * *

Ree and Gavin arrived back at the café at about 10.30 p.m. and decided that Ree would stay over because of Pixie's earlier black mood. When the alarm clock loudly announced the new day at the ungodly hour of 6 a.m. they both groaned and couldn't believe how quickly the morning had come around. Reluctantly the pair dragged themselves out of bed and began their respective days, Gavin banging on Mark's door and waking him up and Ree quietly making her way back to her own flat after taking great delight in informing Gavin that she was going back to bed for a couple of hours.

Pixie felt as if she had hardly slept all night when Ree knocked on her flat door at 9 a.m. with a cup of tea. She let herself in and carefully placed the cup on the table next to Pixie and sat on the bed beside her.

'Pix, come on, I know you're not asleep. Tell me what's wrong.'

Pixie turned over and sat up, plumping her satin and lace pillows into a comfortable position. She looked as tired and worn as she felt, her eyes filling up with tears as she tried to find the words to explain to Ree what had happened. Colin had warned Pixie not to discuss the blackmail with anyone, until they had decided what to do, but Pixie was so distraught that she had to speak to someone and there really was no one after Colin and Martin she trusted more than Ree.

Ree was stunned; horrified that someone could even contemplate doing something so evil. What sort of terrible people walked the earth? Why the hell couldn't everyone just leave each other alone? Fucking parasites!

'I'm going to pay him, I don't care what Colin says. There's no way I'm going to let anyone fuck our plans up and this piece of shit can have his twenty fucking grand. We've only got to live like this for another year then Colin retires and we can just go. If this fucking blackmailer comes back for more then we'll be long gone, babes.'

Pixie made it sound so easy but somehow Ree didn't think it would be that simple. Half an hour later Colin turned up and, always honest, Pixie admitted that she had told Ree everything. Colin was furious at first, not because he was ashamed or embarrassed but because he was a very proud man and was used to being in control. Ree made yet more tea and the three of them sat on Pixie's bed wondering who the hell could do such a terrible thing, who on earth knew and how the hell had they managed to take the photos in the first place.

Pixie changed the subject and tried to be more upbeat, asking Ree what film she had seen. Ree laughed and told them about the lovely meal they had had, the crappy film they had seen and how smelly Gavin was each day after work.

'Actually, I think that working in that bloody café with all that grease is making him lose weight. If he's not careful he'll end up like that skinny git with the pointy face, you know, Jimmy wotsit. Saw him yesterday, creepy sod. He comes in the café all the time, never eats anything. Gav says he's bad for business! He's always in that pub across the road too, the Tanners Arms. He's never with anyone – just sits and watches everybody.'

Realization dawned on Colin and Pixie simultaneously. Who else hated Colin enough? Who else hung about like a bad smell?

'What do you mean Ree, love, sits in the pub?' Colin asked her cautiously.

'Well you know, I seem to see him everywhere. Bump into him in the shop when I get milk, see him in the café. He's always at the pub and just reads a paper and watches out of the window. Always on his own. Bad sign that ain't it, when a bloke's got no friends? There's something really nasty about him. I know he works for Harry, and it's his job to be a tosser, but he's sort of worse than the rest. Do you know what I mean?'

Colin knew exactly what she meant and both he and Pixie were positive they now knew who the blackmailer was. But what they should do about it was another matter.

Chapter Eleven

Propping himself up on his bed, leaning against the shabby faded floral headboard, Jimmy thought of how he would spend Pixie and Colin's money. He was earning a more than decent wage working for Happy Harry, and to have a large lump of cash would be fantastic, but the icing on the cake for him would be to see Colin the Cunt suffer, just like he had. Actually, it was no longer about money – just making Colin squirm – humiliating him the way that he had been humiliated during his years inside. Jimmy blamed Colin for everything. He was the man responsible for all his problems and James Sidney Watson couldn't wait to wreak his revenge.

Oddly enough, Jimmy was not the product of a broken home or an abandoning and neglectful mother. His parents lived in Beckenham now and were decent people although they had grown up in the Southwark area which was where Jimmy was born and had lived until he was twelve. Ironically the family had moved to Kent when Jimmy had started senior school in order to give him a good education and take him away from the trouble in London. At his first opportunity though, their son had returned to the big smoke and courted trouble, only returning to Beckenham when he needed money or a place to hide out in between his various and repeated holidays at Her Majesty's pleasure. Some people are a product of their environment but Jimmy was just born inherently bad.

Colin and Pixie rarely talked about anything else but how to stop Jimmy, for by now they were convinced he was the blackmailer. He was the only one that would stoop so low and had been placed nearby. How could Ree, fairly new to the area, have spotted him while both Colin and Pixie had failed to see the shit on their own doorstep? They spent hours going over and over different plans and scenarios. Pixie was sure that if they just paid Jimmy he would go away and no one would come to any harm – no one would ever know and they could all just carry on with their lives – a bit poorer but happy.

Colin, however, knew Jimmy for what he was and realized that he would never be satisfied. Once he had had a taste of the money and, more essentially, the power it gave him over Colin, he would unquestionably be back for a second helping, a third and the equivalent of dessert and coffee. After a day and night spent talking, crying, arguing and finally agreeing, Colin took charge and told Pixie he would deal with it. She was to forget the whole episode once it was over and never mention it again. Colin's solution was drastic but he had made his mind up. Jimmy would have to die. Pixie was horrified but gave in to Colin because she knew he wouldn't accept any other course of action and this evil man had placed in jeopardy every good thing in her life. It was as good as done, all that remained was just that, to get on and get it done! They would wait for Jimmy to make contact with Pixie and tell them where and how to pay the money. Aware that he was being watched as well as being a watcher, Colin tried to carry on as normally as possible and that meant going to work, going home, staying overnight with Pixie every other Wednesday – just doing normal Colin stuff.

Over the years he had had dealings with some very nasty people, evil, vicious bad people and an awful lot of them owed him favours. Colin was an old-fashioned copper; he had joined the force aged nineteen, when the Krays still ran London and no one mugged old ladies. He was of the old school and was highly respected by his fellow officers and by the criminal fraternity. Pacing his office, he considered the possibilities – who could he trust enough to ask? He could certainly find someone who could remove the Jimmy problem and he knew a good few who would enjoy doing it, but if the guy was caught then he'd be responsible for someone going down for doing him a favour and the shit could really hit the fan. No, Colin decided, he'd have to do his own dirty work; so first he had to get a gun – the quickest and easiest way to sort the bastard out. So, who could he lean on to obtain a clean weapon? Buying one was not an option and 'borrowing' one from the evidence cupboard was out of the question.

Shaking his last cigarette from the packet of Rothmans on his desk, he blew the smoke out in rings, thinking hard. Who owed him big time? Who hated Jimmy enough so that if anything did go wrong they would keep their cool and say nothing? If it all went wrong and he was front page news and banged up for murder then the gun would have to be totally untraceable – the last thing he needed was some guy after him because of a link to a dodgy shooter. Who would rejoice in Jimmy's death? There were plenty of villains who fitted the bill. An image entered Colin's head – a guy he'd not seen or heard of in years. Grabbing his jacket and car keys he almost ran out of the building, side-stepping his sergeant who was about to enter.

'Hi Lance, something's come up, will be a couple of hours, talk when I get back,' Colin shouted over his shoulder as he raced down the front steps.

Twenty minutes later, he was knocking on the door of a very respectable looking building in Dean Street in London's

Soho. Colin studied the brass plaque screwed into the wall. He chuckled to himself at the outward appearance of the place which seemed to suggest respectability but in reality hid a network of drugs and prostitution. He smiled as he spoke into the intercom.

'Open the fucking door Sid. I need a favour from you, for a change.'

Jimmy had cost Sid three years of freedom many years ago. He knew a man who could assist Colin and absolutely no questions would be asked, there would be no enquiries as to why Colin wanted the gun and Colin knew that if by some stroke of bad luck it all went wrong and Sid read about the death of either a Met copper or saw a nasty face in his daily newspaper one morning while enjoying his cornflakes and a cup of tea, well, his lips would remain sealed tighter than if his cereal bowl was full of cow shit. The gun would be untraceable and if things did go badly for Colin, Sid would have no connection to anybody or anything to do with the matter. Sid and Colin both also understood that any debts Sid owed to Colin would be satisfied, paid in full.

* * *

The very idea that Colin would have worked out the identity of his blackmailer had never occurred to Jimmy who had been careful not to encounter Colin or Pixie for months now. He returned to the pay phone outside London Bridge Station which miraculously still hadn't been vandalized and dialled Pixie's number.

Pixie had sat next to the phone for days, waiting for the call, placing all her years of love and trust in Colin. Each time it rang and it turned out to be a punter wanting an hour of pleasure, she passed the phone to Ree to make the booking for the following week. Normal, Colin had instructed – carry on as normal. At 6.15 p.m. the phone rang and Pixie's heart raced in fear and anticipation as it had done every other time she had heard the trill of the phone that day. This time it was him.

'Just listen to me. I want the money left at Victoria Station in a locker at the left luggage centre at the back of the station on the right. The number of the locker is 197. The locker will be open, put the money inside and push the door shut, turn the catch and its self-locking. And I want the money there by 5 p.m. this Thursday or the lovely Rita will get a very nasty shock when she opens this envelope and looks at some very entertaining photos of you and her old man. Another set will be on the desk of Detective Chief Inspector Carson, who will get to see more of his esteemed colleague than he has a care to. Don't fuck me around. Not there by five on Thursday, then my letters will catch the last post.'

'But you said Friday. I need until then to get the cash together.'

'My game lady, my rules. Thursday or you and your boyfriend are fucked and not in a good way.'

The line went dead, Pixie didn't move, still holding the phone to her ear as the tears began to fall yet again.

Chapter Twelve

The man stood before the bank of left luggage lockers, took a key from his pocket, opened the locker numbered 197, removed a canvas holdall and left the key in the lock, the door gently swinging to and fro. Gripping the holdall tightly and without pausing to check its contents, he strode through the crowds disappearing down into the chaos of the Victoria line. It was exactly 5.15 p.m., on Friday, twenty-four hours and fifteen minutes since Jimmy's deadline had passed. Twenty-four hours and fifteen minutes of pure torture for Jimmy, knowing from a kid happy to watch the locker for a few hours in return for a bag of weed that a Greek-looking guy had left the bag as instructed. Malc having collected the bag would not dare open it fearing retribution should anything be amiss. Harry was that sort of man, his reputation preceded him and anyone with half a brain showed respect. So Malc carried out the job ordered by Harry's henchman and asked no questions.

Jimmy sat on the bed in his sparse flat in Vauxhall Bridge Road enduring the agonizing wait until Malc arrived at the appointed time and place of their meeting. Malc had instructions to get on the Victoria line in the first instance and spend about three hours jumping on and off trains, changing direction and tube lines to ensure that he wasn't followed. Jimmy was terrified of failure as it had all been like clockwork so far – he'd got the pictures easily enough and now just needed to wait for his reward. He'd send the pictures to Rita and the Met on Saturday – did Colin the Cunt and his girlfriend with the penis really think that he wouldn't? Yes, Detective Chief Inspector Carson and the lovely Rita's week would start very badly indeed.

* * *

Colin called in help from everyone he could remember who owed him the slightest favour. He didn't need to explain himself and no one had a clue if what they were being asked to do was official but they guessed that it probably wasn't. As a man of integrity, Colin inspired everyone involved to do as they were asked without as much as a second thought as to whether this was kosher or not. Colin was Colin so you did as he asked because he commanded respect.

Pixie had remained at her flat, business as usual, getting back to normal, just as Colin had told her. Telly had not known why he was making the journey or what was in the bag. He had been asked to take a holdall to Victoria and drop it in a locker, click the door shut and return to the café. He understood his instructions and knew that there were reasons that he had been selected for this task but he had no intention of being more involved than that and did not want to know more. He just did as his friend Pixie had asked and intended to forget that the trip to Victoria had ever taken place.

A few days' prior to Telly dropping the bag at Victoria, Colin had sat in the private back room of a pub in Pimlico and told the nine other occupants that at 4.30 p.m. on Friday a bag would be left in locker number 197 at Victoria by an associate of his whose identity was irrelevant. The landlord of the Leather Bottle would swear in the highest court in the land that he did not know Colin and had never seen him nor any of the other attendees of the meeting that night or indeed at any other time in his life. Colin described the bag to his assembled guests and explained that he wanted to know as soon as it was collected and that whoever collected the bag was to be followed even if he went to Timbuktu. When the chase stopped, Colin said, he needed to know where it finished and their job would be done.

* * *

Jimmy was far from stupid but his bitterness and greed were clouding his judgement and making him sloppy. He had taken the bet that Colin and Pixie would pay up and disappear from South London virtually overnight. Sure, the pictures received by Rita and the DCI wouldn't have as much impact, but it would be enough to know that Colin's secret life had been exposed. Malc had been waiting around at Victoria Station's various cafés and bars watching to see if he could spot a watcher. He saw the tramp, he saw the men opposite having a drink together before they went home, he saw the girl kissing her boyfriend as she waited for a train but he didn't see them all watching him. As he boarded his first underground train of the evening he had no idea that there were nine people ready to do the same.

* * *

Sitting in the car park of an Indian restaurant at Elephant and Castle Jimmy shivered in anticipation. He had stolen the nondescript blue Austin Allegro he was sitting in about an hour ago from a hotel car park in Charing Cross having watched its occupants check in, dump their cases then leave again for the theatre across the street. The car wouldn't be reported as missing for hours yet and he would be long gone by then.

Pulling his scarf over most of his face and keeping his collar up, Jimmy constantly glanced at his watch, the minutes passed excruciatingly slowly. Agony.

Colin's radio crackled into life.

'Elephant and Castle tube. He's early by the looks of things. He's still got the holdall with him. We'll stay with him until you tell us to go. No sign of anyone else but he's staying put.'

Jimmy could see Malc standing just in the entrance of the station trying to stay warm as it was cold outside, but he was about thirty minutes early so he decided to sit and wait to be sure that there was no funny business by anyone. If his courier had opened the bag and it had the money rather than being stuffed with Pixie's dirty lingerie then, Jimmy reckoned, the space outside the station would have been empty and Malc would be buying rounds all night at some seedy strip joint. He watched as Malc shifted his considerable mass from leg to leg, banging his gloved hands together in a futile effort to keep warm. He saw a young couple emerge hand in hand from the station, walk past Malc and enter the Indian, sit down and order drinks while they considered the menu. Not once did he see them look out of the window or look at him in the stolen car. Some City boys went into the pub next to the restaurant, they were laughing and joking; he could see them through the brightly lit windows chink their pints together and drink. They gestured towards the dartboard and began a game. Then four half-cut blokes came around the corner and entered the chippy on the other side of the pub. They leant against the high stainless steel counter as they chatted to the buxom blonde taking their order. One of the men left the shop, crossed the road and had a piss behind a pillar about six feet from where Jimmy sat. When the man saw Jimmy sitting there he grimaced and shrugged his shoulders. Jimmy returned the smile with a half grin in understanding and acknowledgement – bloody pubs and their 'toilets are for customers' use only' rules. As the man returned to his friends, another of the men weaved across the road – he looked more drunk than his mate. Jimmy watched as he leant against a nearby car and urinated against its rear wheel. He registered a mild envy as he noticed that the man's penis looked particularly large.

Colin watched Jimmy from the back of the car as the guy made a show of finishing his piss – milking the last drops onto the ground. He whispered to Colin and the woman inside, confirming the exact location of the man they had followed.

Marcia got out and locked the door, shaking her head in disgust. She crossed the road and entered the chippy.

Jimmy had glanced up and seen the woman then dismissed her just as quickly. 'Got a bit of an eye-full there girl eh?' he thought.

Colin crawled into the driving seat and slid down as low as he could without being seen, holding the spare set of keys in his hand, anticipating that the man his friends had followed would either approach Jimmy's car on a signal or at a prearranged time. It was five to nine. Colin had guessed right. Five minutes later Malc walked away from the station and straight to the car park. Jimmy flashed the interior light of the car on and off twice, Malc opened the passenger door, placed the holdall on the seat, shut the door and walked back to the station. Jimmy could hardly breathe and, despite the cold night air, his sweat made his shirt stick uncomfortably to his skin. Colin knew that he would have to follow Jimmy and take the first opportunity to use his gun and retrieve the cash.

Jimmy started up the engine of his car, stalling before driving out of the car park. Colin watched him drive away and take a left turn disappearing into the light traffic. Pulling on one of Pixie's long black curly wigs he followed Jimmy at an unnoticeable distance. Jimmy's head was spinning and at the first opportunity he yanked open the holdall's zip and, shaking, flicked through the twenty pound notes. 'I've done it,' he said. 'I've fucking done it!'

He desperately wanted a drink, his pulse was racing and his heart was thumping. He needed to calm down and also needed to dump the car just in case it had been reported as stolen. The last thing he wanted right now was to get stopped and have to explain away twenty grand. He abandoned the car at the top of Southwark Street, leaving the keys in the ignition. He had worn gloves at all times and never once had his bare hands touched the interior. He walked around the corner, past the shuttered café and turned brazenly into the front bar of the Tanners Arms directly opposite Pixie's house. Where better to celebrate than in the pub where it had all begun? Colin could not believe what he was seeing – was Jimmy completely mad or was he about to approach Pixie? He parked the car. He sat. He waited.

* * *

When the large brandy arrived, Jimmy paid for it with one of Pixie's twenty pound notes. He threw the drink back in one mouthful and ordered another which quickly followed the first down the throat of the celebrating crook. Gavin and Ree were sitting in the saloon bar with a few friends listening to the explicit lyrics of the latest song by Frankie Goes to Hollywood. They were a little shocked by the words coming from the juke box. Knowing that Colin was sorting their problem out, Pixie had claimed to have one of her headaches and had taken a couple of sleeping tablets before going to bed. It was gone ten o'clock – past Gavin's usual bedtime even on a Friday night. Ree stood up and yawned, Gavin doing the same as they put their coats on.

They were planning on staying at the café and, calling goodnight to Gus the landlord, they walked arm in arm into the street. Jimmy stood before them, having left the public bar at the same time as the pair. He was calmer now because of the brandy but seeing them so happy riled him.

'Well, well, well. The young lovers,' he said mockingly. 'I'm going your way, you can keep me company.'

Colin stood in the shadows and watched nervously from across the road as Gavin, Ree and Jimmy all turned left and started to walk. Could the three of them be in it together? No, he decided, remembering Ree's comments, it could only be a coincidence.

Given that the café was only three or four minutes' walk away Ree and Gavin made a grimace at each other but decided to tolerate Jimmy and they walked in silence until Ree suddenly noticed the holdall.

'Where'd you get that bag? It's Pixie's! See Gav? See? It's got her initials on it. What are you doing with Pixie's bag you bastard?'.

From the doorway Colin saw Ree turn and face Jimmy, the street light illuminating all three faces.

'Fuck!' Colin uttered aloud as he heard the raised voices.

Ree reached out for the bag and then her face turned into a mask of terror as Jimmy's free hand flashed out of his coat pocket holding a gun. Colin ran towards Pixie's friends and shouted.

'It's got fuck all to do with them. Leave them Jimmy! You two fuck off, now!'

Totally confused and shocked to see Colin appear as if by magic, Jimmy panicked and turned his gun on Colin who took quick aim and fired. Jimmy fell still clutching his gun and firing at Colin as they both hit the pavement. Gavin threw Ree to the ground. Seeing Colin lying motionless she crawled over to him.

'Tell me what to do!' she screamed. 'Tell me what to do!'

Gavin ran to the pub for help and, as Ree lifted her head to scream again, she registered Jimmy propped on one elbow lifting his gun and pointing it at her. Ree grabbed the gun from Colin's hand and, without hesitation, shot Jimmy full in the chest. Gavin saw her do it – half the customers in the pub saw her do it. A pretty mouse of a girl lifted a gun and pulled the trigger.

Chapter Thirteen

Gus, the landlord, had been staring at the proceedings in disbelief. When he thought about it afterwards it was as if it had all happened in slow motion, it was all very clear, etched on his mind but surreal. Gavin had come running into the bar shouting for help but Gus had already heard the shots and was on his way out. He saw Ree pull the trigger, saw Jimmy's chest explode and watched Ree as she held Colin, cradling his head like a baby, the blood covering her hands and clothes. Gavin was shouting, gabbling incoherently.

Gus hated Jimmy because he couriered drugs and Gus hated drugs, so Jimmy was scum in his book. But Jimmy worked for Happy Harry and Gus didn't want his pub torched. Gus could hear the faint whine of sirens growing louder – someone must have called the police – he knew he had precious little time Colin, who he knew was a copper, was said to be involved with Pixie. Everyone had heard the rumours but Gus wasn't interested, preferring to keep his nose out of that kind of business. Tonight was different, this was serious; a crook was dead and a policeman was seriously wounded. He could just about comprehend from Gavin that it was something to do with the bag Jimmy had been carrying and that the bag belonged to Pixie. He gripped Gavin's arms and shook him.

'Listen to me son, Pixie is my friend and whatever is going

on I don't want to know. Jimmy pulled a gun on Colin, got that? You two just got caught in the middle and Ree acted in self-defence.'

'Now Ree, listen to me, darlin', listen to me, you got that? Nothing about a bag and Pixie. Do you understand me? Say fuck all. Do you understand me Gav, Ree, nothing, don't say a fucking word.'

Gus told the spectators to make themselves scarce and forget everything they had seen. They all understood him loud and clear. The tacit understanding between the occupants of the pub and the main players meant that the whole incident would have not one witness amongst the twenty odd people who had seen Ree shoot Jimmy. No one saw the mouse of a girl pull the trigger. Gus shouted for his wife Christine. He told her to take the bag over to Pixie, tell her what had happened and stay with her until he contacted her again. She was not to let Pixie out of her sight. Gavin fumbled in Ree's coat pocket for her keys and passed them to Christine.

'She'll be out cold,' said Gavin. 'Sleeping tablets.'

Taking the bag and the keys, Christine ran across the road and quickly let herself into Pixie's house. Gus pulled his hands through his hair in despair. 'What a fuckin' mess,' he said, as Ree passed out in shock and fear. 'What a fuckin' mess.'

* * *

Moments later blaring sirens announced the arrival of an ambulance, which was waved down by Gus. He shouted at them.

'That skinny fucker's dead I reckon, but this one's 'angin on, just.'

'OK mate, thanks. What's his name?'

'Colin and the girl is Ree.'

'Colin, can you hear me mate, I'm Paul and I'm a paramedic.' The red-haired giant of a man and his slight female companion knelt beside Colin and did all that they could for him while radioing into the nearest hospital to warn them of their imminent arrival. More sirens could be heard in the distance but there was not one onlooker, not one bystander there to watch. Ree came to and thought that she had had the most awful dream but, as she focused, reality slapped her hard and she replayed every horrible memory from the moment she walked out of the pub with Gavin. The tiny woman paramedic was gently calling her name, leaning over her as a police car pulled in with screeching tyres.

'Can you hear me love, hello, Ree, talk to me love.'

Ree tried to sit up but was told to lie still. She was put in the back of the ambulance.

'Are you hurt? Do you have any pain?' the paramedic asked.

'OK,' she said over her shoulder, 'all yours.'

A woman police officer moved into Ree's field of vision.

* * *

By eleven thirty Jimmy's body was in the mortuary, Colin was in intensive care and Gavin was drinking another cup of tea while going over his statement with a young sergeant. Gus had given the briefest of statements – no one else had seen a thing. Not a twitched curtain, not a man walking his dog, a car driving past or even another drinker from the pub.

'Funny that,' thought Sergeant Nigel Clayton as he rubbed his fingers over his eyes and wished he was at home in bed asleep beside his gorgeous wife instead of being stuck in the interview room with a scared kid who had just had the shock of his life. The girl was a wreck. The landlord at the pub had seen little – pretty normal for that part of South London considering who was involved.

Jimmy was scum and wouldn't be mourned by anyone but Nigel wanted to know why Colin, a highly respected and popular senior officer, had pulled a gun on Jimmy who was now dead and exactly what, if anything, the young lovers had to do with it. The girl said it was self-defence, so did the boyfriend, but until Colin came round with his explanation then the poor cow was going to be in for a rough time.

* * *

The digital display on the teasmade said 9.14 a.m. As she stretched and yawned, feeling slightly muzzy-headed from the tablets, Pixie reached out and hit the start button, dozed for the five minutes the whole process took then sat up in bed sipping at the scalding cup of tea. Christine had slept on the sofa in the lounge and had left the door ajar. On hearing the buzzer on the teasmade then the noise of the radio jingle, she realized that Pixie was awake. Christine had woken a couple of hours before, had already very quietly made herself a cup of strong coffee and folded away and returned the blankets she had found in a cupboard.

Christine had been a South London pub landlady for some twenty-five years and had seen it all, stabbings, gangland killings, broken bottles pushed in faces, but this time it was worse because she knew it was just bad luck, a lovely girl being in the wrong place at the wrong time. All the other stuff was part and parcel of what went on – this wasn't. Dreading what was about to come, Christine tapped on the bedroom door, calling out to Pixie as she did so, full of sadness at the news she was about to deliver.

'Pixie, it's Chris from the Tanners; all right love, I won't come in till yer tell me to but Gus sent me. Are you decent, can I come in love?'

Nearly dropping her tea as she heard Christine's familiar but totally out of place voice, Pixie jumped out of bed and grabbed her dressing gown and wig, putting both on before opening the bedroom door,

'Chris, what's the matter? What's going on?'

'Look Pix, Gus sent me, sit down love and I'll tell you what I know.' So Chris relayed the horrific events of the previous night to a stunned and agonized Pixie who collapsed in misery.

Chapter Fourteen

The woman police constable held Ree's arm as she led her from the ambulance to a waiting police car. The rain started to fall soaking her to the skin but Ree hardly felt it. Just as she hardly felt the hands pushing her into the back of the car or the handcuffs that had been placed around her wrists. She squeezed her eyes tightly closed in a futile effort to stem the relentless flow of tears. The drive to the police station only took a matter of minutes, hastened by the lateness of the hour. The hands led her into what she was told was a custody area. A man introduced himself as the custody sergeant, a fact which Ree only barely acknowledged with the slightest nod of her head. Other hands removed the cuffs, voices spoke, sometimes directly to her – demanding responses. She felt detached. She felt nothing. She felt everything.

The woman police constable reappeared, led Ree to a cell, opened the door and guided Ree inside.

'Take your shoes off please, and I'll need your belt as well.'

Automatically doing as she was told, Ree watched the woman, who was only a few years older than her, taking the items, leaving the cell and locking the door behind her. Ree had been told so many things, given so much information but all she could remember was Jimmy, bloody, lying on the pavement, a gun in his hand then his chest exploding and Colin, poor Colin.

Policemen and women talked at her, not to her because Ree did not absorb any of the words. They told her she had the right to have someone informed of her whereabouts; she had the right to see a solicitor and the right to read a code of conduct whatever the hell that was. She was barely able to accept the invitation to have a cup of tea. All she wanted was to sleep, to go to sleep and wake up back in her bed with Gavin in Pixie's house. But the police kept telling her to do things, kept bringing her back to reality, back to the tiny cell, back to the cold of the early hours of this summer morning in which she had killed a man.

* * *

Janice Hales had come on duty that night at 10 p.m. Half an hour later she was driving like the clappers to a pub near London Bridge in response to a 999 call. Bruce, her partner, had just bought them both a coffee and a jam doughnut from a tea bar by the station and the pair of them were taking the piss out of the drunken commuters running on unsteady legs for their trains when the call came in on the radio. They called in their location and were told to make the short drive to the Tanners pub and make it fast. Janice was twenty-six and still on probation but she loved her work and was already a fair and good copper, despite having only been in the job for some fourteen months. When she and Bruce arrived at the pub an ambulance was already there, and two medics were putting a drip into what looked like a corpse. Doing a swift double take, first she and then Bruce recognized Inspector Colin Arnold as the man being treated and she hurriedly radioed the station. An injured copper was serious stuff. That done, she turned her attention to the other body lying on the pavement. This one she was absolutely positive was dead.

Despite her inexperience, even she recognized Jimmy who seemed to have a surprised look on his face as if he died wondering why his chest had exploded. But what the hell had DI Arnold been doing here? Where was his back-up? A smalltime but still well-known crook dead, a senior police officer alone and wounded and a young girl white as a ghost who kept saying 'I shot him.' Who had she shot? What the fuck was going on? Where was the rest of Colin's team? Surely he wouldn't have been here on his own? Feeling completely out of her depth she radioed in asking for back-up while Bruce busied himself with the quivering young girl who was clinging to the equally shell-shocked young man beside her.

Assistance arrived in the form of half the local nick as one of their own was involved in what could only be described as serious and strange circumstances. A DI was barking orders at everyone and the slip of a girl was cuffed and taken to the station.

'What a surprise, no one saw a fucking thing,' the DI later told his sergeant.

At the station the custody sergeant was concerned that the girl in front of him was in a state of shock and called for a medic to give her the once over. Janice stayed with the girl and explained that she had to remove her clothes as they'd be needed by forensics and that swabs would have to be taken along with her fingerprints. The girl was silent, just the occasional nod which led Janice to wonder if she was on drugs. As the girl undressed and handed over her clothes, Janice had a look at her arms. No track marks which led her to presume correctly that her charge was in a deep state of shock. She gave Ree a white paper suit to put on, which she did silently, without question.

Ree had said 'I killed him' several times. Gavin had given

a statement, taking in what Gus had barked at him about the bag and Pixie, saying that Jimmy had approached them and what Ree had done was in self-defence. He confirmed that Ree had shot Jimmy. There was absolutely no doubt in the mind of the young DI that this was the truth. As to why, he hadn't the faintest idea and could not make sense out of Gavin or Ree or Gus who had also been brought in for a statement. He knew Gus would be a complete waste of time as he was an old school landlord who, come hell or high water, would stick to the very first version of his statement, no matter how many times he was asked the same questions in various different ways. The DI sat back in his chair and wondered exactly what Colin had been up to. Was it even worth delving into or would it just cause more problems further up the line? Something smelt wrong but until Colin came round, they would never know just what had happened.

⋆ ⋆ ⋆

At 5 a.m. on Saturday morning, The same month Margaret Thatcher came to office, Ree was charged with the murder of one James Sidney Watson. She listened as she was cautioned, tears falling down her cheeks, not making a sound.

The magistrates were not particularly interested in the young girl who stood before them. The list seemed to grow longer each day. What was the world coming to? They tutted as they drove their expensive shiny cars to their expensive shiny homes at the end of their tedious day. The duty solicitor had told Ree that she would probably eventually be dealt with at a Crown Court and this was all a formality. She was remanded in custody until a date could be fixed for the trial. She barely acknowledged the proceedings, staring the whole time at Gavin who sat stiffly in the court and cried openly for her pain.

Alan Dixon sat at the back of the court room watching his beloved Ree, the agony etched on his face. The hurt he felt inside over the terrible situation the two people he loved most in the world were now in was almost unbearable. He could not have come to the court as Pixie as that would have drawn unnecessary attention so, as Alan, a middle-aged smartly dressed man, he watched the proceedings and no one gave him a second glance. The policewoman led Ree back to the holding cells underneath the court where she had waited for two hours before she had been called. She was locked in the cell with a couple of other girls who seemed to know each other. One of them produced a tissue from the pocket of her jeans and seemed to know all about Ree.

'You shot Jimmy didn't yer? Me mum heard about it. Fucking tosser 'e was, well rid o' the cunt if you ask me. You 'av to stop fucking snivlin' though luv 'cos where we're goin' they'll take the piss if they think you're soft. Shut up an' calm down, OK?'

By the time the heavy metal door to the cell was unlocked five women were sharing the room which was about fifteen square feet. They were handcuffed and led outside to a white van with high windows which was parked, but with the engine running, in a courtyard at the back of the magistrates' court. The women were led into the van and sat in individual cubicles which were locked behind them. The cubicles had seats of moulded white plastic and nothing else. The drive through the rush hour traffic seemed to last for ever and Ree's stomach churned for the duration of the journey. Finally coming to a standstill and feeling the engine being cut, Ree heard muffled voices then a key being turned in the lock to her cubicle. She was led out of the van and stood with her travelling companions inside the forbidding walls of Holloway Prison.

Chapter Fifteen

'Take your clothes off, including your shoes, but leave your underwear on. Take this pot. I want you to pee in it then return it to me.'

Ree did exactly as the doctor instructed then took the seat that was offered to her. Question after question about her medical history was asked of her and recorded on a form being completed by the doctor. Personal, intimate questions were asked loudly and without any compassion, within easy earshot of the whole room. Was she a drug addict? An alcoholic? Any sexual diseases? Was she a prostitute? A lesbian? A nurse passed the sample back to the doctor who unscrewed a tube, took out a stick of what looked like paper and dipped it in the liquid. Having glanced at the colour of the paper, the doctor washed his hands then scrutinized the form before him.

'Why didn't you mention that you were pregnant?'.

'I can't be! I ... I mean I'm not … I didn't know …' she stammered.

'Well you're not exactly the Virgin Mary are you and now you know. You'll have to come and see me tomorrow for a proper medical examination in the presence of a midwife.'

The doctor called a prison officer over and dismissed his patient.

'Take her to medical wing. Next!'

'Stop crying love, won't do you any good at all here,' said the prison officer. 'Save your energy for your baby. Now, you are going to the medical wing for now. After that, once you've seen a doctor tomorrow we'll move you to D Zero which houses pregnant inmates, the older ladies, the very young and the posh ones who haven't got a clue what's hit them.'

The prison officer gave Ree reams of information about prison routine as the pair walked along the musty corridors. She wasn't listening – her mind was in turmoil – she was pregnant! They had been so careful. Poor, poor innocent baby to be born into this.

'How the hell do I tell Gavin?' she thought.

Her life was crumbling around her and waves of self-pity surged through her body. The prison officer rang a bell and another officer stood on the other side of a wall of metal bars, unlocked a door and told Ree to follow her. A folder with Ree's name written across the top of it was handed to the second prison officer. The door clanged shut behind her and she heard it being locked with an ominous clunk.

The new prison officer opened the door to a room painted a stark dirty white. It was about ten square feet, part of which was taken up by a semi-partitioned toilet and basin in one corner. There was a single bed in the centre of the room pushed back against one wall and a locker, which occurred madly to Ree, looked as if it had come from a hospital, next to the bed.

'The government must buy them in bulk, multipurpose,' Ree thought to herself, it was almost funny.

She had seen no one other than prison officers and guessed that it must be past the time for locking the women in their cells. She was horrified by the severity of it all and tried in vain not to cry. The prison officer told Ree to sit on the bed. Immediately she did as she was told. The prison officer asked if she was injured in any way, if she was on medication; more and more questions until the final one:

'Do you feel suicidal?'

Ree almost laughed and barely suppressed an ironic smile as she quietly replied that no, she was not suicidal.

Satisfied at having gone through the motions, the prison officer left Ree and locked the door to the tiny cell. Ree sat alone with her thoughts and the life growing inside her. She was very frightened. She was in prison. She was pregnant. She had killed a man. There was no one to hold her hand, no one to hug her to sleep, no one to talk to, just the automatic words of a prison officer who had been through all this before and who was really too tired, cynical and overworked to care. She lay on the bed in the darkness listing to the alien sounds around her. The noise was unbelievable – women were calling out to each other, singing, telling one another to shut up. Eventually she drifted into a deep sleep – a physical and emotional wreck.

* * *

Telly and Pixie stood on either side of the bed, Pixie gently stroking the back of Colin's hand. George Hill, the consultant, wearily rubbed his eyes and then began his explanation of Colin's condition once again. He had been through it all a couple of hours ago with the wife and the daughter and an officer from the Police Family Support unit. Now here he was, about to explain Colin's condition to a man who claimed to be a very close friend but who didn't know the patient's wife. Tim, George's lover of some ten years, would be impressed that he had broken protocol to support a 'sister'.

'The bullet entered Colin's stomach, which in itself is bad

enough, but the angle at which it entered the body meant it also clipped a rib. As you know, the ribcage protects the heart and this has complicated the operation to remove the bullet and repair the damage. In itself, this is not that bad, but as Colin fell he seems to have hit the back of his head. This is why he remains unconscious. He has a large bleed on his brain – he had extensive bleeding from the ears when he was brought in and his pupils were different sizes. He could remain in a coma for some time. The bleed will very gradually be absorbed but as I say, it will be very gradual and may take a very long time. Quite how long we can't say right now. We'll keep him on the ventilator to help him breathe and will feed him through this tube. He has a catheter and this drip here will keep him hydrated. I am sorry I can't tell you much more right now. We all will just have to wait.'

Pixie, as Alan, put an oversized white handkerchief to his eyes.

'Will he ever come round doctor? Does he know that we are here? Is he in any pain?'

George was struck by the stark contrast in the behaviour of the man before him who was quite clearly overwhelmed with grief for his lover and the woman he had had the same discussion with earlier. She had not displayed a drop of emotion or even compassion. She had not asked a single question whereas Alan Dixon was obviously distraught.

'I really can't give you many answers at the moment. I can tell you that Colin here is very heavily sedated and that rest and time are great healers. Talk to him, tell him about your day, remind him of past happy times, your plans for the future, anything at all really. On many occasions, when a coma patient regains consciousness they reveal that they have been aware of conversations around them and the presence of people close to them. He is in the best possible hands here,

I can assure you of that. He will have physio, we will scan his brain on a regular basis and continue to monitor him most closely. I promise you we will do our utmost to aid his recovery.'

Shaking hands with Telly and Alan, he invited them to stay with Colin for as long as they wished. After he had left the room, Pixie sobbed and Telly hugged his old friend, trying vainly to think of something comforting to say.

⋆ ⋆ ⋆

Ree was startled awake by the clanking of metal upon metal and an unfamiliar voice calling her name.

'Lovell, time to get up. Its seven o'clock and I'll be back in fifteen minutes to fetch you for breakfast.'

As she slowly realized where she was Ree sat up in bed. She looked around her and it occurred to her that the metallic scraping sound must have been the cell door being unlocked. She stretched and yawned, exhausted from the poor sleep in the unfamiliar bed and the strain of the previous day. Gathering her thoughts, she focused on doing as she had been instructed by the unseen voice. A bang on the door jolted her to her senses.

'Get up, get dressed, collect your breakfast stuff and get in line. Move yourself!'

What was her breakfast stuff? Where was the line? Those and a thousand other thoughts flew through Ree's head. First and foremost however she knew that she had to try to obey her orders. No chance of having a wash at the sink even. She dressed in the clothes she'd been given at the police station. She felt dirty and unkempt – she had no toiletries, not even a tooth brush. She remembered a prison officer telling her that if a friend or relative wanted to bring a small bag to the prison with her personal things, once it had been thoroughly searched, she would be allowed to have them. In the meantime she would have to make do with the clothes she was wearing and she was quite capable of washing her knickers through and leaving them to dry overnight, wasn't she?. As Ree slowly emerged from her cell, feeling like the new girl at school, she watched the other prisoners collect a plate, fork, spoon and finally a mug. All the implements were made of plastic. The 'fork' barely resembled a fork as the prongs were flattened plastic and very pliable – Ree correctly guessed that this was done so that it could not be used as a weapon. She joined the end of the queue and felt the tears welling up in her eyes yet again. A heavily pregnant young black girl waited behind her.

'Get in last night did ya? First time? Scared? Shut up and get yer food and keep quiet. You'll be all right if you do that.'

Two butch women walked along the queue and pushed in front of Ree. The girl behind Ree prodded her in the back, shook her head and took a step backwards to make room for the two women as did all those behind her. Ree stepped back and kept her eyes firmly on the ground. The food was disgusting and Ree could hardly bear to eat or drink a thing. She forced down some water and took a couple of bites of dry toast. The black girl had sat next to her.

'Are you pregnant?' Ree nodded her head. 'Eat for the kid's sake. I know it tastes like shit but you'll soon be hungry.'

A woman the other side of the table asked if she could eat what was left on Ree's plate. The lump in her throat grew larger and Ree knew she would only cry again if she tried to talk, so she merely nodded. A bell sounded. The women stood and threw their scraps into a huge metal bowl and their dirty crockery into another even larger one. The black girl told her they would all go back to their cells now until it was time to be unlocked again for the next meal. Silently, Ree walked back to her cell and watched as the heavy steel door robbed her even of the freedom of the breakfast room.

* * *

Taking his jacket off and lifting his arms, Gavin was searched as he entered the prison. He was even asked to open his mouth to allow a prison officer to look inside. Kids were running around while adults tried to control them. 'What a terrible place to bring a child,' Gavin thought to himself as he was told to empty his pockets into a locker and signed for the key. The kids seemed oblivious to the fact that they were in a prison – brothers and sisters were calling out to each other and saying hello to friends that they must have made here.

Finally, after what seemed like days but was in reality only half an hour, he was led into a room and told to find a spare table. Gavin heard Ree's name being called then saw her appear through a doorway a couple of minutes later. He was shocked at her greasy lank hair and the creased grubby clothes she was wearing. He bit his lip. He wanted to grab his girlfriend and magic her away. Ree's eyes found him across the stuffy, crowded room and she wanted to run to him but of course, she couldn't. The prison officer stood back and told Ree to go to her visitor as she indicated table number seventeen. Gavin rose to his feet and the pair hugged each other, both crying and whispering soothing words. Pulling away only to sit down, Ree held Gavin's hand tightly across the table.

'Colin?' Ree whispered.

'Still hasn't come round. I've been in to see him, even met his missus. The doc just said he's stable. Don't worry love, he'll pull through and will be able to tell them exactly what happened. You'll be home soon.'.

Ree took a deep breath.

'Gavin, I'm pregnant,' she said. She had to tell him, she couldn't keep it to herself any longer and desperately searched his face for a reaction.

'Oh Christ love, how bloody wonderful! Timing's shit, but bloody hell, I love you so much,' and he took her face in his hands and kissed her wet cheeks again.

'I don't want our baby to be born in a prison!'

'Sweetheart, don't be so bloody soft. Soon as Colin comes to he'll tell them what happened – that it was self-defence, a spur of the moment thing. He'll tell them everything. He'll make it right. When our baby is born we'll be taking him or her home to our home, not here. Please love, believe me, it'll be OK, I promise.' His words spoke of a hope which he was not sure he fully believed but, he thought, 'I'm going to be a dad! Dads are strong!'.

A bell sounded and the prison officers called the room to order. The hour long visit had passed in the blink of an eye and Gavin held Ree until he was told he really had to leave. The door from the visitors' room was being held open and the prisoners contact with the outside world was severed for another week.

* * *

Ree was led back to her cell and, as the door slammed shut behind her, she heard the key scraping metal against metal in the lock before she fell onto the bed and wept. Eventually, a light fitful sleep in which she was tormented by Jimmy's long thin face sneering at her took her away from her cell for a few hours. She heard the explosion of the gun a thousand times and felt the kick-back a million times more. When she woke with a start her tears were already running down her face.

The doctor who had carried out the crudest of examinations on her when she first arrived was today stationed in an office on the medical wing. He clearly had no recollection of Ree and the amazing news he had imparted to her on her arrival at HMP Holloway. She was a nothing to him, just ten minutes' worth of his day. A nameless, faceless nothing.

'Are you going to have the baby or do you want an abortion?'

His directness astounded Ree who stammered her response, overwhelmed and emotional, strained and not coping at all with the incarceration.

'I'm, I'm, we're, I mean yes, I want my baby.'

'Right, you seem perfectly fit and healthy so you'll be moving off this wing when someone has the time to supervise you.'

That seemed to be his dismissal and the midwife told Ree she would see her in a week's time on her new wing. A prison officer took her back to her cell where the now familiar slam of metal on metal was still as cruel as the first time she'd heard it. She would never get used to that noise and prayed hard that she would never have to.

The night passed identically to the previous one; the noise, the endlessness, the helplessness, the lack of any control or free will. The following morning after breakfast, Ree was locked in her cell once more. The two butch women had again taken their places in front of Ree and again she had been unable to eat anything more than a mouthful of barely cooked toast. A prison officer unlocked the cell door later and informed Ree that she had to attend a meeting for all new prisoners, including those on remand. Ree stood and followed her jailer. Recognizing two other women from breakfast that morning and even raising a faint smile from one of them, Ree sat where she was told. A male prison officer gave them a lecture about the three Rs as he so wittily called them, Rules, Rights and Regulations. They were everything in this place, he told them. Never be afraid to ask for clarification about anything concerning the three Rs. Ree was numb, barely taking in a word, on the verge of tears all day, every day. Not wanting to speak to anyone, she just wanted return to her world, where she belonged.

Coronation Street blared on the TV in the communal lounge as Ree stared at the screen, sipping her plastic beaker of water. She didn't hear the words or take in the pictures - just sat there wondering how the hell her life had come to this. Her lovely happy secure life with Pixie and Gavin and Telly and Nikki and Mark and Gary. Even some of Pixie's clients came to mind. She thought about all the people who made up her world as tears tumbled down her cheeks.

'Lovie, that won't help, come on now.'

Ree looked up as a heavily pregnant girl pressed a handful of tissues into her hand and sat beside her on the sofa.

'Thanks', Ree whispered as she wiped her face.

'Are you pregnant?' the girl asked and Ree told her that she had seen a midwife that afternoon and been told she was about twelve weeks. For a few moments Ree almost forgot where she was as the two of them sat there talking about their pregnancies. Ree asked the girl her name and where she came from.

Chrissie was eighteen and from Norwich. Inevitably they asked one another why they were in prison. Chrissie didn't bat an eyelid as Ree told her she had shot a man in self-defence and was being held on remand. Chrissie had been living with her boyfriend, her baby's father, who was a pot-head. What she didn't know was that he had a coke problem too and in order to support the habit had started to deal. The night Chrissie was arrested her boyfriend had hidden ten grammes of the drug in Chrissie's handbag and when they were arrested she didn't have a leg to stand on. She was currently two months through a lengthy sentence. Her baby would be born in prison, or at least in Whitechapel hospital and then come back to prison with a very uncertain future.

Ree shuddered and wondered for the thousandth time that week what fate had in store for her. Chrissie's lawyer had told her she would be moved up to the mother and baby unit once the baby was born. They'd stay there for a couple of months then be transferred to another prison equipped for kids. The child could stay with Chrissie until it was about eighteen months old, providing she behaved herself and there were enough resources. After that the baby could be looked after by relatives or would go into care. Ree couldn't imagine anything so terrible, all the experiences a toddler should have, walks in the park, days at the seaside, playgroup, none of those lovely days would be theirs – they'd just have the walls of a prison. Chrissie was kind to Ree and helped her understand what was going on through the day. The routine varied only slightly and was mainly centred around meal times, exercise, work or study, queuing up to use the telephone, and a few hours of television in the evening. Ree hardly ate any of the food as it was so disgusting and of such poor quality. She was given a piece of fresh fruit every day because she was pregnant and was sorry that she hadn't savoured the taste of such things when she lived with Pixie. The women she was incarcerated with had sad tales to tell, but strangely, some of them didn't even realize that there was an alternative or quite how horrible a life they had led as they had never known any better. Many of them were there for drug-related crimes – used by their boyfriends and husbands, just like Chrissie had been. Some of them were there because of the appallingly abusive lives they had led as children and teenagers, seeing no alternative but a life of petty crime, drugs and prostitution.

All Ree could see was a sea of vulnerable people, dumped on by society. Women locked up for shoplifting food from a supermarket, or a pair of shoes for their kids. The only real danger to society, Ree thought, were the magistrates who did the sentencing.

Chapter Sixteen

A blonde receptionist wearing a power-dressing jacket and just a little too much make-up ushered them into a highly polished room containing a table and chairs, a sideboard and a drinks cabinet. One wall was covered in shelves with row upon row of leather-bound books. The room had an air of expense and class, expectation and desperation. The woman asked them to sit and wait for Mr Wells who would not keep them for more than a moment. A TV and video cabinet sat at one end of the room and pads of lined paper proudly bearing the company logo with matching pencils were neatly positioned at each of twelve places. They sat side by side on the left of the table each consumed with fear of the unknown, the unfamiliar surroundings serving only to compound their discomfort.

Martin Wells entered the room a few minutes later with a colleague he introduced as Lionel Asher. The three seated men rose to their feet and Telly, Pixie and Gavin introduced themselves to Lionel. Today, Pixie was Alan Dixon and he and his friends were praying for a miracle.

Martin explained that as he specialized in private client work it would not be appropriate for him to defend Ree as it was not his field and he had no expertise but his partner Lionel Asher, who was a criminal lawyer, would be happy to handle the case. The very words made Gavin feel appalled;

Ree was not a criminal, and he felt those familiar stabs of hatred for that disgusting man, Jimmy, who had caused this wretched mess in the first place.

Lionel looked hard at Alan and said that he needed to know everything, absolutely everything. Baring his soul, Alan started at the beginning, leaving nothing out, pausing only to take small sips of water. Telly and Gavin had not heard the whole story and were staggered at what they learnt. Lionel's face betrayed nothing. He displayed no emotion as Pixie explained what she did for a living and how she had been blackmailed, that Colin had said he was going to kill the bastard and she believed that he had procured a gun . A consummate professional to the core, Lionel merely said thank you when Alan stopped talking. He had been taking extensive notes throughout the conversation and asked a few pertinent questions. Turning to Telly, Lionel asked him about Ree's character, how Telly was involved and his delivery of the holdall. After more note taking and questions, it was Gavin's turn. He went through the night at the pub and how he and Ree had met Jimmy as they left. He gave every detail, every action he could possibly remember of that terrible night, reliving it second by second.

Lionel knew that the outcome of a trial could be very different for Ree if Colin died or was not able to confirm events – events which the police only half knew. If he died, he would obviously not be in a position to exonerate Ree although it was clear from forensic evidence that two bullets had entered Jimmy's body and the traces of gunpowder found on both Colin's and Ree's hands confirmed that they had both handled, and probably both fired, the same weapon. The question was whether the Crown Prosecution Service would decide that there was enough evidence to suggest that Ree killed Jimmy maliciously or whether it was self-defence as she claimed. Did she shoot Jimmy because he had shot at Colin and was she enraged or was she protecting herself? Lionel explained that in cross-examination the most confident and positive witness could be made out to be a liar and ridiculed. Lionel had not yet visited Ree in Holloway although an application had been made for him to do so. Speaking to Martin Wells after the three men had left the office Lionel doubted very much whether Ree would stand up to cross-examination. Apparently she had been heard to say several times to various police officers, 'I killed him.'

* * *

Telly, Gavin and Pixie left the smart office in the City and wearily made their way back to their everyday lives, which felt as if they were on hold. Gavin had another visiting order to see Ree the following day and, as much as he was desperate to see her, he was dreading telling her about the visit to Pixie's lawyers.

Chapter Seventeen

The unexplained disappearance of her daughter in January 1980 had obviously always bothered Laura but as Adam had told her at the time,

'She'll come home when she's good and ready,' knowing all along that nothing would induce the girl to return.

Laura took comfort in the fact that Ree was a bright girl, had taken clothes with her, had planned for her escape and had taken her Post Office book too. She wasn't stupid, she'd be OK. At the time Laura had assumed that Ree was staying late at school as she normally did but when there was no sign of her by 10 p.m., even Adam was beginning to fear the implications of her disappearance. What Laura interpreted in Adam as anxiety for Ree's well-being was in fact his fear that maybe his step-daughter had gone to the police. Laura was fed lies as Adam told her he would report Ree missing and would do his utmost to find her. After a couple of days Adam's fear abated – surely they would have come for him by now if the young bitch had gone to the authorities? Swallowing hard, Adam walked up the steps of the police station and spoke to one of the officers manning the front desk.

Wiping the beads of sweat from his top lip then forcing his eyes to fill with tears, he took a deep breath.

'I want to report a missing person.'

'OK sir, we'll have someone with you in a few minutes, if you'd like to take a seat please.'

And so the charade began. Adam answered all the questions posed by the tired, overworked constable. Oh yes, she was a very wilful girl, but he loved her very much, in fact he had brought her up as his own, spoiled her, she didn't want for anything. Had it all planned, packed a case, most of her clothes were missing, taken her Post Office book too. She'd run away loads of times, but not stayed away like this before. Shouldn't wonder if there wasn't a boy involved, she was very, well, he hated to say it but, promiscuous. Of course, it was nothing to do with her upbringing, oh no, they were very strict with her, had to be didn't you? But, well, they just couldn't do a thing with her – she was a very wllful madam.

Closing his notebook, the policeman sighed. He'd heard it all before – bloody kids and the trouble they caused. Decent bloke like this, so upset he was, doing his best, raising someone else's kid, little cow just threw it back in his face. PC Curran would circulate the photo Adam had brought with him and in the meantime he should try not to worry too much, kids today don't know how lucky they are.

'She'll be back, tail between her legs, back by the end of the week. Mark my words,' he said with what he hoped was a kindly smile.

The photo Adam had picked out was a slightly blurred terrible likeness of Ree. The last thing Adam needed was anyone actually finding the little runaway. Shaking his head sadly at Laura on his return home he comforted her.

'Don't fret too much love, they are doing everything they can to find her. I'll keep popping into the nick and keep them on their toes.'

Adam had never heard from PC Curran again and although he told Laura on many occasions that he had been into the station and enquired as to any progress made, the reality was that he had no intention of doing anything to help the police find his wife's daughter.

* * *

Nearly choking on his ketchup-smothered sausage sandwich, Adam read and reread the newspaper article. Ree, in prison, up for murder.

'Can hardly believe the little cow had it in her. Well, well, well, fancy her turning up there after all these years,' he thought.

Laura sat opposite him but hadn't seen the paper; she never really read the papers or watched the news – her husband and the boys kept her busy. She pushed a fresh mug of tea towards Adam.

'Are you OK? You look like you've seen a ghost. Drink this, you'll feel better.'

She watched him anxiously, never wanting anything to upset Adam for fear of his terrible temper. Taking a mouthful of tea and folding the paper away at the same time, he told her he would be out for a while, but would back for dinner at the usual time.

'Steak and chips tonight. Make sure that the meat is cooked the way I like it and if we run out of beer again you'll be well sorry.'

Taking the remains of his breakfast, Adam waddled to his car. He had put on a lot of weight over the years and got pleasure in seeing his wife's disgust when he crushed her frail frame as he forced her to have sex. He drove to the nearest useable telephone box he could find, shaking with excitement at the untold riches he imagined he was about to earn from his betrayal of his step-daughter.

* * *

Unsteadily dialling the phone number at the bottom of the newspaper column Adam asked for the article's author, Geoff Harris, and was put on hold. Eventually a loud northern accent came on the line and asked Adam what he wanted.

'I'm Renee Lovell's father. How much?'

Geoff Harris couldn't believe his ears. OK, he was a scummy news reporter for a tabloid newspaper, but even he couldn't believe his luck. Big news story like this, a gorgeous bird up for murder and here was her old man out to make a killing while making a hack very happy indeed. What a sick world this is, he thought with a mixture of pleasure and loathing. Always wary of cranks, Geoff asked Adam some personal questions about Ree then arranged to meet him later in a wine bar just off Villiers Street.

'Have you spoken to any other journalists?' he asked.

Sensing an opportunity to make even more money from Ree's situation, Adam was cautious and said that he would see what Geoff had to offer before he made any decisions or was forthcoming with any information of any kind. After reconfirming their meeting, Geoff said goodbye then found his editor who made a few calls before he gave Geoff his top price for the story. Grabbing his jacket, Geoff made for the Embankment already working on the headlines in his head.

* * *

Adam had only called the one newspaper as he had no idea quite how much momentum the story of his step-daughter was gathering until he stopped at a newsstand outside Charing Cross Station. Collecting a handful of newspapers Adam asked for change then headed for the bank of telephone boxes nearby and arranged several more meetings with equally excited journalists.

Nursing a warm pint of bitter, Geoff waited for Adam cursing his lateness. After deliberately keeping him waiting for half an hour, Adam entered the wine bar and soon saw a man on his own holding a copy of the local paper open at Ree's story. Ironically it was placed above a story speculating that the new pound coins were about to make holes in the nation's trouser pockets. The wine bar was thick with cigarette smoke which was being pushed around by a largely ineffectual ceiling fan. Adam wandered over to the man who seemed to match the description Geoff had given of himself. They introduced themselves and Adam, who considered himself a shrewd businessman but in reality was a small time gofer, con man and spiv, came straight to the point.

'Exclusive, everything from school photos to the sobbing mother. How much?'

Geoff named a figure; Adam laughed and stood as if to leave, picking up his now discarded jacket and the packet of Rothmans and his lighter from the table. He slipped them into his pocket, sneering at Geoff.

'Bringing me all the way over 'ere, don't waste my fucking time.'

'All right, sorry, you want my top price?'

'Look mate, I got loads of you scum bags want this, so don't fuck me about. Highest bidder gets the lot. So, let's start again. How fucking much?'

Geoff told him the sum; Adam merely nodded, saying that he would consider the offer. He wrote the figure down in a newly purchased notebook alongside Geoff's name and telephone number and left the pub without a flicker of emotion betraying his feelings. As he turned his back on the bemused reporter, a cruel grin engulfed his fat face.

'Fucking amazing. You beauty!' he muttered to himself as he re-emerged into the daylight and prepared for his next meeting. He hadn't imagined in his wildest dreams that he would even be offered half the amount proposed by Geoff. With some time to kill, he sat on the steps at Trafalgar Square with the late edition of the *Evening Standard* and caught up with the most recent events of his now lovely step-daughter's life.

Chapter Eighteen

Gavin had caught a bus to take him to the prison but could not cope with his fellow passengers – they all seemed so normal, happy even, so he decided to get off and walk the rest of the way. He cursed his predicament for the hundredth time that day.

This was his third visit to the prison and he was by now horribly familiar with the procedure upon his arrival. He produced his visiting order and stood in line.

After the entire contents of his pockets had been locked away he sat on a hard orange moulded plastic chair and waited for Ree. He recognized some of the faces from his previous visits; it wasn't just the individual features he picked out but more the aura of desperation and despondency that filled the room. It was almost tangible; the sheer hopelessness of everyone's lives.

As Gavin glimpsed Ree standing in the line waiting to be told to go ahead and sit down, he saw how worn and tired, grubby and even scruffy she appeared. Her clothes were very obviously not clean on today, her hair, normally so shiny and bouncy was dull and lank, tied back from her face with an elastic band. Blinking away his tears and plastering a huge smile across his face, Gavin shared the feeling of despair of those around him.

Ree was given the nod and eagerly clasped Gavin's hands

as they sat at the small table. Apologizing for her appearance Ree explained that she hadn't been able to have a bath the previous night as there had been a problem, some kind of fight between some women on her wing. Gavin wanted to wrap his arms around her and whisk them both away from all this filth but for now had to be content with making jokes about her being smelly and bringing her in some soap.

Ree knew he was doing his best, as was she, but coupled with the acute morning sickness, she was feeling the jokes were more than strained. Without really needing to ask she understood that there was no change in Colin's condition. Gavin shook his head and gave her a quiet no, no change. They talked about how awful Ree felt in the mornings, how wonderful it would be when she stopped feeing quite so sick. She was still having problems eating the terrible food in the first place and Gavin could see how gaunt her face had become. All too soon the hour was over and they each went back to their own despair, alone.

⋆ ⋆ ⋆

Laura could hear the phone ringing but she was at the top of the stairs with the hoover in one hand and a duster in another. Each day the routine was the same, she started at the top and worked her way down, polishing, dusting, wiping, until it all gleamed – until there was nothing her husband could pick fault with. He always tried of course, the odd sarcastic remark here and there but she was used to it, resigned to it. She even had got used to being beaten – it was preferable to having to have sex with the repulsive man.

'Sod it, they'll call back if it's important,' she thought to herself as she lugged the hoover to the bottom of the stairs ready to vacuum the lounge.

As she bent over to plug the machine into the socket, the shrill ring of the telephone seemed to insist that she pick up the receiver. It was only ever for Adam – probably one of his dodgy mates with yet another too-good-to-miss scam. She didn't answer the phone when her husband was at home, he didn't like her to. When he wasn't around she had to take a message making sure she got all the details right, or there was hell to pay. She picked up the receiver.

'Hello?' she said in her usual timid voice.

'Laura, hi, it is Laura, isn't it?' The man talked as though he had known her all his life.

'I'm Geoff, your husband may have mentioned me? I was the lucky guy who won the bidding for the story. Anyway, we need to fix up dates for the interviews as soon as poss. Photos too love. Have you had a chance to pick out some decent ones from the family album?'

Wondering what on earth this loud man was talking about, Laura asked him for his telephone number and just as she was repeating it back to him, Adam came through the front door.

'Who are you talking to?' he demanded.

Passing the phone to him Laura walked quietly away, going to the kitchen to make tea for Adam as she knew he would expect a cup immediately he finished the call.

'I said I would call you,' Adam angrily told Geoff Harris.

Rather bemused by all the secrecy, Geoff explained that he needed to get the interviews done as soon as was humanly possible, to keep the interest going, just in case the copper came round and it was all over.

'We need to get our money's worth out of you y'see. We're going to pay you a bloody fortune so we'd best get cracking.'

They agreed that Geoff would come to the house that evening, with a photographer. Adam had not yet told Laura about her daughter or his plans to sell their story.

Finishing the call, he walked through to the kitchen sitting himself at the small bistro table. Laura placed a mug of tea in front of him, and anxiously asked if he wanted anything to eat or if there was anything she could do for him. She hoped he would not force her to give him a blow-job. He took delight in pushing her face down onto his rancid, unwashed penis and today, the very thought of it made her sick to the core.

'Sit down Laura, I need to talk to you about our Ree. You remember how the ungrateful little cow just upped and left without a word, broke our hearts she did, well, I want you to read this and just you see what she's been up to in the last few years.'

Hardly able to believe her eyes Laura read the newspaper detailing Jimmy's death, the copper with his life hanging in the balance and her daughter on remand for murder.

'What we have to do now love is to set the record straight, tell everyone what a good girl she was. We'll be helping her, doing it for her benefit; we'll not get a thank you from her, the ungrateful bitch, but we'll do what we can.'

The article said that Ree was in Holloway on remand, awaiting trial, that witnesses saw her kill Jimmy and that she had admitted it. Laura had thought about her daughter every day since her sudden departure. She felt overwhelmed with guilt at the neglect of the child, the weakness she had shown as a mother and how she was sure that Adam had more to do with Ree's leaving than he cared to admit. Laura had seen the way he looked at Ree as she developed into a woman – a tall, slim, beautiful young woman.

Just before Ree had left, Laura had been lying in bed pretending to be asleep to avoid sex with her husband when she felt him get out of bed then heard him trying the door handle to her daughter's bedroom. A few days later Ree had gone and Laura was sure she knew at least part of the reason. So many conflicting emotions swept through her, not least of all revulsion for Adam as she continued to read through the article. And now he was telling her that she had to talk about her missing daughter to a reporter. For the first time in her life, Laura stood up to Adam.

'I need some air. Leave me alone, just leave me be!'

Grabbing her coat as she dashed for the back door, Laura could hear Adam shouting after her to come back, to do as she was bloody well told. But she ran as fast as she could. Trying to collect her thoughts and sort through the jumble of her mind, Laura took herself back to the day that Ree didn't come home. Adam had gone to the police station, said he didn't want her to have to cope with it all, it would be best dealt with by him. Her mind clearing, she wondered just what Adam had done. What had he said?

As she turned the corner Laura passed a newsagent's where she bought a copy of the *Evening Standard*. The paper was full of the story of the young girl who had run away from home, got into a bad crowd and why she might have killed a known villain. Columns and columns speculated on the outcome of the forthcoming trial. Laura decided that she had to know just what Adam had told the police so, summoning every ounce of confidence she had, she walked up the steps of the police station and pushed open the heavy outer door. The officer at the desk looked up.

'I am Renee Lovell's mother. Can I talk to someone about my daughter?'

The young man looked hard at the woman in front of him and asked her to sit and wait.

He telephoned his immediate superior officer. Presently, a woman of about thirty asked Laura to follow her, then took her to a tiny room.

'My name is Sergeant McKenna, Carmel McKenna. How can I help you Mrs Lovell?'

'It's Mrs Jackson. It's like I told the bloke outside, I'm Ree's mother. She ran away years ago and I need to know why. My husband reported her missing but we never heard nothing of her ever since. Why didn't you look for her? She might not be in this mess now if you had of done.'

Laura's tone was accusatory but she knew where the blame really lay and her share of it was almost too much to bear.

Carmel asked Laura for some form of ID but the best she could come up with was her library card. Carmel could see the likeness between the woman and her imprisoned daughter and also the desperation etched on the face of the cowed woman so, despite the usual protocol, was satisfied.

'Look, it may take me a while to find the notes from the time but if you wait here, I'll get someone to bring you a cup of tea and I'll see what I can do.'

Barely nodding, Laura was afraid to speak lest she should cry. She waited for what to her seemed an eternity but which was in fact only about fifteen minutes. Walking briskly to her office, Carmel brought up the file which she knew was there. She knew because she had looked at it when Ree was first arrested – the missing persons report had been flagged when a background check was done. The fact that she had been reported as missing several years before at this station had been checked by a colleague and had even been remarked on over lunch in the canteen. Carmel flicked through the computer notes and printed the file off. Taking the papers with her, she found Laura with tears streaming down her face, hugging her mug of tea.

'Sorry I was so long. OK, here it is. Look, when kids run away and it's not the first time we don't place quite the same priority on it as say an abduction or if we think the child is at risk.'

'What do you mean, not the first time?'

'Well, Ree was reported missing by Adam, your husband, yes? He says here that she had run away several times before and was always in trouble, and you were both very concerned as she was very promiscuous. Promiscuous was the exact word he used.'

Laura was staggered that Adam even knew the meaning of such a word and could hardly believe his deceit.

'That's not true! Ree never gave us the slightest bother, worked hard at school, never ever in trouble and had never run away before. She was never later home than she was allowed for God's sake. What the hell has he told you that for? Christ, I think I know why she went, will she ever forgive me, my poor poor girl!'

Carmel's years of experience told her that Laura was telling the truth about her daughter and she let her continue talking.

'Ree isn't his kid. He's her step-father and he always hated her, right from the off. But he knew, see, that if he took me on with a kid then we'd get a better chance of a council house. All I wanted was to get away from the bloody chaos at me mother's, away from the other kids and 'ave a bit of space. First bloke that come along he was, and I bloody jumped at the chance didn't I?'

Rambling, Laura continued, Carmel wondering where all this was going.

'Told me he'd sort it out, when Ree ran off. That he'd deal with it. I always do what Adam tells me to do 'cos he has been known to give me a whack if I don't. And look at the choice I've got, no bloody choice. Where would I go? What would I do with the boys? I can't go back to me mother's. She's got plenty of problems of her own. So I just walked away from her, didn't I? I didn't even ask if he'd been in to see you lot again and find out how things were going 'cos it would've just got him all worked up see, really annoyed like. So pathetic cow that I am, I just abandoned my daughter. She took her clothes and had money. Bright girl she was so I just thought she'd be all right, better off even without us. God, I'm a terrible mother, aren't I? Don't deserve to 'ave kids, but I'm weak and he's a bully. He scares me. I'm sounding even more pathetic, aren't I? Trying to make excuses for meself now.'

'You're not pathetic at all,' Carmel whispered.

'Just a victim of neglect, abuse and years of bullying, like so many others I see day in day out,' Carmel thought, recalling the women she saw regularly, battered and bruised, bones broken and scared for their lives, but who went back because it was all they knew, because every drop of self-confidence had been drained from them.

Gently, Carmel, following her instincts, looked at Laura.

'I think I can help you. Will you trust me Laura? Will you let me help you?'

Chapter Nineteen

Stroking his hand, Pixie gazed at Colin who appeared to be in a peaceful sleep. Every day she came and sat with Colin, willing him to live, to wake up from the coma and tell the police what had happened. In her mind it was all so simple, as soon as Colin woke up, he would tell them that Ree had shot Jimmy after Colin had been shot and Jimmy had pulled a gun on Ree. The police would understand and Ree could come home, have the baby and everything would be wonderful. If only life were that simple she thought to herself as she prepared to leave the hospital.

At first she had been afraid to come, worried that she would bump into Rita, or one of Colin's kids. She knew that Rita came every afternoon and sat next to Colin, hardly sparing him a glance. She would flick through a magazine, drink a cup of tea and leave after about half an hour. The nursing staff were very discreet and realized that there was much more than just friendship between Colin and the smartly dressed middle-aged man who visited him each evening. Pixie always came to the hospital as Alan. He didn't want to create a stir and was more than aware that meeting Rita would be awkward enough if their paths were to accidentally cross. He knew times had changed since he was growing up but he and Colin were a product of their age and Pixie would not do anything to draw attention to his feelings for

Colin. He rightly guessed that George Hill had seen through his 'close friend' story and held the consultant's compassion close to his heart. He kept an eye out for Rita or an unscheduled visit from anyone else and got on well with the nursing staff – they knew which of Colin's visitors really cared for their patient.

Pixie said goodnight to the young nurse sitting behind the desk at the reception area. They exchanged sad, secret smiles and Pixie summoned a taxi at the main doors of the hospital. She hated the journey home to her empty flat, no Colin, no Ree. Tonight Pixie really did not want to be alone so she asked the cabbie to take her to Telly's house where she could at least be herself with an old friend. Climbing wearily from the cab, she paid the driver then walked up the path to Telly's house. As she stood on the door step, cringing at the old *Starsky & Hutch* theme tune of the bell which Telly refused to change, Pixie thought again about all the hopes and dreams she and Colin had shared – blown away by the greed and misplaced loathing of one very evil and now very dead man.

Telly greeted Pixie with open arms, wrapping her in his embrace.

'Stay here tonight Pix, you don't need to go home for anything. I think you need a bit of company right now.'

Alan or Pixie, it really didn't matter to Telly, as he closed the door behind his old friend and Pixie felt the warmth and love of true friendship envelop her.

Chapter Twenty

'Lovell, your turn.'

Ree had been daydreaming of happier times when she heard her name being called by the prison officer.

'Come on, he hasn't got all day to wait for you. Dr Khan is a busy man.'

Hurrying to her feet, Ree tapped on the cold metal of the doctor's door and entered his office. Ree had seen Dr Khan twice before and although he was quite kind and answered her questions fully, she felt his constant disapproval of her and her situation. Today she was going to have a scan and hopefully get an accurate date for the baby's birth. Pining for Gavin but having trained herself not to cry, Ree sat where the doctor told her and answered his questions while he jotted her responses on her notes. There were no pretty pictures on the walls, no smiling faces of new babies, just the bare walls, painted the same grey as every other surface of the prison.

She knew that had life been normal Gavin would be with her, at the local GP's, as excited as she would be. She wouldn't be doing this alone.

'How have you been feeling? No more nausea? Eating properly? Let's take your blood pressure.'

They went through the motions of a normal antenatal appointment then Dr Khan asked her to lie down on the examination table and lift her tee shirt and jumper.

'I'm going to pull the waistband of your trousers down and tuck this paper into them to stop the gel getting on them. Right, the gel is cold I'm afraid.'

Ree turned and faced the small monitor to her right and watched intensely as the doctor wiped the gel over the end of the ultrasound probe and then over her stomach.

'That's the heartbeat, these are legs and arms, spine all OK, yes, all fine, no problems …' His words were lost on Ree as she gazed at the tiny black and white, barely discernible, image on the screen, her baby, hers and Gavin's child. Ree's good intentions got the better of her and the tears cascaded down her cheeks.

'So, according to the scan you are seventeen weeks pregnant; only another twenty-three to go. Any questions? No? Right, all looks absolutely fine. I'll see you again in four weeks. Tell the officer to send the next one in please.'

Ree was dismissed, not unkindly, but this was not at all how she had envisaged her antenatal appointments as being. Not this stark grey room, just her and the doctor, brisk, hurried even, just another statistic and burden on the state. She had dreamt of the time when she and Gavin would have children – the planning, the togetherness of their being married, buying their first house then taking the huge step of having a child. But now all those beautiful plans were lying in tatters as she was reduced to being summoned by her surname and given the most basic of care.

Having wiped the sticky gel from her stomach Ree thanked the doctor and delivered her message to the officer. She was instructed to wait with the other women who had already been seen and was told she would eventually be escorted back to her wing.

* * *

Gavin thought about Ree all day, as he did every day. He knew that this morning, at around 10 a.m., she would be having an antenatal appointment and was itching to see her tomorrow to hear all about it. He was heartbroken that he couldn't be with her to see the ultrasound scan for himself and was confused about the best way to behave in front of her. He certainly did not wish to upset her even more by saying how much he regretted not being able to be present for the scan but on the other hand he did not want his girlfriend to think he was uncaring by neglecting to mention it. He talked his dilemma over with Telly, asking the older man for advice. Telly was almost as upset as Gavin, thinking about poor sweet Ree locked up, pregnant, alone and scared for the future not only for herself but for Gavin and their child. Putting a fatherly arm around his shoulder, Telly choked back his own tears as he told his friend just to wait until tomorrow to see Ree and be as positive and bright as he could bear to be.

'How can anyone know what to say mate? Nothing could possibly make this situation any better other than Colin coming out of that coma and telling everyone the truth – that Ree grabbed the gun and shot in self-defence. Then we can all just move on from this terrible mess and Ree can come home to us, where she belongs.'

The remainder of the day passed slowly for Gavin. Every day weighed heavily on him but knowing Ree was having the scan made it worse. He went through the motions with the customers, hardly smiling and not engaging in any of his usual light-hearted banter at all. The regular customers were well aware of the situation and gave Gavin all the support they could, but despite everyone's best wishes, nothing could alter the fact that Ree was in prison.

Gavin and Mark closed the café and went through the familiar routine of cleaning and locking up. Mark's friend

Gary arrived just after the last customer had left the café and greeted Gavin with his usual cheeriness. Gary knew the sad circumstances of Ree's absence but had no idea of the special significance of the day. He was full of his and Mark's impending night out in the West End and all the fun they had planned. Gavin tried to be happy for them and their enthusiasm but found it hard to focus on anything other than Ree's predicament. Gavin told Mark to stop work and that he would finish off on his own.

'Go on. You get yourself ready. I'll finish off here – have a great time and be sure to have a couple of beers for me. God knows I could do with something!'

'Cheers mate, see you in the morning then, I'll give you a knock.'

Gary and Mark disappeared upstairs and Gavin continued to mop the floor. He was happy that he was going to visit Ree the following day but totally devastated that he had missed his baby's scan. Sad and lonely, he collected the laundry bag and put it in the back of the van which was parked at the rear of the building. He dumped the sacks of rubbish in the same place that he did every night to await collection and locked the doors behind him. Satisfied that all was in order, he wearily climbed the stairs and called out to Mark to see if he had finished in the bathroom.

Mark peered around Gavin's door a short while later, dressed in his finest, ready for a night on the tiles.

'Here mate, a couple of good films in case you feel like it tonight. I'll try not to wake you when I get in. Sorry Gav, I know how pissed off you are and I know there's really not much I can say. Take care mate.'

Gavin nodded in acknowledgement of his friend's kind words and, not trusting himself to speak without his voice betraying him, half-smiled at Mark who left the room, quietly closing the door behind him. He lay on his bed, tired and miserable, thinking only of Ree. He showered, dressed and decided to take Telly up on his invitation to come and eat with him that evening as he really could not face another night alone. Closing his bedroom door behind him, Gavin made his way downstairs and left the café, locking the shutter door behind him. He decided to walk to Telly's house – the cold night air would be refreshing.

Telly was his usual effusive self and tried his utmost to console Gavin but also realized that nothing really mattered to him other than having Ree back home. After supper, the pair watched *Bergerac* on television and for an hour or so were both lost in their own little bubbles of escapism, shutting out everything other than the ridiculous but nonetheless gripping storyline unfolding before them. Once the programme had finished Telly made them a cup of tea and Gavin decided it was time to be heading home. A five-minute discussion concerning a visit to the wholesalers ensued after which Gavin left Telly, deeply grateful for his friend's kindness. Pulling his coat tightly around him, he slowly walked home, dreading even more than usual the loneliness of the night ahead but feeling desperately guilty in doing so because he at least had his freedom.

He put his key in the shutter door and was surprised to find that it was unlocked – he was sure that he had shut it when he left but he had been distracted. He pushed at the café door, it too was not locked. 'Shit,' he thought.

'Please don't let anything have happened. How would I explain it to Telly?'.

'Oh well, no harm done,' he thought. The shutter had looked as though it was locked to passers-by.

He pushed the door closed behind him. Everything was just how he'd left it. Feeling the effects of the Metaxa that

Telly had insisted he should drink before leaving, Gavin climbed the stairs to his room and fell fully clothed on top of his bed.

He lay there and was thinking about his evening when a noise disturbed his thoughts. There was someone in the café, he was certain of it!

Moving very slowly and quietly, Gavin got up from his bed and crept onto the landing. There were no lights on but he could see in the gloom that the door to the street was still shut and the shutter door was also closed. Had he locked an intruder in?

He stood still and listened. The noise was in Mark's room – but he was sure Mark wasn't in – he always threw his coat on the banisters as he climbed the stairs.

'Mark, is that you mate?'

There was no answer. Convinced that he could hear an intruder inside the room, Gavin took a deep breath. He flung open the door and flicked the light on.

'Come on then you bastard!' he shouted, ready to unleash his fists on the burglar he was sure was inside.

'For fuck's sake Gav – what you doin'?'

It took a few seconds before he actually registered what was happening. Gary was on top of Mark. They were on the bed. They were naked and having sex! Horrified, Gavin stumbled backwards out of the room. Never in a million years had he suspected that Mark was gay. He retched into the tiny sink in the bathroom – the strength of the revulsion he felt for the two boys shocking even him in its enormity. What right had he to judge Mark for doing what he was doing? Was Mark gay? Was he being forced into doing something he didn't want to do? What the hell did it have to do with him anyway? Gavin's mind was reeling, taking him back to the night he had sold himself for money, to the night when he was ready to try anything to start a new life. The night when he had been as good as raped by his first punter. As he dashed back to his room he despised Mark and Gary. He despised everything to do with what he had just witnessed. He suddenly felt hatred even for Pixie and everything he or she was. More though, he despised himself for giving into the weakness of financial need on that night long ago – he'd not gone to a clinic afterwards, not had tests for anything. What if he'd given Ree more than a baby? What disease might the baby have? Consumed with guilt and angst, he had succeeded in scaring himself half to death and knew that all he was doing was adding to the huge worries about Ree he already tormented himself with. Pouring himself a large measure of brandy from the bottle in his room he fell onto his bed.

'Gavin, mate. You OK?' asked Mark.

'Fuck off you fucking queer,' Gavin sobbed, wondering how he was going to face the guy who he thought of as a brother when they had to work together tomorrow. He cried himself to sleep.

Chapter Twenty-one

For a few seconds as Laura absorbed the unfamiliar surroundings, she panicked, wondering where she was. The amazing events of the last twenty-four hours flooded back to her as she sat up in bed, registering that this was the first day of the rest of her new life. Carmel had given Laura the confidence and the practical help to leave Adam, to escape his bullying, his intimidation and his abuse.

The refuge was paradise to Laura, she was finally free but she was also ashamed to think that it had taken Ree's incarceration to bring about this change. This was a second chance as far as Laura was concerned and she would not waste another minute of her life. Adam was an evil man who, far from rescuing her, had pushed her further and further into a life of drudgery and despair with his fists, his cruelty and sordid sexual demands. She pushed back the pale pink bedspread which was clean but had definitely seen better days. The carpet was very thin in places and she could feel the outline of the floorboards under her feet as she crossed the small room to the window. As she drew back the curtains and opened a window on the new day, she felt free for the first time in her life.

* * *

Gavin's alarm clock screeched at him to drag himself out of bed. He had slept badly, a combination of guilt, despair and brandy. Turning the shower to cold, the water woke him up and made him face reality. He dressed and shut the door to his room behind him, meeting Mark on the stairs as he did so. Awkwardly the men faced each other.

'I had no idea.' Gavin stared at his work mate desperately trying to suppress the urge to punch him. He clenched his fists, but kept his hands by his sides, amazed at his own feelings of revulsion for this man he regarded as his best friend.

'Don't know why mate, and don't know what the big deal is. We are what we are and I thought it was pretty obvious how me and Gary feel about each other.'

'Well …'

'Look mate, you've seen me naked before! Bit embarrassing for us to have you walking in and all that but get over it eh?'

All Gavin could remember was the punter and Johnny who had laughingly counted out the twenty pound notes afterwards. All he could feel was the pain, the humiliation and the loathing. He knew that Mark was not that man but irrationally he lumped him in the same category and felt nothing but loathing for him.

'We've got to work together Mark, let's just get on with it and stay out of each other's way. OK?'

Gavin stomped down the stairs and Mark followed as they began their daily ritual of opening up the café. The strain took its toll on both of them and when Telly came to the café in the afternoon he instantly detected an uneasy atmosphere.

'You boys been fighting over the bathroom again? Whatever it is I don't want to know but get over it – it's bad for business.'

* * *

Mark could not understand what Gavin's problem was. So what that he was gay? Big deal, who gives a damn? And Ree was Pixie's maid. Pixie a cross-dressing male prostitute. He didn't realize that Gavin was revisited by the horrors of his first and only experience of gay sex – an experience brought home now every time he looked at Mark. Gavin knew deep down that it was unfair, wrong even, but life was unfair. As the day wore on Gavin's irrational anger increased and his animosity towards Mark intensified.

★ ★ ★

Pixie stubbed out her first cigarette of the day and drank the last mouthful of her cup of tea. Wrapping her dressing gown around her she decided to give the flat a good clean. She stripped the bed, put the sheets into the washing machine then turned the mattress before fitting clean sheets. She scrubbed the bathroom, cleaned the windows, hoovered, dusted, polished and ironed. Finally satisfied, she headed for the shower then set about making herself ready to face the world. A little tartan skirt with thigh length boots. Something to eat at the café, some shopping, supper with Telly then changing into Alan before going to the hospital. She had stopped seeing clients, there really was no need from a financial perspective now she'd got the twenty grand back, though she'd rather be poor than live without Colin, her soulmate.

She walked into the café and Telly gestured to her to join him at his table while he finished an irate phone call with a supplier.

'Nah mate. Same price as usual or forget it!'

He put the phone down.

'He told me to forget it, the bastard. I tell you Pix, sausages are the bane of my life right now.'

The pair sat in contemplative silence, each with their own sad thoughts, waiting for Gavin to bring over a couple of mugs of tea.

'What's up with Gavin?' Pixie asked. 'Is Ree OK?'

'He's had a row with Mark I think – no idea what about. Life's too short eh Pix love?'

Whatever it was, he had no interest in the squabble.

Gavin banged the mug of tea on the table in front of Pixie, slopping some over the rim and onto the table as he did so. Shrugging it off as the stress and strain of the whole sorry state of affairs, she left the café in order visit to Tesco, then the greengrocer's and the butcher's and complete her other chores. Gavin watched her leave

'Fucking pervert,' he mumbled under his breath.

'Right, that's enough, Gavin, out the back, now.'

Telly took the plates of food out of Gavin's hands and told Mark to take over for a while. It was nearly four o'clock so he would easily cope.

'I heard what you said about Pixie and you've been treating Mark like shit all day. Now, you better tell me just what the fuck is going on because this is my place and I won't put up with all this crap. I know you got a lot of stuff going on at the moment but what's this all about? Being a shit to the people who care about you is totally out of order.'

Telly looked at Gavin expectantly, waiting for some sort of explanation.

'It's everything,' Gavin mumbled, 'just everything. Mark and I had words about nothing and I'm just missing Ree so much and I suppose seeing everyone carrying on as normal just pisses me off.'

Telly instinctively knew that he was being fed an excuse but told his friend to finish for the day and get a good night's sleep. Maybe he would feel better in the morning.

* * *

Pixie dumped her groceries in the kitchen, unpacked and put them away then poured herself a large gin and tonic before switching on the TV. The early evening news told Pixie all the events of the day but she wasn't interested, she just stared into space, thinking of the dreadful things occurring in her life at that moment, wallowing in a rare moment of self-pity. Snapping to, she downed her drink and composed herself.

'No fucking point in all that now is there girl,' she told herself.

Later, as Telly and Pixie ate their supper they discussed Gavin and his bad mood. Telly had spoken to Mark who had given him, albeit very reluctantly, an outline of the previous evening's events. Telly was well aware of Mark's sexual leanings and had long ago realized that Gary was much more than just a friend to Mark. Pixie was not totally convinced, why should Gavin have such a strong reaction, and why to her too? And why now?

* * *

Gavin wandered through the park, trying to put his thoughts into some kind of perspective. Telly was right. He was being a complete tosser. Mark was entitled to be who he wanted to be and just because he had had a nasty experience he had no right to have any bad feelings towards either Pixie or Mark. He would go home and find Mark and Gary and apologize. Pixie also deserved an apology for his surly behaviour. Then he would go to the doctor and get himself tested. Every drop of logic within him told him that this was the right thing to do – the grown-up and decent thing to do. But he couldn't quite manage it when he returned to the café, the memories of

Steve the punter – yes, he even remembered his name – came flooding back as soon as he saw Mark through the window of the café, smiling at a customer as he placed a plate of chips on the table.

* * *

Carmel sat in the small room waiting for Ree to be brought to her. She had twisted a few arms and called in a several favours to be allowed this visit. She was incredibly nervous on Laura's behalf, totally unsure as to how Ree would react to her request. Over the last few weeks, she had seen Laura emerge as a much stronger person, no longer afraid of her own shadow, ready to face her daughter and explain her actions and ask her forgiveness. It was a bloody tall order Carmel thought to herself as she watched through the slats in the blinds covering the glass walls a prison officer approach the room. Ree was quite obviously pregnant now. She must be more than five months, Carmel thought as the small blonde girl was ushered into the room.

She asked the prison officer to wait outside. The woman hesitated momentarily then agreed. Carmel asked Ree to sit down then introduced herself.

'I'm nothing to do with the case against you Ree and please don't worry. Nothing is wrong. There is no more bad news or anything like that.'

The relief on Ree's face was almost tangible.

'However, I am here on behalf of someone who would very much like to come and see you – your mother.'

She waited for a reaction but Ree just lowered her head.

'She came to see me alone Ree. She's left Adam because she found out that he lied to the police about your disappearance. She's living in a hostel now and she just wants the chance to come and see you, to explain for herself. Maybe you will understand and find it in your heart to forgive her.'

Ree couldn't speak as she was so overwhelmed with emotion and shock. Laura had been pushed to the far corners of her mind. Her mother was a buried and forgotten piece of her past. But here she was, wanting to see her, to talk, to try to plaster over the deep wounds of Ree's pathetic childhood.

'Can you just think about it love, and if you do decide you can see her, then send a visiting order to her at this address. You don't owe her anything Ree, remember that, but life is very short and don't do anything you may one day regret. You're about to become a mother yourself, and might need a hand from your own mum. Take your time love. Think about it – it really is entirely up to you.'

Ree remained silent as Carmel caught the attention of the waiting officer.

Trying to think of some meaningful words of comfort but failing miserably, Carmel said, 'Best of luck love,' and left the room.

Ree was escorted back to her cell and the range of emotions flooding through her left her totally exhausted. She fell into a deep dreamless sleep but awoke feeling drained and tired; she didn't need anything else to complicate her life right now. Desperately wanting to be held by Gavin, she realized with sadness that she had another five days to wait before he would visit her again. Never before had she felt so lonely, so achingly alone.

Chapter Twenty-two

'This is all great Adam, but the deal was an interview with your wife. We agreed. We need to speak to your wife.'

Geoff was growing increasingly impatient with Adam's evasiveness and did not realize that the man had no idea where Laura had disappeared to. She had taken nothing with her, just the clothes she was wearing the day she had slammed out of the back door. She didn't really have any proper friends, just a few women she occasionally went to bingo with. He'd scoured every local bingo hall and watched outside the pub she'd cleaned each morning. He'd even been to see his mother-in-law but there was not a sign of his wife – it was as if she'd vanished off the face of the earth. Adam could see all the money vanishing with her.

'Look Adam, nothing is really happening with this case now. It's stagnant because the copper is still out for the count and Ree's been banged up. We need this in the paper in the next couple of days or the deal's off and you can kiss goodbye to any payment. We need the family photos, the tragic interview with the mother. Call me within the next twenty-four hours or just forget it. You've got my number.'

Geoff slung his mac over his shoulder and saw himself out of the back door thinking of the next big deal while Adam threw his empty mug across the room in frustration and, as it smashed against the wall, he cursed Laura again and again.

* * *

Squeezing her hands, Gavin took in Ree's words.

'Your mum? What a turn up for the books! Do you want to see her? You know you don't have to, don't you? You don't have to do anything you don't want to. You know that, don't you?'

Gavin was as shocked as Ree had been as he listened to her recounting Carmel's visit.

'So this copper really reckons that your mum honestly believes that he had reported you missing and was trying to find you? Are you sure that you want to do this now? It's a lot for you to cope with love, on top of the baby and well, just dealing with being here.'

'I've decided to hear it from her myself. I'll send her a visiting order and see what she says; I'll give her a chance. You don't know what he was like, to her as well as me, she was weak and just wanted peace, I understand that. It doesn't mean that she doesn't deserve a fair hearing now does it?'

Gavin spent the rest of the precious hour telling Ree all out about Mark and Gary and how he had walked in on them.

'You mean you never realized?' Ree asked. 'I don't believe it, surely you must have cottoned on. I thought everyone knew that Mark was into blokes. It don't matter though, does it? I mean, Gav, why should it bother you? '

'Oh no love, what I mean is I was just surprised. I mean he doesn't exactly look like one, does he?'

'Bloody hell Gav, listen to yourself! What do you think a gay bloke looks like? It's not something bad – people are just people. Look at Pixie. She's just a person, just a bit different from you and me.'

Gavin cringed in embarrassment, ashamed with himself

for his prejudices. He had momentarily let one bad incident from his past cloud his judgement, even to allow it to potentially damage his relationship with people who were his friends, his true friends.

The bell sounded and visiting was over for another week. Gavin and Ree both reluctantly stood and then watched each other go to their separate parts of the room, mouthing 'I love you' to each other until Ree was led away by a prison officer. This was the hardest part for both of them – the separation, the waiting for the following week. Gavin left the prison and walked slowly back to the bus stop, head bowed, eyes brimming with tears. How the hell was he going to put this right? He had hurt his friend Mark, not to mention having had some terrible thoughts about Pixie who had only ever been a wonderful loving friend to Ree. He felt bad for not telling Ree everything too. As he threw a handful of change at the conductor, he thought about how kind and generous people had been to him and resolved to put things right as much and as soon as he possibly could. He got off the bus at Elephant and walked the short journey to Telly's house. Unsure of how to begin or where to start, he pushed the door bell and prepared himself to confess his massive secret to the man he thought of as a father, loved a million times more than his own. Telly knew that something had been bothering Gavin, something pretty serious by the look on his face. The two men sat facing each other over the kitchen table, each clutching a mug of tea.

'Come on then mate, spit it out. What the fuck is going on in that pea-sized brain of yours?'

Telly was nothing if not direct and soon Gavin had done exactly what Telly wanted. He started at the beginning and told him everything. He was drained by the time he had finished and Telly could see how deeply the experience had affected the runaway who had become part of the family.

'OK, let's just get this into perspective. It was all a long time ago and on a serious level all that really matters is that you didn't pick nuffin' bad up and give it to Ree or the baby. Nothing else matters and no one else needs to know, unless you decide to tell them. I think Ree probably has enough going on at the moment so maybe this little gem is one we can leave for another day. But, you know what secrets are like, they fester and grow and can turn into something nasty that bites you on the arse. So one day soon, tell her, OK? But that's your call. As for Mark, well, he's a good lad and I've got no problem with what he's doing. I've known for a long time and it's no problem for no one. It's his life. I just told him to be careful and not tell everybody 'cos not everyone is as wonderful as me!'

Gavin laughed loudly. Telly always had a knack of making things seem so much better. Now all he had to do was to find Mark and make his peace with him before the whole thing was blown even further out of proportion. Feeling ten times lighter, Gavin thanked Telly and walked back to the café, feeling as though a huge burden had been lifted from his shoulders.

* * *

Penny had managed the refuge for fifteen years but was always moved by the plight of the sad women and children for whom she cared. She knew that for every woman who took shelter at this refuge for abused women there were ten more who remained in their homes, still suffering. She sorted the post and frowned as she saw the letter for Laura, worried that the newcomer had given her location away to someone who might tell her husband. This often happened and when it did all hell broke loose. Keen to know if there was a potential problem, Penny found Laura in the kitchen peeling potatoes for that evening's supper.

'Hello love, this came for you. Look, I'm not prying but you have been careful haven't you?'

Laura wiped her hands dry on a tea-towel and looked at the envelope with horror.

'I haven't spoken to no one, I promise you. I haven't hardly been out of here.'

Trembling with fear, Laura tore at the seal and pulled out the contents of the brown envelope. Realization of what she was holding hit Laura like a steam roller and Penny just about caught her as she fell forward.

'It's my Ree, she wants to see me! Oh my God! Oh my God … thank you, thank you …'

* * *

Rita sighed loudly as she flicked through the glossy magazine. Occasionally she glanced over at Colin; the mix of emotions she felt for him and the situation she was now faced with filled her with self-pity more than anything else. She had always felt that Colin was having an affair, maybe even a string of them or he was keeping a mistress. He was more than generous with the housekeeping but kept his financial affairs to himself so it was a possibility. Before he was shot it had not bothered her one little bit, she almost felt it was an occupational hazard – one that a wife of some thirty years coped with. As long as it reduced the demands in the bedroom, let her get on with her life and she wasn't kicked into touch in favour of a floozy, then it was fine. The most important thing was that, to outsiders, her life was seen as perfect – nice house, successful beautiful children, deliveries made from prestigious companies when she knew the neighbours were in. Sure, it meant that her friendships were based on her snobbery but she enjoyed the envy she was sure she engendered. She got pleasure out of being in control – she knew so much about her friends' worries and troubles but made sure that she never shared anything private in return.

It was the need to be in control, to know things, that consumed her. Why did Colin never answer the phone when she did her monthly visit to her mother's? Did he really take the opportunity for an overnight, overtime shift?

Out of curiosity she had followed him one day; well actually it had been on several occasions. And, at first, that's all it had been, curiosity – having a look at the competition. Rita knew it wouldn't be easy to follow her husband, after all he was a DI in the Met so not entirely stupid but then again, neither was she. She used her friend Moira's car, and even borrowed an old coat and headscarf so as not to make it too easy for her husband to spot her. She followed, she watched and she waited and was rewarded by seeing her husband use a key to go into a house in a small road off Southwark Street. She took refuge in the pub opposite and was able to witness Colin leave the building an hour later. Some five minutes after that a good-looking blonde opened the door and headed down the street. She wasn't that great to look at – someone in the City maybe – thought Rita.

She felt that she had been a good wife, overall anyway. True, her dad had been livid when she and Colin had told him that she was pregnant and that Colin was standing by her. Colin was a very young copper on probation then and the last thing he needed in his career was a scandal. So they were married, quickly, and a forced and artificial respectability was enjoyed by all. The baby duly arrived and everyone cooed, publicly ignoring the fact that she was an eight-month baby but privately loving the gossip. Accepting of her lot in life, Rita produced another two children and settled into her domestic role quite happily, keeping herself busy with bridge, tennis and a part-time voluntary job as the children grew older and more self-sufficient. The marriage was a bit of a sham, but that was the norm these days – many of her friends were in the same position. Oh yes, outwardly it was all a bed of roses but they hid the horse manure that made them blossom. They went to the ladies' nights at the masons' do's together, the golf club dinner, anything to do with the children but at home, alone, it was totally different. Hardly bothering to speak to each other, other than the bare necessities, they carried on their separate lives.

On bad days, Rita toyed with the idea of waiting outside the house off Southwark Street. She could confront the blonde, tell her to back off and leave her family alone. Then she would tell Colin that she knew about his mistress and that her conditions of an easy divorce would be that they waited until their youngest daughter had finished university. Colin would then sign the house over and provide her and the children with a healthy monthly allowance.

That had still been her plan but, last night, she decided that she needed to know where she stood now. Would she be OK if Colin stayed in a coma? What about his pension? Pouring herself another glass of red wine she had climbed the stairs to Colin's study. This was his sanctuary, his private place. Having looked through the desk drawers and finding little more than clippings about high profile cases that Colin had worked on she turned her attention to the wardrobe where her husband kept his dress uniform. It was there that she found the safe. She tried various combinations – Colin's birthday, the date of their wedding, their daughters' birthdays. Nothing worked. Finally she tried his police number. Success. Inside were the papers she was looking for which she put to one side to look at later. Underneath was a photograph. It was of Colin kissing someone who was obviously a man in a dress and a wig. She turned the picture over with shaking hands and found the caption made out of letters cut from newspapers – DI Arnold and his lover Pixie.

She retched then vomited her red wine on the cream carpet.

'You bastard! You shitty pervert! How could you do this to me?' she screamed, knocking over the glass as she ran out of the room.

She was stunned, shocked and sickened to the core by her discovery. How would she and her daughters cope if this got out? How would her friends react if it became public knowledge that her husband had been cheating on her with a tarted-up, full-blown transvestite?

Now, here he was, in a coma, fighting for his life. Only if he died would she be spared the indignity of what would follow if he recovered. She had no doubt that if he ever came to then he would retire and leave her to be with that thing, that excuse for a man, that travesty of a woman.

'Mrs Arnold? Hello, Mrs Arnold ...'

Rita came out of her deep thoughts, suddenly aware that her name was being called. A nurse was asking her if she wanted a cup of tea but Rita didn't want tea, she wanted blood.

'Does she come here? Does my husband's lover Pixie come here?' Rita asked the young nurse.

'Sorry, Mrs Arnold, not sure that I understand you. Does who come here?'

'Don't play games with me, the thing, the transvestite thing, does she come here?'

Rita spat the words out with venom. The nurse guessed

who Rita meant but being the sole of discretion just smiled.

'It's been a very long day, why don't you go home and get some rest. You're no good to him tired out. Come on now, I'll walk down with you.'

Rita couldn't believe that she had actually publicly acknowledged her husband's perversion but she was determined that she would come out of this the totally innocent party, and with as much money as possible.

* * *

Ree had posted the visiting order addressed to her mother with a shaking hand. She let go of the envelope and heard it drop softly into the post box at one end of the wing. She stood there, looking at the small slit in the metal and immediately felt her mouth go dry and her heart race. Now all she had to do was wait to see if Laura turned up. She knew the next week would pass by painfully slowly but she had an antenatal appointment to go to and her job in the library which she really enjoyed.

She felt quite well now and had even adjusted to her life in prison, shutting out the negative and concentrating on the positive aspects, despite these being very few and far between. Working in the library was definitely the best part of prison life. Having been very bright at school she loved to read and now she could read as much as she wished. But the one thing that gave her the most pleasure was helping others. She had been stunned to realize how high the illiteracy rates were amongst the prison population so, armed with her love of books and the gift of patience, she opted to work on the literacy programme. There were several volunteers who came to the prison a couple of times a week to help out along with a paid librarian but the demand far outstripped the help available and Ree found herself being constantly sought out by inmates who knew she would always patiently help them write a letter home or aid them read a letter they had received. For Ree, it helped to pass the time, to fill the hours and stop her dwelling on her own situation. She thought about Gavin every second of every day, and also of the day that her baby would be born, of Colin coming out of the coma and the day when she could walk out of this terrible place, free.

Chapter Twenty-Three

As the two old friends sat either side of Colin's bed each lost in their own thoughts, the arrival of the young nurse broke the silence. She stood there nervously, hesitating and trying to find the words to express what she wanted to say. She looked at Pixie, or Alan as she was today.

'Um … excuse me, but do you think I could have a word with you please, maybe in private please?'

'Darling, there's nothing you can't say to me in front of Telly. What is it love? Come on in and sit down.'

Pixie had been coming to the hospital every evening for months now and Telly often came too. This young nurse was completely familiar with the 'situation' and was the same nurse Rita had spoken to earlier in the day.

'Look, I know this is none of my business and the sister told me not to say anything, but I can't just sit back and see any more hurt. His wife was here earlier, and she said she knew about you, not just that Colin was having an affair but about you, um, that your name is Pixie and you are a ... um...'

'It's OK love, I know what you're trying to say. Thank you. It was very brave of you to tell me.'

Pixie gently stroked Colin's hand and the nurse slipped silently out of the room. Telly stood and walked to the window, covering his face with his hands for a moment, then rubbing his tired eyes. He watched an ambulance stop outside the Accident and Emergency department and the ensuing action as doctors and nurses flocked to the stretcher. He watched another ambulance speed away, siren screaming, lights flashing. Turning away from the window, he looked at Pixie. 'How much worse can this get?' he wondered to himself, shaking his head at no one in particular.

'I dunno what to say Telly. I had no idea that she knew. Col definitely never let on if he knew. He reckoned that she thought he was having a fling but they never talked about it. I wonder how she found out? Let's call it a night, I'm all in.'

They said goodnight to Colin and Pixie kissed him tenderly.

'We'll be all right love, see you tomorrow. Come back to Pixie lover, please come back to your Pixie. I need you with me. Love you.'

* * *

The two railway workers slipped off their donkey jackets and sat at their normal table. They spread their crumpled up copies of The Sun over the table and glanced at the headlines before turning to the back of the paper and the football news.

'Two full English please Gav, and get a fuckin' move on this morning, took bloody ages yesterday, we'll want it on the 'ouse if we get docked for being late on account of you!'

'Sod off you cheeky buggers, not my fault you're so bloody slow at eating, must be your age, you are getting on a bit now aren't you!'

Telly, Gavin and Mark worked quickly and efficiently, cooking, serving, preparing, cleaning. The morning rush eventually subsided and Telly made three mugs of tea for them all.

'Right, you two bloody twits, out the back and sort it out,

and bloody quickly too. I don't pay you to get the arse with each other on my time so piss off and sort out whatever it is.'

The two boys picked their mugs up and Telly busied himself with a regular customer – telling him all about his new grandson.

Gavin opened the door to the yard and walked out into the fresh air, or as fresh as it ever got in this part of London. Mark followed him, feeling awkward and embarrassed, knowing this was going to be the most difficult conversation they had ever had.

'Mark, mate, can I just say how sorry I am. I was a twat, am a twat! I'm so, so sorry.'

'Why did you get so pissed off though, what's the bloody big deal? I'm not happy working here with you, living here too knowing that you have a problem with me. So tell me. I'm gay but what the hell did I do that got you so worked up?'

'It's not you. You didn't do anything wrong and you've got to understand that I don't have a problem with you at all. It's … well, a long time ago I was in a situation and what I saw the other night just brought it all back to me. It was crap of me to take it all out on you but I did and I can't change that and I'm not proud of myself about it. Please believe me Mark when I say it was really nothing personal. I've got my head around things now and promise you that it won't happen again.'

Mark was wise enough not to push the matter as he guessed that Gavin could have experienced any number of situations which he had no wish to revisit.

'Mate, if you ever want to talk about it, well you know where I am. Shit happens when you come from the sort of places we started out. It happens wherever you start out but well, we've been through enough crap to keep us going for a lifetime. That hostel, living on the street, it's all shit and we know what can happen there. But that was then and this is now so let's think about the future and all the good things, not all that shit from the past.' Grinning, Mark opened his arms wide.

'Shall we kiss and make up now then?'

After calling his bluff and planting a big wet kiss on Mark's cheek, the two boys walked back into the café and shook hands with Telly.

'Now do some fucking work for a change will you? And that time is coming out of your breaks!'

All happy once again, Telly whistled to himself and the day continued with one less problem.

* * *

Adam felt as if he had walked up and down every street in the country, not just London, in his search for Laura. He still couldn't find her anywhere. He had been everywhere that was familiar to her, and everywhere that wasn't. All he could think about was the money disappearing before he even laid his hands on it. The fact that his wife had left him was not the issue, all he was bothered about was the money; as far as he was concerned, Laura could rot in hell but only after she'd given an interview and pictures to Geoff Harris.

* * *

Ree sat in the small holding cell with the other women who were waiting for visitors. She chewed her nails thinking again about the last time she had seen her mother, the memory hazy and vague. She clearly remembered the harshness of home and Adam and his cruelty to her mother but Laura was more of a non-event in Ree's life – a background figure, pathetically sad. The baby shifted inside Ree, kicking her hard under her ribs as it turned around. She stood and rubbed the base of her spine, trying to bring some relief to the ache she had felt slowly growing sharper over the past couple of hours. The door opened and two names were called; Ree froze with the realization that in the next few minutes she would meet her mother for the first time in over three years. She walked into the main hall and instantly recognized the anxious worried look on Laura's face. Laura stood and blinked back tears as Ree sat at the table opposite her and held the outstretched hand that was offered.

'Hello Mum, been a long time hasn't it? It's OK, Carmel told me what he did. I don't blame you, you know.'

'Oh love, I've been so terrible to you! Such a terrible mother, all these years and now look where you are.'

The two women held hands and caught up with each other's lives, both feeling overwhelmingly miserable. Ree bore her mother no ill-feeling and just wanted to start again, if that's what Laura wanted too. Laura explained that she had left Adam and that address for the visiting order was a refuge. She said that she was determined to start her life anew, make up the lost years to her daughter and hopefully be a grandmother to the baby. Ree was happy to have at least one part of her life going well. The hour passed quickly and she was sorry to see Laura leave.

'I'll send you another order as soon as I can. Don't worry about me. I'm fine here. It's not my first choice of hotel, but honestly, I'm OK. Thanks for being brave enough to come Mum, I do love you.'

'Oh love, you have no idea how much it means to me to hear you say those words. I'll see you soon, soon as I can, I love you too.'

Both women went back to their own worlds.

* * *

Penny handed Laura a mug of tea and looked at her worn tired face, the stress and strains of the day clearly showing. They sat at the vast scrubbed pine table in the kitchen of the refuge, peeling potatoes for supper.

'I can't begin to think how difficult it must have been for you. Well for you both. Carmel seems to have done a wonderful job for you, what a lovely girl she is. Lots of my guests come via her; she sees such terrible things in her job, doesn't she? Still, as long as there are committed people like her around to help, the world will be a better place eh?'

'Penny, I can't believe I have wasted so much of my life with that monster, missing out on so much of my daughter's life – believing that she had just run off the way he told me and that he'd been checking the police progress. How could I have been so stupid?'

'It's not being stupid love, its being bullied, being lonely, being scared. Didn't exactly have much of a start in your own life, did you? There's no use crying over what's been and gone. You have the chance to start again, not just with your relationship with Ree, but for yourself. You're still young you know, you've got every chance of happiness. Look, you've already taken the first step by seeing your daughter.'

'Thanks Penny. I am so relieved to be here, to be away from Adam and feeling so scared all the time. Wondering what mood will he be in? Will he hit me? Will he be angry or will it be OK for a change? I just wish I'd been stronger and been able to stand up to him when the kids were younger and we stood a bit of a chance. Look at us now: I'm here in a refuge, the boys are monsters just like their dad and my lovely girl is in prison. I have to start all over again with everything. I've no home, no money, not even a change of clothes that I can call my own. What a bloody mess.'

'Yes love, but you aren't scared any more are you and surely that's the best feeling in the world. We'll help you from here – to get somewhere of your own to live, help you with a job or maybe get on a training scheme. It's not all bleak love, just think of it as me time! You can do anything you like now!'

Penny gave Laura a hug and threw a tea-towel at her.

'Right then lady, let's get these spuds finished then deal with that huge pile of dirty dishes, just for a change!'

* * *

Ree lay on her side on the lumpy mattress, alone in her cell. She couldn't sleep, just tossed and turned, thinking about Laura, Adam, her brothers, the day she left home. She knew how upset Laura had been when they had met earlier that day, and she vividly recalled just how weak her mother had been against Adam and his evil ways. Adam had one hell of a lot to answer for. She slept badly and felt sick when she woke up the following morning. She informed a prison officer as soon as the woman banged on her cell door and after being examined was sent to see the doctor.

'Your blood pressure is slightly higher than it should be but a little rest should sort that out. Bed rest, OK? Right we'll have you taken back to your wing and you can stay in your cell for a couple of days. I'll see you on Friday. You may go.'

Dr Khan was not unkind, just overworked and harassed; and he also knew that many of his patients were just trying to pull a fast one.

Back in her cell, Ree tried to sleep as she knew that was what the baby needed. She sat propped up with the extra pillows she had been allowed and read for a while before eventually falling asleep. When she awoke it was to the sound of an officer calling her name,

'Lovell, come on, you have to eat something now. Maybe go out for some exercise afterwards if you want to.'

Ree drank the mug of lukewarm sweet tea and ate a sandwich. The officers were good to her, considering she was facing a murder charge and there was a copper still in a coma. It wasn't so bad if she closed her eyes and pretended.

She walked around the gardens with the other expectant mothers. The gardens were the only normal part of the prison, pretty and well kept, the only colour in the grey world she now inhabited. In particular, Ree walked with Chrissie, whose baby was due at the end of the following week. She told her new friend about the visit from her mother. When she had finished Chrissie was quiet.

'At least you know your mum and you know that she loves you. I can't remember mine. She dumped me in a care home when I was three and I never saw her again. You wanna try living in care. Compared to that, you've had the life of a princess.'

Ree smiled sadly.

'Ree, it's OK. It's done, it's over. Shit happens! At least you know it wasn't all her fault. I don't have any answers, haven't got a clue who she was or why. Wish I had a mum, you lucky cow.'

Ree put her arm through Chrissie's and squeezed her hand.

'I don't intend to let her go again, don't you worry. I tell you what, we'll share her.'

Quiet with their thoughts, the two girls carried on walking.

Chapter Twenty-four

Lionel Asher rubbed his eyes and slammed the file shut. The CPS had a bloody good case against Ree and he would have to perform a miracle to keep her from getting a stiff sentence. Right now though his eyes were tired and the rest of his body was feeling the same way. Renee Lovell was so far removed from his usual clients that the whole case was fascinating from a human point of view. Usually, Lionel worked on multimillion pound fraud cases, high profile celebrity stuff often involving drugs or a kiss and tell news story. The media had been all over him like a rash when this case came into his hands. He knew that as soon as Ree came to trial or, please God, Colin regained consciousness, the vultures would be back.

Leaning back in his chair, he replayed the whole story in his mind, minus the blackmail because as far as he could see there was no point in dragging that up. It had nothing to do with his client's motives, Pixie had the money back, Jimmy was dead and the police knew nothing about it. So, the kids came out of the pub, Jimmy was there, Colin was there …

'Sod it,' he thought, 'I'm going home and will think about it all in the morning.'

He knew that his client was incredibly timid and would find the strain of the cross-examination difficult to cope with, especially now that she was already seven months pregnant.

Time was ticking by and it was looking increasingly like she would have had the baby by the time the trial came along. Poor kid, he thought, what a start for the baby. Holloway wasn't exactly noted for its child-friendliness. He drained his coffee cup, stone cold and disgusting and realized just how late it was. As he threw a few papers into his brief case he thought about Martin Wells and the first approach his colleague had made concerning the case. He knew it was great publicity for the firm but, only if they won, which he fully intended to do. Martin had explained that Alan Dixon was an old friend, a very good, trusted and loyal friend for whom the firm had acted for thirty-five years. Loyalty was everything to men like Lionel and Martin and they would do their utmost for Ree. Alan's alter ego, Pixie, would have to stay a secret from the press. It would lead to sensationalism and the focus would be concentrated on a streetwise girl who worked as a maid for a transvestite prostitute instead of a young girl who helped out in a café and sometimes worked as a volunteer at a shelter for the homeless. The whole case could be lost if Pixie's secret was to become public knowledge. He shuddered as he imagined the headlines, said goodnight to the security guard at the reception desk and walked to the underground car park. Retrieving his Jaguar, he drove to Gants Hill and his safe, secure, white-bread world.

* * *

Adam stood in the doorway, hidden by the darkness of the night and the crowds. Piccadilly Circus was manic at 10 p.m. and tonight was no exception. He couldn't believe his luck, there she was, sitting in the window of the coffee-shop, with some blonde tart he had never seen before. He had met up with a couple of mates, arranged to buy some nicked portable

TVs they were flogging, and was celebrating his projected profits as he already had a buyer lined up. Having called it a night, he had turned left out of the pub and there she was across the road in the window of the café. She was laughing, and she looked different. He watched his wife pull her fingers through her hair and could see that she looked happy, relaxed. He was close enough to see that she wasn't wearing her wedding ring. Her greying hair had been cut and coloured and she was wearing a different style of clothes than she normally did. She looked younger, prettier than he had seen for years. He felt totally out of control and the anger boiled inside him. She was deliberately taunting him.

'Fucking bitch! I'll knock you into next bloody week if you think you can get away with losing me all that money and walking out on me and the boys too. I'll fucking kill you.'

'Come on, it's well past bedtime, let's make a move. Great to get out for a change, isn't it? *Never* Say *Never Again* was great; we must do it again soon,' said Penny, reaching for her bag.

'Do you know, I haven't been out in the evening with a girlfriend for, well, I don't think I ever have since I was a teenager. Adam never really let me go out except to the bingo and even then he drove me there and picked me up. He only let me do the cleaning job because it meant he didn't have to give me housekeeping money and the last time I mentioned going to a do at Christmas with the girls from work he slapped me and told me I was a selfish cow to even think of it.'

'That's the past and, like I said, you can do whatever you want to now. No one has the right to treat another human being the way he treated you. Come on love, let's go. Bloody hell, Sean Connery in the film was fit, wasn't he? Now he is someone who could tell me what to do anytime!'

The two women put their coats on and left the café, oblivious to the fact that they were being followed. They disappeared down the steps of the tube station and Adam, keeping a safe distance, jumped onto the same carriage as the doors were closing. He watched them get off, change trains at King's Cross and was still with them when they emerged at Islington. He continued to follow them, keeping well back and trying to stay in the shadows as they walked down the quiet residential road before they turned up the path to one of the houses. The blonde one unlocked the door and shut it behind them.

'Gotcha, you bitch,' Adam gloated and planned his revenge on the way home.

Chapter Twenty-five

'You can keep the book for a week, it's good, you'll love it.'

Ree stamped Jackie Collins' *Hollywood Wives*, took the library card out and placed it in the card holder. The library was a haven of peace and quiet; she could forget herself here, forget the real world as she checked books in and out, put them back on the shelves and read them when she had the time. She pushed the trolley to the shelf marked A and took the first book in the line from the trolley to put it away. As she reached down to take another book, a sharp pain stabbed her in the back and travelled around her front. She cried out in shock and instinctively grabbed her stomach. Another pain shot through her and she fell to her knees, gripping the sides of the trolley. Sheila, the librarian, rushed over to Ree, pushing the panic button around her neck as she did so. Two prison officers came running into the library expecting some kind of trouble. The older of the two quickly assessed the situation and realized that Ree was in labour.

'Shit! Sheila, call an ambulance and see if Dr Khan is here today. Ree, it's OK, I think you're early, aren't you? OK, we're not far from the hospital so we can get you there in no time. Shelia, tell them she's early, how many weeks are you Ree?'

Desperately trying to breathe through the fierce contractions, Ree felt warm liquid seeping between her legs.

'I'm about eight months now. I think my waters have broken.'

Dr Khan came running into the library and took control. He timed the contractions and told Ree that they were seven minutes apart.

'Ree, the ambulance is at the main gate, we'll have you in the hospital within about ten minutes You're only a few centimetres dilated so don't panic too much, we've got time. You'll be at the hospital before your baby is ready to be born!'

The paramedics arrived and scooped Ree into a wheelchair. Putting her in the back of an ambulance, they soothed her as she fought back the pain of another contraction. A prison officer climbed in while Ree was puffing and panting, breathing through the contractions as she had been taught. She wondered if she would have to go into the hospital handcuffed.

'Gavin, can you tell Gavin, please, I need him with me, they promised he could be with me. Please can you ring him.'

'I'll check in and see what the arrangements are and will contact him if that's what has been agreed.'

'For God's sake, please! I'm having a baby here, not robbing a bank, or mugging an old lady. I'm having a baby, please just help me!'

Another sharp pain made Ree catch her breath as she cried out for Gavin, saying his name over and over, quietly whispering, whimpering. The ambulance arrived after the promised ten minutes although Ree felt the world was passing her by in slow motion and the journey had taken hours. As they pulled to an abrupt halt outside the maternity suite, Ree felt her arm lifted and a handcuff snap around her wrist. It was the worst moment of her life. The paramedics looked at each other in disbelief.

'For pity's sake, is that really bloody necessary? The poor girl is in agony and about to have a baby, have you no compassion?'

'Procedure, that's all. May I remind you this "poor girl" is on remand for murder and I'm just doing my job.'

'Can we stop arguing about this and just get in there please?'

The prison officer marched beside the stretcher-trolley and into the delivery room still firmly attached to her prisoner's wrist. A white-coated doctor entered the room and took one look at the scene. He exploded with rage.

'Get that off my patient's arm and get out of here, now! And before you start babbling about procedure or any other such rubbish, just don't bother, get it off and get out!'

The prison officer opened her mouth and began to protest as the doctor interrupted her loudly and very firmly.

'I said get it off. Get it off now!'

'I'll be right outside and will notify the prison of this,' the prison officer said as she backed out of the room.

The doctor winked at Ree.

'A couple of calls to make then I'll be straight back.'

A nurse hooked Ree up to a monitor and put a wide strap across her belly with sensors attached to the belt. A small screen came to life, blinking numbers and lines moved across the monitor.

'Hello my love. My name is Hannah Fisher and I'll be your midwife for the time being,' said the nurse, introducing herself before explaining that she would take care of Ree until the baby was born or her shift ended, whichever came the sooner.

'OK love, now, I know you're in agony. I've had three of my own, but to make this as easy as possible for you I need you to focus on the instructions I give you. You'll be a little while yet so I'll try to make you as comfortable as possible. And don't think that just because you've come from the prison we care about that in any way, that is nothing to do with us at all and all the time you are here you will just be my patient. OK? Any questions at all? Anything I can do for you now?'

The door opened and the doctor reappeared.

'Just spoke to your young man, and to your mother, both are on their way. Somehow I didn't think the prison authorities would rush to let them know. It was all in your notes. Let me introduce myself. My name is Dr Hollis, and as I'm sure Hannah here has informed you, to us you are an expectant mum, just the same as everyone else on the ward. Though you appear to have a rather persistent uniformed friend! So, shall we have a look and see what's going on?'

With that the grinning doctor carefully examined Ree and reassured her that all was well.

* * *

Telly had answered the telephone call at the café in his usual gracious style.

'What d'y'want? It's lunchtime and I'm busy.'

As he put the phone back on its cradle he grabbed Gavin's jacket from the back of the door and opened his wallet. Thrusting a handful of notes into the bewildered boy's hands he pulled his apron from him at the same time, yelling.

'It's now, its early, quickly, quickly. Ree – she's having the baby, get a cab, she's at the hospital, go, go, go!'

Gavin could hardly comprehend Telly's instructions and could only think that something terrible must have happened as this was four or five weeks too early. Amid cheers from the regulars, he stumbled from the café and onto the pavement, waving like a maniac at every cab he saw. A bright pink taxi saw him and swung around in the road as Gavin sprinted to it, shouting instructions at the driver. He trembled as the car approached the hospital, every minute felt like agony and each red light and traffic hold-up made him want to scream. The cabbie recognized the signs and regaled Gavin with bloody tales of his own children's births, cheerfully describing the carnage to his very green passenger. Finally, throwing far too much money at the driver Gavin ran into the old Victorian hospital, desperate for a sign to the maternity ward. An elderly man approached and asked if he could help him. Gavin barely registered the laminated volunteer badge pinned to the man's pullover, but asked him for directions to the maternity ward before running off at breakneck speed. As he ran through the maze of corridors, he tried to compose himself, knowing that he needed to stay calm for Ree and the baby. Their baby. Pushing open the swing doors to the ward, he approached the nurses sitting around a couple of desks at the entrance.

'Please can you tell me where I'll find Ree, um … Renee Lovell, I'm her fiancée, Gavin Cooper.'

'Ah, Ree, yes love, we'll have to get past Hitler over there first, hope you're ready to be frisked!'

The nurses laughed and Gavin saw the very bored looking prison officer sitting on a hard plastic chair outside a closed door.

'We gave her the most uncomfortable chair we could find,' said one of the laughing nurses with a wicked twinkle in her eye.

Ree burst into tears when she saw Gavin enter the room.

'Thank goodness you're here; she might hurry up and get on with it now!' said the nurse taking Ree's blood pressure.

Gavin held his lover in his arms, stroking her hair and whispered quietly to her.

'I came as quick as I could. I love you babes!'

* * *

At the opposite end of London, Laura was also trying to get to the hospital to be with Ree as quickly as she possibly could. She cursed the traffic and, as she finally jumped out of the cab at the hospital entrance she was transported back to the day Ree was born. She wanted to weep as she found her way to the delivery suite, wishing with all her being that she could turn back the clock, but knowing that she couldn't. She wiped the tears away and was determined that this baby would have it all, would be happy, secure, loved and cherished, all the things that every child deserved.

'Ree's fiancé is with her right now and she's doing just fine. She's very tired but I'm sure she would love to see her mum. Why don't you go and get yourself a cup of tea and I'll let her know you're here. It really should only be one visitor to a bed, especially at this stage, but well, I think these are exceptional circumstances so I'll pop you in to see her as soon as possible.' The beaming midwife pointed Laura to a waiting area then, braving another scowl from the prison officer, gently knocked on the door and walked in. Gavin was sitting on the edge of the bed with his arm around Ree. who was still having contractions every five minutes or so. The last examination had revealed that she was now about six centimetres dilated so was cooking nicely as Hannah had put it.

'Ree, you have a visitor. Your mum is here; would you like to see her?'

Ree nodded and a few minutes later Laura was hugging her, while Gavin stood awkwardly by. By any measure, these were very strange circumstances for the pair to meet. They stood either side of Ree's bed, each holding a hand while the Hannah carried out another examination.

'OK my love, you are nearly there now. About eight centimetres dilated and doing great. Try and breathe through the contractions. I know they hurt like hell but take in a big slug of the gas and air and you won't feel a thing. Right lovie, another one is coming, come on now, big breath in …'

Ree let go of her boyfriend's hand and held onto the mouthpiece of the Entonox, concentrating on breathing through the pain. All she could think about was how hot the room was.

'It's November and I'm hot, so hot, it's bloody November and I'm so hot,' over and over again as the contraction passed and the gas and air muddled her thoughts and dulled the pain.

'What is it?' she thought to herself, 'What day is it?'

She knew what the date was as she had been stamping it in library books that morning. Concentrate on the date.

'It's 26 November,' she said to the bewilderment of all in the room.

Hannah helped Ree onto her side, telling Gavin to hold Ree's leg on his shoulder.

'Ree, you are ready. You're ten centimetres, next time you feel a contraction you have to push for all you are worth, OK? Here it comes, now push sweetie.'

Ree pushed, groaning with pain, tears and sweat falling from her face as she looked at Gavin and he looked back at her feeling helpless as he watched the agony on her face.

'Hey, fabulous honey, I can see the head, you are doing really well. Now rest, and when the next contraction comes push and we'll have this little beauty out. That's it now, come on Ree, nearly there love, that's it, a little shoulder and … there, oh darling you done it! A little boy, a beautiful baby boy!'

As Gavin and Laura helped Ree lie back on the bed and

propped her up with pillows, Hannah wrapped the tiny bundle in a towel and gently wiped the blood and mucus from its face. Hannah had delivered hundreds of babies but the wonder of it was still just as special as it had been the very first time. As she passed the baby to Ree, she watched the three adults smiling broadly, overwhelmed with happiness. The baby instantly found Ree's nipple and suckled gently.

'Gavin, look Gavin, he's so perfect, so wonderful, I can't believe it.'

Laura watched the little family, praying that they might have the happiness she had never had. She kissed her daughter softly and left the room.

Chapter Twenty-six

Telly didn't hear the phone ringing at first over the noise of the packed café. A huge robbery had taken place early that morning and news of it had just broken. The robbers were fairly well known in the area and the fact that they had nicked millions of pounds worth of gold and got clean away was quite spectacular.

Grabbing the phone, Telly shouted for quiet then a huge smile spread across his face as he replaced the handset.

'Shut up everybody, I gotta tell you, shut up! It's a boy, Ree's had a baby boy, and they are all doing fine!'

A huge cheer instantly erupted from the customers while Telly swelled with pride and love as if he had just become a dad again. Mark produced an empty bucket and placed it on the counter,

'Come on you lot, Ree and Gavin are going to need all the help they can get, dig deep and we'll find out what they want for the baby.'

Gavin was hugely popular and it seemed as if every customer was immediately on their feet, opening wallets and handbags, only too happy to give something for the baby. Telly had whipped off his apron and was already out of the door and striding up to the florist a few doors away to order a huge basket of blue and white flowers. Mark, ever thoughtful, phoned Nikki and gave her the good news.

'Oh wonderful, that's just wonderful. How much did he weigh?

What's his name?'

'Oh, umm … I don't know! I'll get Gav to ring you as soon as we see him.'

'Bloody useless,' thought Nikki as she excitedly dialled Pixie's number.

'Pix, it's Nikki, Ree's had the baby, it's a boy. Isn't it wonderful? And typically, Mark didn't even know the baby's name or weight, but as soon as I know I'll call you. Got to go, kids are screaming at each other, lots of love, bye.'

Pixie put the phone down and thought about the little girl who had come to her looking for somewhere to live. The little girl who was now a woman, a mother, and would hopefully soon be a wife living a normal life. Happy tears filled her eyes as she decided to find Telly and toast the happiness of the people she counted as her closest family. Smiling for the first time in months, she put on her best dress and high heels, made up her face and walked to the café where Telly greeted her with a huge grin and even bigger hug.

It was now well past four o'clock but the café was packed. Several bottles of champagne had been opened and poured into the mugs which only ever normally held coffee and strong sweet tea. The happiness was infectious and Pixie was glad she had left her flat to be with her friends. An enormous cheer made Pixie and Telly look up as Gavin and an older woman opened the door to the café. Gavin was overwhelmed by the good wishes and hearty handshakes as he found Telly and Pixie who both brought fresh tears to his eyes with their loving congratulations.

'Pix, Telly, I'd like you to meet Ree's mum, Laura.'

After the introductions were completed and mugs of champagne pressed into empty hands, Nikki appeared.

'Well, Dad, I bet you still haven't asked. What did the baby weigh and what are you going to call him?'

* * *

Ree was totally exhausted by the day's events and with her beautiful baby asleep in his cot beside her bed she had gratefully fallen into a deep sleep. Gavin was coming back to the hospital when visiting started again for the evening so she took the chance to grab a well-earned rest.

Gavin gently opened the door of the side room, ignoring the steely glance of the prison officer who was still sitting on the hard chair. A nurse followed him into the room and spoke quietly to him.

'They are both shattered, but I think baby will be waking up soon for a feed. Shall I take those beautiful flowers and find a vase? Sit here and have some peace while they both sleep.'

The nurse took the bouquet Gavin had been holding and came back a few minutes later with two vases full of the various blue and white flowers. Gavin had also brought a blue teddy bear with him. The day after he had been told that he was going to be a father he had bought a pink and a blue bear from the street market.

'The pink one will have to wait,' he thought as he placed the toy gently at the end of the small clear plastic cot.

'You are going to have the best of everything, but most of all your mum and me love you and will do every day of your life for as long as we live. This is the first time I've told you that I love you, my beautiful baby boy, my son.'

Chapter Twenty-seven

One day Adam had followed Laura and Penny for three and a half hours until he was at the end of his tether. He had muttered and sworn under his breath, seething to himself that he hadn't managed to catch his wife alone. Everywhere she went that other bitch had gone with her. They had been to the council offices, to the job centre, to the local adult education centre and then they had sat down in a café drinking bloody coffee. He had been furious to see that Laura was doing things for herself, without him, without his permission; how dare she! She was arranging things, moving on without him.

From the sheltered doorway of a Midland bank he had watched the two women pay for their coffee and put their coats on. They had headed towards the bus stop and jumped on the first bus that came along. He had guessed from the number on the front of the bus that they must be on their way back to the hostel or refuge or whatever they bloody called it.

'She'll be so sorry she ever crossed me,' Adam had told himself as he watched the vehicle disappear into the heavy traffic. 'I'll make her so fucking sorry.'

He never saw her on his own. Then his chance came.

* * *

The bus stopped at Oxford Circus and Laura jumped off,

completely unaware that Adam had been sitting at the far end of the deck, hiding behind a newspaper. As she made her way through the shopping crowds she felt truly happy for the first time in her life. Everything was falling into place for her. She'd had a great deal of help and encouragement from Penny who had shown her how to take control of her life, how to think for herself but she'd had to find the courage to be her own woman. Today she wanted to buy some clothes for her grandson, such a wonderful little boy, still without a name poor little mite at three days old. So she had decided to do some shopping in Oxford Street, on her own. She walked into John Lewis, through the perfumery where she smiled when accosted by several young women caked in make-up inviting her to try this new fragrance or that one. As she turned to walk towards the lift hall Adam stood in front of her, blocking her way. The blood drained from her face and she felt faint and nauseous at the same time. It was a feeling she recognized so well – the feeling of pure fear.

'Hello Laura, having a nice day out, are you?' Adam sneered at her, sensing her fear, enjoying her anguish.

He took a step towards her and grabbed her arm, pulling her even closer to him. Quietly, he spat the words into her face.

'Think you could just walk away from me, did you? Think you could disobey me and cost me a fucking packet? Well I'll tell you what you are going to do. You are going to walk out this shop with me, come home where you belong and give that fucking interview to the paper and do exactly as I tell you. Do you understand me? I am going to teach you a lesson you will never fucking well forget. Just you wait, oh yes, you'll never dare disobey me again.'

Petrified at the thought of returning to her old life and losing everything she had recently gained, Laura summoned every drop of strength she had and spoke loudly and clearly as she pulled away from her husband.

'Let go of me, who the bloody hell do you think you are?'

Adam was astonished. Laura had never ever dared to answer him back or question his orders and here she was, speaking to him as if she was the boss!

At that moment a shop assistant walked over to them, wondering what the raised voices were about and not wanting a fuss near the other customers.

'Are you all right Madam? Sir, you look a little flustered and I couldn't help but overhear loud voices …'

'This man is threatening me and is scaring me,' Laura said.

She had rarely been so frightened in all her life but she had learnt so much about herself and the kind of life she could have that she was damned if she was going to give it all up to this bullying ogre of a man. The shop assistant stood between them and turned to Adam.

'You are quite safe here Madam, I can assure you. Now Sir, I must ask you to leave instantly or I will call for our security officers who will restrain you until the police arrive. Do I make myself clear?'

Sweat ran down Adam's forehead, as he angrily clenched his fists and marched out of the shop, stunned at the change that had come over his previously timid wife.

Laura, burst into tears with relief, overwhelmed with the fact that she had finally after all these years of intimidation stood up to and beaten Adam and she'd done it on her own.

Gerry, the shop assistant, was in fact a floor manager and had seen Adam block Laura's way. He had seen the reaction on Laura's face and had made his way over to the pair as quickly as possible without alerting anyone else. He now sat opposite Laura in his office, having called for a cup of tea and a box of tissues. Laura explained that Adam was her husband and she had recently left him, that she was living in a refuge and was looking for a job, a new start. Gerry told her that Adam was just a bully and bullies picked on weaker, defenceless people. Laura dried her eyes and thanked him for his kindness, still amazed with herself that she had finally found the strength to stand up to her husband and was not ashamed to tell of the life she had left behind.

'We're always looking for staff in one department or another you know. You don't need any qualifications but it often helps if you know the floor manager!'

Gerry chatted to Laura about several vacant posts and, when she was finally relaxed and over her frightening confrontation with Adam, he asked her if she would like him to send her an application form.

'Do you know what? I think I would,' Laura said, amazed at herself, astounded at the transformation and determined to never allow herself to ever be bullied or intimidated again. She left the store having given her address to Gerry who promised to send her an application form.

'Whatever you decide, drop in and see me next time you are passing? I'm always up for an excuse for a break! You could join me,' Gerry said as she was leaving. Walking into the weak sunshine Laura resolved to do just that.

Chapter Twenty-eight

Rita threw the magazine onto the sofa next to her, unread, and stared unseeingly at the wide bay window before her. She had initially taken her anger and frustration out on the house, cleaning and washing even more than usual, bleaching the already gleaming toilets and taking down the nets, cleaning the windows, changing the beds, dusting, forever dusting. She picked up the cup of tea and pulled a face as she sipped at it – the liquid was stone cold. She stood up and took the cup and saucer to the kitchen. Tipping the cold tea down the sink she flicked the switch on the kettle and reached for a clean cup. Running the tap, she rinsed the tea from the sink wiped invisible splashes from the work surface and folded the dish cloth, placing it in the washing-up bowl. As the kettle boiled she tapped the grey marble-effect Formica work surface with an immaculately manicured blood-red painted finger nail.

What the hell was she going to do? How the hell could she emerge from this with her dignity intact and be the innocent party? Her life would be over and she would be a laughing stock if everyone found out that her husband had been having an affair with a bloody transvestite. If he came out of the coma what state would he be in? Would she be expected to look after him?

The switch on the kettle clicked off as the water reached its boiling climax. She automatically reached for the tea caddy and dropped a tea bag in the cup. Only her, she couldn't be bothered to use the pot. What would he be like? Would he be a cabbage or whatever the term was? Would Colin be some drooling thing she had to look after twenty-four hours a day, wiping his arse for him, feeding him like a baby. Christ, she must have been a bloody bad person in a previous life to get lumbered with all this.

Pouring milk into the cup she squeezed the tea bag between her long fingernails and dropped it into the bin. Why the hell hadn't he had the bloody decency to just die and save them all from this charade? If he died that would be the end of it and that bloody man-woman thing would disappear too. She could be a tragic widow and could hold her head up at the bridge club. She sipped the hot tea, yes, that's what would be best; hopefully Colin would die.

* * *

The two visitors at a time rule seemed not to count as far as Ree was concerned. She was still in the side room, with a prison officer constantly in position outside the door on a hard chair, although sometimes a cushion and a cup of tea were found when it was the turn of a decent prison officer, one who displayed a kind side and treated Ree and her family and friends like human beings. Telly and Pixie sat either side of Ree, gazing at the baby sleeping in her arms. Laura and Gavin looked on.

'It really is about time this poor child had a name,' Telly said as he stroked the baby's cheek.

'Max, that's a good name, what about Max?'

Ree and Gavin had argued for hours, unable to reach a decision, and now everyone else was chipping in with suggestions of their own.

'Max Cooper sounds like a car or a comedian and Max Lovell sounds like a toilet roll!'

Ree laughed at Telly, who took the sleeping bundle from her.

'Poor thing, what a wicked mother you have, poor child, laughing at your Uncle Telly like that.'

There was a tapping at the door and the doctor whom Ree had met when she had first arrived at the hospital peered into the room.

'Hi Ree, I've been off for a couple of days, just wanted to check up on you and your son. All OK? How is everything going? I can see you are having a party here so I won't stay.'

The doctor shook hands with Gavin and congratulated him on the beautiful baby. Ree watched the doctor peering over to get a closer look at the baby who had just opened his eyes as his lay in Telly's arms. Dr Hollis, Daniel Hollis said his name badge.

'So, does he have a name yet or is he going to be Baby Lovell for ever?'

Ree looked at Gavin.

'His name is Daniel. It's a name which I will always associate with kindness. Thank you doctor, for everything.'

Chapter Twenty-nine

'He is such a lovely baby. So good. Just does all the things they are supposed to, you know. Sleeps, feeds, and well, I know I'm biased but what a gorgeous thing he is. He's got a shock of very dark hair, and so soft. I'm almost broody – is that possible?'

Pixie laughed as she squeezed Colin's hand. Smiling at the thought of Daniel, she stood stretching her arms above her head as she walked around the room, feeling numb after sitting for the last hour or so. As she leant against the wall, looking over at Colin, she took in the vases of flowers, the 'get-well' cards strung up behind the bed, there were that many of them. Pixie had a routine and, as Alan, came to see Colin each evening at around 8 p.m. and stayed for an hour or two. She would read to her lover, or just sit in silence holding his hand, mulling over the future, reliving happy memories of their past. Sometimes she would tell Colin all the news of the day, chatting about everybody they knew, just in case he could hear something that would bring him back. Tonight all the news was of the new addition to the family as Pixie thought of the baby, for Daniel was the nearest thing she would have to a grandchild.

As he poured himself a glass of water and sat down again, Pixie continued.

'Nikki brought the kids to the hospital to see Daniel and

they loved him, wanting to hold him. Little Telly seemed to think Daniel was a dolly. Won't be long before Nikki's expecting again I don't doubt. Poor Ree, she's looking so tired, little mite is keeping her awake feeding all the time. Even though he was early he's got a great appetite on him and what a set of lungs! Anyway, they are all just enjoying this time they have together as a little family, before Ree has to go back to that bloody awful place. Oh Col, I can't bear that for her. It's there all the time, hanging over them, well, all of us really, but Gavin feels so helpless and he's trying to keep everything together but, you know, he's so upset inside. Come on Col, wake up and tell them what happened. God knows what sort of trouble will come out of it all but nothing can be as bad as Ree being in prison surely? Please wake up Colin, please my love.'

Pixie kissed Colin lightly on the cheek, collected her masculine coat. 'I love you, sleep tight,' she whispered and walked out of the room, softly closing the door behind her.

Telly was waiting in his usual spot for Pixie to emerge through the heavy glass double doors. Asleep, or dozing as he usually called it, with a newspaper scattered around him, the steering wheel and the floor, Telly's snores could be heard outside the car. Pixie tapped on the glass and Telly opened his eyes, taking a minute to register his whereabouts. Reaching across the passenger seat, Telly pulled up the lock and Pixie climbed in the car.

'OK? Want to go straight home or shall we have a nightcap at mine?'

Telly turned the key and started the engine. The strains of the Flying Pickets filled the air with 'Only You' and Telly immediately turned it down until the music was just an indeterminable background noise.

'Take me home please Tel. Come in and have a drink with

me, but I just want to get home. It's been a funny few days. So exciting about the baby, bloody wonderful, but then I go in there and look at him and wonder where will it all end. It's December. Soon be Christmas. Look at us all, Ree will be back in that bloody awful place, having to go through all that process as to whether she can keep the baby with her or not and Colin is another awful place, locked away in his mind. What a mess.'

'OK. Let's get you home. Think about just the good things Pix. Ree is well, Daniel is perfect. Thank God for that, the rest we can leave for another day.'

* * *

Rita's stiletto heels announced her arrival at the hospital. The nurses who were sitting at the entrance to the ward heard the clacking.

'Brace yourselves girls,' one of them murmured to her colleagues.

Three o'clock on the dot; she would stay for about twenty minutes, sitting silently beside Colin's bed, flicking through some gossipy showbiz magazine then leave without so much as a word. She never spoke to any of the nurses or even gave them a smile. When it was necessary for a medic to enter Colin's room and see to the drip or check his catheter she still never said a word not even to ask how her husband was doing. She was a cold fish, they all agreed.

Rita sailed past the nurses' station, her heavy perfume lingering after her. The nurses kept their heads down and wondered about this woman, her husband and the other man who visited every night – the man whose world seemed completely devastated.

Sitting on the armchair beside Colin's bed, Rita pulled a

magazine from her bag. The glossy pages were full of smiling families planning their perfect Christmases. Tips on cooking, decorating the perfect Christmas tree and suggestions for presents only served to make Rita even more livid. She was angry, frustrated and bitter. Closing the magazine, she spoke directly to her husband for the first time since he had been injured.

'Why the bloody hell didn't you just die you selfish bastard instead of putting me through all this? I fucking well hate you for what you've done to me, all this, this show of sitting here playing the devoted wife. All these years you've been deceiving me, seeing that thing, oh yes, I know Colin, I know all about your sordid revolting relationship with Pixie. What is his real name by the way? Is one of these cards from him? Do you think I could guess? Yes darling, I found the photo in your safe. You know the one, don't you, you bastard? The one with you kissing. It made me sick. Not sure I'll get the stain out of the carpet that's for sure. I can just about understand you leaving me for another woman, someone younger, it would at least make sense, but to be having an affair with a man who goes about dressed up as a woman, well that just beggars all belief. You make me feel ill Colin and I hope you die, save me and the kids a great deal of heartache. Have you ever bothered to consider them in all this? What the hell are they going to think if it all comes out? We'll be a laughing stock and I don't expect there will be much of a pension if you resigned. You've buggered everything up. Just hurry up and die you creep!'

Angrily, Rita thrust her arms through the sleeves of her coat and buttoned it up to her neck. She put on her gloves and without a backwards glance stormed out of the room, allowing the door to slam behind her. The noise of her heels could be heard all the way down the corridor to the lift hall.

'I saw her talking to him, I could see through the blinds, she was actually talking to him, didn't seem that happy mind you,' a student nurse reported to her mentors.

Chapter Thirty

Gently placing a kiss on her baby's forehead, Ree laid the satiated sleeping bundle in his cot and sank back against the pillows, closed her eyes and slept. She was exhausted, completely drained with the constant breastfeeding which lasted an hour at least each time, every three or four hours. Gavin tiptoed into the room and silently closed the door behind him. He sat in the comfortable worn armchair between the two sleeping loves of his life. A wave of happiness washed over him as he momentarily forgot all the problems in their lives and concentrated on the short time his family was now sharing together. Daniel screwed his face up in his sleep then let out a tiny sigh as Ree began to snore softly. Gavin looked at the cards strung above the bed and all over the place. The room was awash with flowers, mainly shades of blue and white but plenty of everything in between. The gifts from the customers at the café had amazed him. Men whom he served breakfast to every morning brought him in hand-knitted cardigans and bootees, mitts and blankets from their wives. Meg, a fixture of the café and who had been a customer for years before Gavin arrived and learnt that she came every day at 11 a.m. for a coffee and a teacake while she took a break from her stall in the market, had only that morning handed Gavin an envelope full of cash telling him that the stall holders had had a whip-round for them. He had

had no idea that he and Ree had so many friends and had been staggered by the generosity of even casual acquaintances. Teddy bears and cuddly toys of every kind were piled on a chair in the corner of Ree's room and she had been overwhelmed by the number of visitors she had received. As Gavin watched his sleeping family his eyes filled with tears of love for them and helplessness at the situation. He knew that before very long, a few more days in fact, Ree would have to go back to the prison with the baby, which would be the worst moment of his life.

A prison welfare officer had come to the hospital to see Ree the previous evening. She had explained that Ree's application to keep the baby with her had been successful and for the time being at least they would be sent back to Holloway where they would, in the first instance, spend time on the mother and baby unit. Once a place was found for her in a dedicated mother and baby unit at another location she and Daniel would be transported to wherever that was. There weren't many of these places or, indeed, vacancies available the officer had gone on to explain. It was, however, thought that there would soon be a spare room at the prison in Durham. The thought of Ree and Daniel being so far away horrified Gavin but the main thing was to concentrate on now, to enjoy every second that they were here, together, and just hope they would all find the strength to cope with whatever was thrown at them. He watched his girlfriend and his son as they slept, and savoured each precious moment.

⋆ ⋆ ⋆

Geoff impatiently tapped his biro against his teeth as he waited for Adam to answer the phone. A nameless source had informed Geoff that Ree had given birth to a son and now he was desperate to have one last attempt at putting a story together. This was lovely juicy human interest stuff which the readers would lap up, if only Adam would get his act together and sort his wife out.

Adam had been nearly asleep, dozing in front of the TV, waiting for the boys to come home from football and make him something to eat. They stayed out more and more lately, the older one talking about going into the army. Bloody good riddance to another mouth to feed was Adam's view.

The persistent ringing of the phone had startled him and it had taken a few moments to register. He hauled his grossly overweight body from the chair and rushed as fast as he was able to the hallway grabbing the phone from its cradle. Breathless, he barked into the mouthpiece.

'Yes, who is it?

'Adam, mate, its Geoff. Look, we've heard that Ree has had her baby so I really do need to strike while the iron is hot. Have you managed to get anywhere with your wife? Laura isn't it? Look, if you can get some happy family pictures in the hospital and all that, well, we'll up the money. Another five grand for pictures of the new mum and baby on top of what we already discussed. What do you think mate? Is there really any chance do you think? And this really is our final offer. Adam, are you there mate, Adam, hello, hello?'

Adam felt the pain shooting down his arm as he staggered backwards and clutched his chest.

'The money, that bitch, the money ...'

He could not breathe as he sank to the floor, dropping the receiver as he hit the carpet. He was vaguely aware of some faraway, tinny voice calling his name then heard nothing at all as the agony of the scorching in his chest drove him to unconsciousness.

Geoff could hear a rhythmic banging as the receiver

swung backwards and forwards like a pendulum; the sound growing fainter and fainter as it lost momentum. He put his phone down and moved his attention to his next great scoop, burying Adam in the recesses of his mind as a total waste of time.

'Strange bloke,' he thought to himself. 'He was the one who came to me in the first bloody place and now he's ignoring me. Oh well. You win some you lose some,' he philosophically decided.

* * *

Laura held her grandson, cooing and clucking to him, stroking his tiny face with the tip of her finger. The special new born smell filled the room and she etched these treasured few days on her memory for ever. She had tried to explain to Ree what life had been like when she had been born, how difficult things were and how she was not ready to be a mother, still really a child herself. She told her daughter about the cramped tiny flat, the council estate and the poverty. Ree had never really talked to her mother before, could never remember having a conversation like this, about things that actually mattered.

Laura was overwhelmed with guilt for her treatment of Ree and now her daughter understood a little more of her own upbringing and the loveless way she had been raised. Ree was not angry with her mother, just sad at the circumstances and determined that Daniel would never experience the feelings of isolation that both his mother and grandmother had experienced.

There was a tap at the door and Hannah came in, all beaming smiles and happiness.

'Just got to do the usual check-ups my love. On you, not

baby. You stay where you are Grandma, baby looks very happy to me.'

She had that way of talking which regressed everyone back to three years old and at nursery school. She was a lovely lady, full of energy and enthusiasm and obviously loved her job.

'I hate to ask love, but when will you have to go back to Holloway?'

Laura had been dreading asking the question but wanted to make the most of their time together. Ree felt her eyes pricking and looked away, out to the grey winter sky. It was the moment she did not want to contemplate, walking back into the prison, with her baby.

'I think I stay here until Daniel is about ten days old.'

Hannah chipped in, with one of her big smiles. 'Ree, do you know I have a feeling that when baby Daniel here is ten days old well, he might just be a touch jaundiced. Obviously, you will both have to stay here under observation until he is better … could take a week ... may even be able to string it out to Christmas, but don't get your hopes up too much. Now, rest, do as you're told or I'll send you back pronto!'

Winking at Ree, she clipped the chart back on the end of the bed and left the room.

'She's an angel! Now, you heard her, rest,' smiled Laura.

Daniel, still sleeping, was placed back in his cot. Laura kissed Ree and left her to rest. As she came out of the room, gently shutting the door behind her, Laura saw the midwife sitting in the ward office, pen in one hand, mug of tea in the other. Smiling at the very pleasant prison officer whose turn it was to be on guard, Laura took a deep breath and approached the office.

'Hello my love, what can I do for you?'

'Look, what you said earlier, do you really think you can

delay Ree's return to the prison? I mean, I know you mean well, but I don't want her to get her hopes up ...'

'Come on in and sit down. Well, certainly I can let them know that we think Ree and the baby need to stay here for a little longer but in all seriousness, I think we can probably keep them for another week. So make the most of it. I'd get shot if I was caught, but she's such a lovely girl and it will do her the world of good, and the baby too, to be here, in a calm relaxed environment rather than in a prison. We'll do our best, I can promise you that.

So, grateful for the extra time with her daughter, Laura left the hospital and took the short journey to the café. Daniel was six days old now and every day had been precious to her. As she sat at the top of the bus on her way to London Bridge, gazing out of the window she saw busy streets full of Christmas shoppers and the first of the early evening commuters on their way home. She thought about all the mundane sights she took for granted, things that Ree couldn't see, wouldn't see for goodness only knew how long. She grieved for her daughter, for the years they had spent apart, for the hardships she had been through and the continuing pain she would suffer. Climbing wearily down the steps from the top deck, she walked down Southwark Street towards the café.

Gavin and Mark had closed up and were going through their ritual of clearing the greasy residue of the day. Gavin looked up and saw Laura as she raised her hand to knock on the glass door. As he unlocked the door and ushered her in, he asked Mark to make just one more cup of tea that day. Laura had dark rings under her eyes and was clearly feeling the strain of all she had been through over the last few months.

'Oh no, I don't want to hold you up, honestly, it's fine. I

just came to tell you that Ree is supposed to go back to the prison in four days. Did you know that Gavin? Only, no one has mentioned it, and well I asked Ree today and that nice midwife Hannah says that they should be able to delay them going back by about a week. Isn't that wonderful? We'll have an extra week. Look, why don't you go and get changed and I'll help Mark finish off here.'

Laura's words woke Gavin up like a slap around the face. Of course he knew that Ree and Daniel had to go back to the prison but it wasn't something he wanted to actually think about, to put into words. He wanted to push it away and make it vanish. He wanted to make believe that they were just a normal couple bringing their beautiful baby home where he belonged. The fantasy was now shattered and he knew that he would have to face up to reality.

Mumbling his thanks to Laura, Gavin pulled his apron off and threw it in the sack for the laundry. He showered and changed in record time and was soon on the bus. It was dark as he decided to walk the last five minutes to the hospital. He could hear rumbles of thunder far away in the distance and hurried on. The first bolts of lightning cracked across the sky and, just as he walked through the heavy glass doors, the rain fell in torrents.

Shutting everything out bar his burning desire to be with his family he hurried to the maternity ward and slid silently into Ree's room. She was sleeping and looked so beautiful, peaceful – free of the cares that he knew were weighing her down like lead weights. The baby stirred slightly, creasing his tiny brow and waving a clenched fist around. Quickly Gavin picked his son up, shushing him, giving Ree a precious few moments' more rest. Yes, he would have to face the fact that this wonderful time would soon be over, Ree and Daniel would be gone and he would have to cope with weekly visits again. But not today, not today when Ree was sleeping and Daniel was in his arms. Not today.

Chapter Thirty-one

The mirror gleamed but still Rita rubbed it, polishing and shining as if her life depended on it. Her visitors were due at 11 a.m. so the house had to be scrubbed from top to bottom. She had been up since six although she had actually woken much earlier. Sleep did not come easily to her these days, in fact most nights she resorted to a tablet to get her off. When she first had the phone call she had assumed that they wanted to talk to her about money – Colin's pension or salary, or maybe a lump sum payment but when it transpired that the officers wanted a chat about what Colin had been up to the night he was shot, well, that really was something entirely different altogether.

The door bell rang and she could just make out the shape of Joe, the window cleaner, through the frosted glass. As Rita pulled off her rubber gloves and hurried down the hallway to open the door for him she checked her watch – 8.30 a.m., exactly. Rita couldn't stand lateness as Joe had discovered to his cost. He had stepped inside the porch to avoid the cold of the December morning and greeted Rita with a wide cheesy grin and very cheery good morning. She was an obnoxious battleaxe and he earned every penny of his wages from this one. He knew a cup of tea was out of the question but on the plus side she was a regular customer, through the winter too, so he put up with the old bag.

'Good morning Mrs Arnold. Chilly but bright! Where would you like me to start today?'

Rita gave Joe her instructions and left him to it. She finished off the bathroom, plumped up the already perfect cushions in the living room and was finally satisfied. After a shower and half an hour with the heated rollers she began to relax. Carefully applying her make-up and selecting a black pleated skirt, white blouse with a frilly, stand-up collar and flat black loafers she felt ready for the grilling, albeit with a gentle approach, she knew she was going to face. She had thought carefully about her answers and decided that she would plead ignorance as to Colin's actions and whereabouts on that fateful evening. She would say that she assumed he was at work and if they brought the subject of Pixie up, if they knew, she would also plead ignorance, be the injured party. She knew it was in her interests for Colin to come out of this in the best possible light. She wanted his pension, not for him to be sacked or dismissed or whatever it was they could do to him.

Joe knocked on the back door.

'Hello Mrs Arnold. All done and ready for you to inspect.'

For the first time ever, Rita opened her purse and paid in full without so much as a glance at the windows. He took the money and ran before she could change her mind.

* * *

Two hours later Rita carried a tea tray into the lounge. Resplendent with three types of biscuit and her finest bone china, the tray was carefully placed on the coffee table and the tea was duly dispensed.

'I wish I could be of more use Inspector, but Colin never discussed his work with me. Of course I knew when there was something really important going on but never any details you understand. So I just naturally assumed he was at work. He is devoted to the job, works hard and now we don't even know if he will survive. Breaks my heart every day when I visit him.'

She twittered at the policemen. Inspector Bruce Grey shared a meaningful look with his sergeant, Pat Vickery, who raised his eyebrows in acknowledgement. They knew that was a lie for a start, having been to the hospital and chatted to the nurses about Colin's visitors. Rita was down to about twice a week for around twenty minutes a time. So, she was lying about the state of their relationship – what else was she lying about?

Chapter Thirty-two

Daniel sucked greedily on Ree's left breast, making her wince in pain as he relieved the pressure with the first few sucks. He had a huge appetite and was growing stronger and bigger every day.

'Welcome to your tenth day in the world my little one. I love you more and more as each day passes,' she whispered to her infant as Hannah came into the room.

'Morning my love, just had the prison on the phone. I think they are missing you, but, and I know this is naughty and may God forgive me, but I told them that you have an infection in your stitches and need to be here until it's cleared up. Aren't I bad? Don't you dare let on now will you?'

Ree looked at the midwife with immense gratitude for the extra time she would have with Gavin and her mum and close friends. Hannah's kindness meant the world to the new mum who was dreading the day that her return to prison could no longer be stalled. As she lifted Daniel onto her shoulder to wind him, she thought about how her life had been turned on its head over the last six months. Would it ever be a normal happy life again?

* * *

Each time Gavin arrived at the entrance to the hospital he dreaded finding that Ree and Daniel had been sent back to the prison and that no one had bothered to tell him. Holding his breath as he waited to be admitted to the ward, he heard the buzz of the alarmed door and pushed it open before going to Ree's room. Breathing out in relief as he saw the bored prison officer outside the door, he swapped the carrier bag he was carrying from one hand to the other and opened the door.

Today Telly had cooked a fabulous moussaka for Ree as he was convinced that all hospital food was inedible and she was wasting away. The meal was still hot as he had packed it in a thermos dish and had driven Gavin at breakneck speed from the café to the hospital to ensure that the new mother had at least one decent meal!

Hannah excused herself and left the family alone together, wondering to herself how on earth the lovely young girl could possibly have anything in common with the Renee Lovell the newspapers had depicted as a murderer.

Producing two forks, Gavin placed the container on Ree's tray table and, as Daniel fed from his mother's right breast, his parents ate every scrap of Telly's delicious offering. Ree told Gavin what Hannah had said and that they would have a few more days at least together, but they both knew that this was only a delay of the inevitable.

* * *

Smoothing the front of her skirt, wiping the moisture from her palms, Laura walked through the swing doors of John Lewis. Penny had given her such a talking-to that morning, boosting her confidence and telling her that of course she was capable of getting a job and doing it well. She had not worked properly for years, not since Tesco when Ree had been a baby, and she had almost not bothered to get off the bus, wondering what the hell she was doing.

'Don't be stupid girl,' she told herself. 'You can do it! You deserve it. You're going to do this to mark a new start. You'll do it for Gavin, for Ree, for Daniel, for Penny, for Gerry. You'll do it for yourself damn it all!'

So here she was, twenty minutes early for her interview as a sales assistant. Gerry had been very instrumental in persuading her to apply for a job. They had been meeting up for a cup of coffee quite often since she had confronted Alan and stood up to him. Two days ago she had passed her completed application form to her newest friend to hand onto the personnel department. Gerry took Laura to his office and dialled an internal number.

'Val, hello, Gerry, ground floor. Can you arrange an interview for me as soon as possible with a lovely lady who I think would do very well for us. Yes, she's just passed me a completed form and is with me now.'

Gerry covered thc mouthpiece with his fingers. '2 p.m. on Wednesday suit you?' he asked Laura, who nodded mutely.

'OK, she'll be with you then, Laura … Lovell,' he said, reading Laura's name from the top of the form he held.

* * *

And now, it was Wednesday, and Laura could see Gerry scanning the floor, talking to customers, directing a group of Burberry-clad very loud Americans to the lift hall. He spotted Laura and smiled at the tourists before hurrying towards her.

'I was so worried you were going to change your mind.

I'm really pleased you are here. Come on, time for a quick coffee before you go up.'

* * *

Laura emerged from the lift and followed the signs directing her to the personnel department. A receptionist smiled at her asking how she could help. Telling the young girl much more calmly than she actually felt that she was here for an interview, the smiling girl asked Laura her name and then invited her to sit and wait for Val Terry who would be with her very soon. The girl made a phone call and went back to her typing. Laura looked around her, taking in the noise of the ringing telephones, the typewriters clicking away in offices she could not see. She heard laughter as two people turned the corner and came into view.

A very tall woman turned to the man and said she would ring him with the figures before the end of the day. They shook hands and the man left through the same doors Laura had minutes before walked through. Laura wondered what she was doing here, with all these people in their smart padded-shouldered suits and busy lives. She wanted to get up and run away, hide in her room in the refuge, go back to where she only had to peel potatoes or wash dishes.

The tall woman turned to Laura and held her hand out.

'Hello, I'm Valerie Terry, and you must be Laura. Lovely to meet you. Please come with me.'

Laura stood and took the woman's proffered warm hand, shaking it and smiling, saying hello and following her as she walked along the corridor. Too late to run now.

* * *

Six days later Hannah conceded defeat and as kindly as she

could told Ree that the prison authorities were insisting that she return to Holloway without further delay. She dialled the telephone number of the café.

'Can I speak to Gavin please, it's Hannah from the hospital, everything is fine, no panic, just need a quick word.'

Hannah heard Telly roar over the noise of Capital London, the sound of a till pinging open and crockery being clattered. The background noise in the café subsided and Hannah, dreading the next couple of minutes, heard Telly tell Gavin it was the pretty young midwife but that all was OK, not to worry, no panic. She gulped and tried to find the words while remaining composed.

'Hannah? Hi, it's Gav. It's OK, I can guess why you're ringing, been expecting, well dreading, your call. It's time, isn't it? They have to go.'

'Yes my love, I'm so sorry. Can you come right away? I've persuaded them to let her return by ambulance. I can give you until about seven o'clock this evening.'

Gavin replaced the receiver and stood with his head in his hands, powerless and afraid. He pulled off his apron and opened the back door to the café, perching on a pile of empty milk crates, gazing up at the sky. Telly gave Gav a few minutes on his own then appeared with a mug of tea for them both.

'Come on mate, you knew it was only a matter of time. Drink this then get cleaned up and over there. Have a few hours with them and make the most of it. There's nothing I can say that will make the slightest difference to how you feel so don't waste any time, just go.'

Handing his mug to Telly, Gavin nodded and within ten minutes was showered and on the bus. He completed the journey on autopilot, oblivious to his surroundings or the people around him. He walked from the stop nearest the hospital and ignored the fairy lights, the shoppers, the snatches of carols. As he passed stores ablaze with Christmas he could only focus on the misery he felt.

⋆ ⋆ ⋆

Ree had packed both hers and Daniel's clothes which were the only items she was allowed to take back to the prison with her. The toys and teddies, cards and flowers still needed to be looked after. Telly and Pixie were coming to the hospital at half past six to collect the bags of gifts and take them back to the flat in Pixie's house which Gavin had been working on to make into a home for his family.

There had been so many flowers and carefully Ree had separated the bouquets and arrangements into vases and asked the nurses to spread them around the ward. Daniel was sleeping in his tiny Perspex cot and the doctor had discharged them both. Snatching the last moments of freedom, she added a cupful of salt to the bath water and, holding onto the rail, climbed into the huge white tub. She sat back and closed her eyes, relishing the peace and quiet, the privacy, the pure tranquillity. Daniel was a very greedy baby whose constant demands for his mother's milk made her incredibly tired and within a few short minutes she was dozing contentedly in the bath.

A gentle tapping on the bathroom door woke her.

'Hello my love, just to let you know that Gavin's here; and its three o'clock,' Hannah announced.

Quickly washing her hair then winding a towel around her herself, Ree returned to her room to find Gavin chatting to Daniel as he cuddled him. Trying not to cry, Ree kissed them both then dressed, brushed her hair through and busied herself with packing the last of her toiletries and clothes. Daniel needed a wash too and Ree sat in a soft cosy chair in the bathroom while Gavin gently undressed his son and carefully lowered him into the yellow plastic bath.

The child opened his eyes and waved his tiny fists around as his father dribbled the warm soapy water over his son's tiny body. Lifting him onto the towel opened out across Ree's lap he then wrapping him securely and warmly in it fluffy folds. The new parents took their child back to the bedroom where Gavin then dried, powdered and dressed him. Ready for his milk, Daniel began to bawl until he was firmly latched onto his mother. Satiated, he promptly fell asleep, completely unaware of the drama unfolding around him.

Supper arrived but Ree could only pick at the food. The unappetizing meal was pushed to one side as she ate a banana from the bowl of fruit on her bedside cabinet.

Seeing Laura through the glass, Gavin opened the door for her and ushered her inside.

'Telly rang me lovie. I hope you don't mind. I just wanted to say goodbye. Oh Ree, I'm so sorry, wish it could all be so different, we'll all miss you and Daniel so much, we'll be thinking about you all the time.'

Laura was crying now and Ree was desperately upset but managed not to let the water fall from her eyes. She was determined to stay composed for Gavin's sake. At least she had Daniel to comfort her, keep her occupied. She felt desperately sorry for her lover who would be going back to his room at the café alone.

There was another tap at the door and Pixie and Telly arrived. Ree knew this was almost time, she had a precious half an hour left with her closest friends and family. After hugging Ree and kissing the baby they left, with Laura, all three of them heavily laden with bags of gifts, hardly saying a word, not knowing what to say. Five minutes later Hannah stood in the doorway.

'I'm sorry my loves, but it's time to go now.'

She picked Daniel from his cot and Gavin took the bags, closely followed by a prison officer. An ambulance was waiting in the courtyard, engine running. On seeing them approach, the crew jumped out of the cab and one of them opened the back doors wide.

'Let me help you up, mind your step. Can you sit there for me please? Great. Now, thanks Hannah, can you pass me the little one please. I'll just strap your little bundle of joy into the cot and we'll be away.'

Hannah coughed and the other crew member turned to the prison officer.

'Erm, could I have a quick word?' he asked.

The escorting prison officer hesitated then followed the medic to the front of the ambulance. Hannah walked closely past Gavin who was standing by the ambulance door.

'You've got two minutes ...' she hissed.

Not needing to be told twice, Gavin hopped into the ambulance, stroked Daniel's face then took Ree's hands in his.

'I love you so much my darling darling Ree. Every second of every minute of every day I'll be thinking of you both, loving you both.'

Ree nodded, unable to speak, desperately trying to be brave and stay composed. Sharing one last kiss, Gavin climbed down from the ambulance as the prison officer reappeared.

The woman smiled at Gavin and strapped herself into the flip-down seat opposite Ree. One of the crew shut the doors behind his colleague then climbed back into the cab. Ree waved to Gavin who stood motionlessly, staring unseeingly into the blacked-out windows. The engine turned over and the ambulance slowly drove out of the hospital.

Hannah put her arm through Gavin's, his hands deeply buried in the pockets of his jeans. They watched the vehicle until it disappeared from view, both were totally quiet. Hannah rubbed Gavin's arm, words failing her, feeling his immense pain and suffering.

Chapter Thirty-three

The short almost sedate drive back to Holloway Prison was in stark contrast to the journey Ree had made a few weeks previously, after her waters had broken in the prison library. Daniel stirred in his cot, screwing his face up then relaxing again, as Ree wondered what he could be dreaming about. Annie, the paramedic who sat opposite her in the ambulance, tried to talk to Ree, asking her about her baby and making cooing noises to him. She was being kind but Ree couldn't bear any of it. Her head was pounding as she knew that every second took her that bit closer to the prison until finally, they were there, driving through the main gates which had been opened wide in anticipation of their arrival. She watched them being banged shut behind the ambulance by two male prison officers as they slid the bolts across and entered a code into a key pad. It was an impenetrable barrier between what should have been her real life and her incarceration.

Annie asked Ree to wait in her seat, a big sad smile fixed in place across her weary face. The back doors of the ambulance opened and the prison officer who had accompanied Ree from the hospital unclipped her seatbelt and climbed down. She told Ree to undo hers and come and stand next to her. Ree did exactly as she was told as she felt the cold metal of the handcuffs slipped over her wrists and clicked shut. Annie unfastened Daniel and carefully picked him up trying hard not to wake him, standing awkwardly beside Ree in the courtyard attempting to shield the baby from the drizzle which was gradually turning to rain. She turned to her fellow crew member and raised her eyebrows. He understood and spoke to the prison officers who had made up the welcoming committee.

'Look guys, this baby is going to get soaked, he's a prem baby as it is and we really need to get him in the warm. I know you have your procedures but can we please get in out of this rain.'

Ignoring him, the officers carried on collecting Ree's belongings from the ambulance then finally turning to their prisoner they instructed Ree to follow them.

'We're ready for her now. We have a job to do and we will do it properly. If she don't like it that's tough shit. Shouldn't have been a naughty girl should she? And now look what she's gone and burdened the taxpayer with. Go on Lovell, move.'

He then addressed Annie directly.

'Take the brat and pass it to the nurse in the doctor's office. Then you are all done here so you can go. We've taken all the crap from the back.'

Dismissing Annie, he took Ree's arm and pushed her towards an open door.

'In there, I will take your cuffs off once the door is locked behind you. You will then strip down to your underwear. Please also remove your shoes. A female officer will come and see you.'

Annie and her colleague watched as Ree was marched off, then followed another officer with the baby, handing him over, as instructed, to a nurse. She bowed her head to hide her shock and her tears as her colleague, Chris, wrapped his arm around her and they walked back to the ambulance.

They climbed into the cab in silence and waited for the dull black steel doors to be opened. Never had Annie witnessed such cruelty in all her years working as a paramedic. Never had she witnessed such disregard for another human being. The doors eventually swung open and, deep in thought, Chris and Annie left Ree and Daniel to the place where they were nothing and nobody, a burden and a waste. Biting her lip, determined not to cry and shame herself in front of the spiteful prison officer who obviously considered her scum, Ree stood in her bra and knickers, barefoot, waiting for the next prison officer to arrive.

'Open your mouth, lift your tongue. OK, put your clothes back on. They've been searched. Go with this officer, your kid is in with the nurse. You will collect it then be taken to the mother and baby unit.'

Dismissed, the woman looked away and busied herself with her notes on the latest prisoner to have come through on society's filthy conveyor belt. As they crossed the courtyard and entered a room, Ree could hear Daniel crying. He was lying on a changing mat, naked, while a prison officer inspected his clothes and nappy.

'He'll be freezing, what on earth are you doing? Why have you taken all his clothes off?'

The nurse quickly crossed the room to Ree, and held her hands.

'I'm sorry love, but sometimes women try to bring drugs in with their babies. I'll wrap him all up warm again in a sec, he'll be fine. I can't begin to imagine how terrible you feel.'

Numb, Ree watched as the nurse was finally given the nod by the officer. Quickly she refastened Daniel's nappy then dressed him, cuddling him and rocking him to sleep.

'Nearly there love, I'll take him up to your room and help you settle back in. Everything you brought back with you will have to be searched too so that might take a while, maybe even tomorrow. We have plenty of things upstairs. Come on Ree, don't cry now.'

The nurse carried Daniel to the mother and baby unit and finally into the tiny room which was now Ree and her baby's home, albeit temporarily. Now fast asleep, Daniel was laid in a cot next to his mother's bed. The plain grey room was cold and hard, no colour in it at all. Ree sat beside her baby, tired and cold.

'Ree, I'm a nurse OK, not a prison officer, I'm a nurse. My name is Sheila. It's OK my love, I know this is all terrible but we have no choice. You have to get through this for Daniel's sake. There are no locked doors on this wing, but you can shut the door at night if you wish. I'm here to help you and baby get through this; whatever I can do to help just let me know. It's hard enough to be a new mum let alone having to do it here, but I'll help in any way I can, OK? Let's go and get a cup of tea and I'll show you where everything is. Your baby will be fine. He's fast asleep and we'll only be a few minutes.'

Smiling, Sheila held open the door for Ree who, after turning to look at Daniel, followed her into the ward.

Chapter Thirty-four

Gavin felt as if his heart had been broken, and then jumped all over just for good measure. After the ambulance had driven away, Hannah had taken him back inside the hospital to the canteen. They sat out of the way in the corner, Gavin still struggling to keep his emotions in check. He bowed his head and played with the sachets of sugar, tipping the contents from one side of the packet to the other. Hannah placed a mug of tea in front of him.

'Drink it, it's hot, you're frozen through. You'll be no good to Ree with double pneumonia now will you?'

Making a half-hearted attempt at a smile, Gavin picked up his mug and gazed out of the window, staring into the darkness of the hospital grounds.

'You'll be able to see them soon won't you? How often can Ree have visitors?'

Hannah did her best to chat to Gavin, to make him think about the positive things in his life and to forget about the terrible things that were going on. Feeling slightly warmer and looking forward to receiving a visiting order from Ree, Gavin told the caring midwife that he had to make a move home. Hannah hugged him as he stood before the entrance doors to the hospital. He was grateful to her for all her kindness and understanding, hugged her in return and thanked her and all the other nurses who had been so caring.

He left the birth place of his first born for the last time. Pulling his coat tightly around him, he turned his heavy steps towards the bus stop and his lonely bedsit above the café.

As he neared the café the rain was falling out of the sky by the bucket-load. He was soaked through to the skin and all he could think about was a hot shower and being dry again. He fished in his pockets for his keys but as he reached the café realized that the shutters had not been pulled down. Through the sheets of rain he saw Telly and Pixie sitting at a table with a couple of glasses and a bottle of wine between them.

Gratefully he pushed the door and stepped into the warm and dry café, shutting out the terrible weather behind him. Telly rushed off to find him a towel while Pixie helped him with his sodden coat.

'We didn't want you to come back on your own, back to an empty room and all Gav. We miss her too you know and the brief thinks that the trial will just be a formality and she'll walk soon as.'

Rubbing his hair and face dry Gavin felt the warm glow of friendship from these two totally different characters who had shown him more love and kindness than he could ever have imagined when he first arrived in London. Telly produced a bottle of whisky and as Gavin sat at the table, wrapped in his toweling bathrobe, enveloped in love, he thought that somehow he would be OK. Somehow, they would all be OK.

Chapter Thirty-five

'He was soaked through to the skin, I felt so sad for him, what a bloody mess this all is.' Pixie stroked the back of Colin's hand very gently as he lay unmoving in the hospital bed; the starched white sheets without a crease, his arms neatly by his sides. She continued to talk to him, telling him all about how beautiful baby Daniel was, how well Ree looked and how sad Gavin was without them both.

It had been a week since Ree had gone back to prison and tomorrow Gavin had a visiting order to see her and his child. Pixie explained to Colin how their friend was looking forward to seeing his family but dreading it too. It was nearly Christmas and what a lousy one it was going to be for them all. How different it should have been.

Pixie continued to chatter and told him of the gifts that she had bought for friends, for Nikki's children and Telly and how they were all going to spend Christmas Day at Telly's house. After an hour or so, Pixie kissed Colin softly on his cheek and said goodnight. As she turned to give Colin one last look she thought she saw his right eyelid flicker, just a slight movement but a movement nonetheless. Not wishing to wake the whole ward, Pixie rushed to the nurses' station, stunned and excited, not altogether sure of what she had seen. Hurrying to his bedside, the nurse examined Colin for any change or sign of recognition. There was nothing. Colin's face was totally devoid of any expression, his eyes were firmly closed and after watching and hoping for a few minutes, Pixie sighed and put it down to tiredness and wishful thinking. The nurse explained that it could have been an involuntary eye movement and that occasionally it indicated some brain activity. The doctors would be told in the morning but in the meantime there was really nothing that anyone could do. The nurse held the door open for Pixie and walked to the swing doors at the entrance to the ward. She reached out for the person she knew as Alan.

'We will call you if there is any news. I promise. I know that he has a wife but it's quite clear to anyone who really loves and cares for Colin. We will call you.

Pixie hailed a cab outside the hospital and sat back into the warmth of the worn leather seats. Rubbing a patch of glass clear of mist, she watched the Christmas lights as the cab made its way down the Borough High Street. She couldn't think of anything worse than trying to put on a brave face over the next couple of weeks as a lonely and sad Christmas had to be endured followed by the inevitable festivities of the New Year.

It was nearly 10 p.m. when she arrived home, tired, lonely and sad. Curled up on the sofa with a large gin and tonic and only the late news for company, she wept. She was oblivious to the voice which was quietly telling her about a bomb going off somewhere in the Middle East. The newscaster was saying good night so she switched the television off and flicked through her records, sinking back on the sofa as Frank Sinatra gently sang her to sleep.

⋆ ⋆ ⋆

Detective Inspector Bruce Grey leant against the coffee and

tea machine as his sergeant pushed buttons selecting warmish wet liquid which loosely resembled tea with one sugar. Pat Vickery was totally fed up with the whole business and wished he'd never heard of DI Colin Arnold.

'Look, we've had a different version or none at all from everyone we've spoken to. Christ knows who Colin got the gun from. We don't even know if Jimmy was the intended victim. If it was meant for Jimmy, then why? None of Colin's gang is going to tell us a bloody thing. Each one of his mates has just given us a big fat "haven't got a clue what you're talking about", so where the hell do we go from here? He's at bloody death's door himself, his missus is playing the perfect wife and the only other visitor to the hospital besides the Greek guy is Alan Dixon who we know is a transvestite whore who was not there on the night and isn't going to say anything. It's a holy mess that's for sure.'

They had reinterviewed Gus, who still claimed to have seen nothing. They had delved into Colin's private life and found nothing untoward. Jimmy Watson was a low-life piece of scum and no one would miss him. It looked like there was a problem between Jimmy and Colin and the girl had got in the way. Fair enough, but what a bloody mess he'd made of things in the process. The dodgy gun for example, untraceable and unaccounted for. Where had that come from? Had Colin pulled in a favour from someone? Did he now owe some crook big-time? Vickery wanted a neat little whitewash, and if truth be told so did he. The boss wasn't interested in any more bad press. All *he* really wanted was for Grey and Vickery to come up with a reasonably plausible tale that tied up all loose ends and in which Colin was allowed to retire honourably – whether or not he emerged from his coma.

'Look guv, we can easily put this one to bed. It's been six

months now. Colin was, well is, a bloody good copper and so what if something got a bit personal. We'll have a word with the CPS new information has come to light or some such. Get the girl out without a trial. I think we can all agree that it really doesn't look as though she had anything to do with it. If she hadn't stayed on the scene we might never have found her. There's other things to worry, about don't you think? Let's get back and see that old bag of a wife of the DI and tell her we are pensioning Colin out on full whack plus maybe a bit extra for acting beyond the call of duty or something. Best all round. We don't need the shit of a trial. Come on, it's nearly Christmas, season of goodwill and all that old bollocks.'

Grey swilled the cold liquid around in his polystyrene cup before dropping it in the bin.

'Yeah, OK, fuck it, it's not like we can prove that Colin did anything wrong anyway.'

Chapter Thirty-six

After over two weeks away from the place Ree had almost forgotten how noisy the prison was. Daniel seemed oblivious to it all, sleeping the most of the day, staying awake only to be fed or bathed. The mother and baby unit was a massive improvement on the previous wing in which Ree had been incarcerated before his birth but it was still an appalling place – full of despair and despondency.

Most of the officers were pleasant enough, but the odd one thought that the babies should have been taken away from their mothers at birth and given to middle-class parents who would love and cherish these children in a way their natural mothers never would. Certain prison officers seemed to take great delight in making life as difficult as possible but thankfully these were few and far between. Some of them were like the nurses – they cooed over the babies and were very kind, helping in any way they could. The atmosphere was very different too. It was much more relaxed and, most importantly, there were no locked doors and there was always a midwife around to give practical help and advice. After a couple of days, Ree had fallen into a routine and all she could think about was Gavin's next visit. When the time finally came, she dressed Daniel in his best blue and white outfit and got him ready to see his daddy. Determined not to let her boyfriend see her miserable and looking how she actually felt, she washed her hair and put on a little make-up, making as much of herself as was possible in the circumstances.

The women who were receiving visitors were taken to a room with sofas and coffee tables, nothing like the austere visiting rooms Ree had been used to. They were told to sit down while their visitors were brought to them. It was in these almost civilized circumstances that Gavin saw Ree breastfeeding the baby who had inconveniently decided it was time for lunch. Overjoyed at being reunited, if only for two short hours, the family cherished every precious moment they spent together.

A prison officer approached them and let her know that the registrar was now ready for them. Daniel's birth had yet to be registered so arrangements had been made for the registrar to attend the prison and, as Gavin and Ree were unmarried, both parents had to be present in order for Gavin's name to be inserted on the birth certificate.

The subject of middle names and godparents had been discussed amid much merriment during Ree's time at the hospital. The registrar was a regular visitor to the prison and treated the new parents with the utmost courtesy just as if they were attending his regular office in Islington. After entering the details of Daniel's birth and parents' names, he asked Ree for Daniel's full name never batting an eyelid as Ree calmly but with a hint of a smile replied.

'Daniel Aristotle Alan Hedley.'

Nikki had laughed hysterically when Ree had asked her for her father's real name as Ree explained that she wanted Daniel to have both Telly's, Pixie's and one of Gavin's names for her baby.

'You'll wish you hadn't you know, poor little bugger. Don't do that to him, it's all right for our lot, we've all got long daft names, but do you really want to lumber Daniel with Aristotle!'

After the registration a beeping sound filled the visiting area announcing that Gavin and other non-residents had to leave. Visiting time was over. Hugging one another tightly, Ree passed Daniel to his father for a farewell cuddle. Kissing them both, Gavin carefully folded the birth certificate and looked forward to showing Telly and Pixie, knowing how delighted they would be. Nikki had been sworn to secrecy. He would be back at the prison in a week's time; it would be his last visit before Christmas. He had already been informed that if he wanted to bring gifts in for his family then normal procedures would have to be followed, which he knew translated into no gift wrappings, no surprises. Not really Christmas at all – just a meaningless spoilt day. Ree had asked him not to bring anything in, to completely forget about Christmas this year because when she eventually left the prison she would take great delight in burning everything she had in an attempt to erase the terrible experience from her memory.

Helping Ree to her feet, Gavin walked with his arm around her to the door, then after one last tearful kiss whispered a goodbye knowing that the next hello would be after a long, painfully lonely, week.

* * *

As she pulled the curtains shut in what Rita liked to call the lounge and Colin always referred to as the front room, she paused and watched her neighbour opposite as he stood on a step ladder fixing Christmas lights to the outside of his house. Sniffing in disapproval at the altogether far too common show of tackiness, she shut out the unwelcome intrusion Christmas had made into her thoughts. She had never really liked Christmas anyway – she had gone along with all the fuss and effort for the sake of the kids and because Colin expected it. 'Well thank God we'll have none of that nonsense this year,' she thought. 'Won't even have to bother to visit the bastard.'

Feeling sorry for her, several of Rita's family and friends had invited her to spend Christmas with them. She had declined all the kind offers telling everyone that it was really all too much for her what with Colin being so poorly. She told her daughters and mother, her friends from the bridge, the golf and the tennis clubs that she was going to a retreat in the country to get some peace and quiet and to think about how she needed to come to terms with the fact that her husband may never recover.

The retreat was a bit of a white lie – the hotel she was actually going stay at for five days, from 23 December' was in Knightsbridge, a stone's throw from Harrods and she had every day mapped out. Facials and manicures had been booked, a couple of massages, then shopping in the sales after Christmas and lots of lovely room service. Smiling at first she then pursed her lips – the short period of indulgence would be over and the whole mess could still jump up and bite her after the holidays were over. She poured herself a large gin and tonic. Automatically adding ice and a slice of lemon from a jar in fridge, she felt that the rather large sum of money in the joint account that she would be spending was the very least she deserved and would go a little way to compensating her for the terrible trauma she had suffered over the last few months. The compensation for the trauma of her marriage over the last few years would wait yet a while.

Switching the television on and flicking through the channels she settled for *Coronation Street* though her state of mind was not much improved as she watched her namesake, Rita Fairclough, cope with a dead husband. 'Lucky cow!' she thought, 'At least your husband had the decency to die with his secrets.'

She turned the volume down when the door bell chimed.

'If that's carol singers checking that I'm in before mauling 'Silent Night', then they are going to be very sorry that they chose my house,' she said aloud as she pushed her feet into her recently purchased fluffy black mules.

Her venom had to be quickly adjusted when she opened the door to Sergeant Pat Vickery and DI Bruce Grey.

'Evening Mrs Arnold. Could we come in for a moment please? We are sorry to disturb you and not let you know we would be dropping by but it is important.'

Grey smiled at Rita as she ushered the two policemen into the lounge and offered them a drink.

'No, thank you,' said DI Grey.

'We just wanted to let you know that in view of the tragic accident that DI Arnold has been involved in, you might like to hear how the financial side of the matter will be sorted out. Obviously we all want Colin restored to health and back at work but, well, we all have to accept the fact that things are looking bleak right now. So we thought that the least we could do was come around and personally assure you that the force will not allow you or your family to face any unnecessary financial difficulties.'

Vickery looked at the floor, inspecting the thick patterned carpet and noting the large gin and tonic sitting alongside a very exclusive, expensive box of chocolates. They confirmed his opinion of Mrs Rita Arnold – she was not hugely upset by her husband's condition, that much was certain.

'Obviously Colin was, is, a marvellous policeman,' continued Grey. 'And as is right, he has continued to receive full pay while he has been incapacitated.'

Silently Rita willed the inspector to get on with it, cut to the chase and tell her how much she was going to get. 'Now, your husband was due to retire next year so what we propose is to bring his retirement date forward and pay Colin's pension starting in the New Year. His salary due up until his expected retirement will be paid in a tax-free lump sum and there will also be a significant payment for being injured in the line of duty.'

Grey watched as Rita failed to disguise the smile that crossed her face. It was not, he thought, the smile of relief, more a smile of delight. Indeed the sort of smile he was expecting to see from his son when the boy found out on Christmas Day that Santa had sent exactly what was on the list he had put up the chimney. He wondered if she understood how differently things could have been.

'Well, obviously Colin has always been a wonderful husband and father. He devoted his life to his work with the police and I was wondering if this would be financially recognized. Indeed, I have been worried about how I would manage. I'm glad you have at least brought my concerns to an end. It's been such a difficult time for me, as I'm sure you are aware and now I can concentrate on what matters. Getting Colin better.'

Grey's thoughts would not be considered charitable at any time of the year.

Simpering at the policemen, Rita asked when the compensation money would be finalized.

Vickery told her that in view of the impending Christmas holidays things would be a little delayed but they would try to hurry things along for her as they didn't want to make things any more difficult than they already were. Taking a tissue from a box on the coffee table Rita dabbed at her dry eyes, sniffing slightly. Vickery thought he would be sick if he had to watch her theatrics any longer.

After wishing Rita a very happy Christmas under the sad circumstances, the two men left the house, solemn in case they were being watched until they had climbed into their car and shut the doors.

'Bloody bitch. Doesn't she realize that she could have found herself married to a vegetable who'd been dishonourably discharged from the force?' DI Grey said, shaking his head in disbelief.

'I know,' replied Vickery.

'Now I can concentrate on what matters,' he continued in a passable imitation of Rita's voice.

'The only thing that matters to Mrs DI Colin Arnold is Mrs fucking DI Colin Arnold!' said Grey, as he started the car.

'She knows that Col was up to something, she knows that things aren't all as they should be so to come away with a full pension and a few extra quid she is laughing. I'm surprised she didn't actually laugh out loud – bloody Ice Queen! I bet she sells up and fucks off quick as poss and leaves Col in a home somewhere. Poor bastard. If I was married to that I think I'd fucking stay in a coma for as long as I fucking could!'

Vickery laughed and turned the heater up to its warmest setting as the pair drove off arguing about which pub to grace with their presence and whose turn it was to get the first round in.

* * *

Alone, Rita swore under her breath as she shoved washing into the machine. Banging the powder drawer shut and punching the buttons hard, she slammed the door to her utility room as she marched about the kitchen, cursing her husband.

'Fucking bastard. I could have got a nice large death in

service payment, something worthwhile. But, no, you have to spoil things for me!'

She would think about selling the house, living on Colin's pension and look into the force paying something towards a home for the shit. She retrieved her gin and tonic and took a sip. The tonic was flat. Pouring the drink down the sink she fixed herself a large refill and returned to the sofa. Kicking off her mules, she selected a chocolate while mentally adding up the value of the house and deducting the cost of one of the new riverside apartments she had seen advertised in the local paper. Adding their savings in the building society, shares, and the seven months' salary things weren't too bad but, she thought, they could have been so much better. The rather smart black dress would have to wait for now. She called the local Indian restaurant and ordered a takeaway then thought over every hour of her impending Christmas break, savouring every forthcoming mouthful and every reward she would enjoy.

Chapter Thirty-seven

Exhausted, Ree sat back on her bed and closed her eyes, hoping to catch a few hours' sleep before Daniel woke her for another feed. What she wouldn't give for eight hours' sleep – a whole night without this little monkey waking her up. Yes, he was totally wonderful but if only he would sleep for more than a few hours at a time. Within minutes she had drifted off but it only felt like moments later that she was awake again, vaguely aware of the noise that was her baby once more demanding attention. Almost crying with exhaustion, she lay on her bed, willing Daniel to go back to sleep. Looking at her watch, she saw that it was gone two o'clock in the morning.

'Everything all right in here?'

Lizzie, the nurse on duty that night, popped her head around the door. In the faint light that was seeping into the cell from the corridor, Lizzie saw Ree, lying back against the pillows, white as a ghost, black hollows for eyes, totally drained of all energy, silently weeping.

Lizzie picked Daniel from his cot and soothed him, cooing to him until he was quiet and making tiny mewing noises instead of squawking uncontrollably.

'I'm sorry Lizzie, I'm just so, so tired. I need to sleep and don't even feel like I've got the energy to hold him.'

Ree was distraught, overwhelmed with guilt and shame.

'Oh sweetheart! Look, I'll take him tonight. No arguments

– I'll give him a bottle and you can sleep. It's not failure, it's called being sensible. If you are that tired then you are no good to him. Now, you sleep and I will take Daniel. I'll wake you in the morning.'

Placing Daniel back in his cot, Lizzie patted Ree's hand then wheeled the child along the corridor to the nursery.

Amid worries such as would her milk dry up and that she was an unfit mother, Ree gently drifted back to sleep.

* * *

Stretching and yawning, Ree shifted around in her bed, pushing the covers back and relishing the dozy warm sleepily feeling. Suddenly remembering where she was and how she had felt the previous night, she opened her eyes and sat bolt upright. She registered the cot beside her, the baby sleeping peacefully, her nightdress soaked in leaking breast milk and lastly the beaming face of Sarah, the duty nurse, reading and drinking a cup of tea.

'Hello lovie. My my, you were tired. Stay there, I'll get you some tea. Any sugar?'

Sinking back in her bed with relief that all was well, Ree smiled and shook her head. Sarah was back in a few minutes with the tea and a couple of biscuits then settled herself in the chair.

'Ree, it's twenty past two in the afternoon. You were completely exhausted, and you are absolutely no good to anyone like that.'

Shocked, Ree looked at her watch in disbelief.

'It's OK, Daniel has had a couple of bottles. Now, he's not long been fed and put down so, drink your tea, get something to eat, have a shower and then come back and be ready for him when he wakes up. There's no shame you know in admitting you need a little help. I'll come back in an hour or so.'

Smiling and leaving Ree no opportunity to protest, Sarah left the room.

An hour later the young mother felt refreshed, clean, and for the first time in what felt like for ever, not the slightest bit tired.

'Well you look better!' Sarah exclaimed as she entered the room with two fresh cups of tea.

'OK, let's have a chat. You don't have to do this on your own you know, we are all here to help you. If you weren't here and were at home, you'd have your mum wouldn't you and your fella. They would help you. There's no shame in getting someone else to give Daniel a bottle now and then so that you can get a decent night's sleep. He won't grow up feeling deprived and neglected and your milk won't dry up because of it. Okay, you could express some milk if you wanted, but your nipples are very sore looking so maybe at the moment that's not such a good idea. We will be watching you young lady and not in a bad way. The first sign of a yawn and I'll be in here tying you down to that bed!

Sarah patted Ree's hand and told her to make the most of the next couple of hours.

'Why don't you go and get a book – there are loads along the corridor.'

Taking Sarah's advice, Ree wandered along the corridor and actually looked around the ward with fresh eyes for the first time. She took in the posters advocating breastfeeding over bottle, the charts detailing the ages babies needed their jabs, the lonely faces of the young girls in the same predicament as she was. She selected a book then returned to her cell. She collected her water jug and refilled it from the kitchen, remembering all she had been told about the need to drink plenty of fluids to keep her milk flowing. With Daniel still sleeping soundly, she sat in the reasonably comfortable armchair in her cell, opened her book and gratefully lost herself within minutes, concentrating only on the words in front of her and forgetting the reality of her own world for the next hour.

Chapter Thirty-eight

Gavin worked hard, offering to do all manner of extra jobs for Telly to make up for the day he took off each week to travel to Holloway. With Christmas now several weeks behind them, Gavin and Pixie worked on the flat in her house – sanding down woodwork, painting, putting up wallpaper and making a beautiful nursery for Daniel. Gavin coped by tiring himself out. He spent every drop of energy so there was no time to think and wallow in the acute loneliness which attempted to fill his mind every day.

* * *

Ree looked after Daniel. She washed his tiny clothes by hand and lovingly ironed them. She fed him, cuddled him and sang to him. She read her books and waited for news. She counted the hours until the next visiting day arrived, proudly showing Daniel to his father and grandmother at every opportunity. She took her baby for walks in the gardens in the pram the prison had provided. She made friends with the other mums and existed, day to day, in her world, suspended in this anxious parallel universe that was HMP Holloway.

* * *

Telly ran the café with Mark and a little help from Nikki when Gavin went on his weekly trip to the prison.

★ ★ ★

Pixie visited Ree occasionally and attended the hospital every night, quietly talking about her day, offloading all her worries to someone who never interrupted or answered back.

★ ★ ★

Mark and his boyfriend moved into Mark's small room which was the cause of much good humoured leg-pulling. Gavin was pleased to have the company and was touched when the boys refused to let him move to Pixie's.

'Stay here mate until Ree and Daniel come home so you can move over there together. We'll manage without a living room until then!'

★ ★ ★

Meanwhile, Rita put the house up for sale and viewed the riverside apartments.

★ ★ ★

Vickery and Grey told their boss a few white lies which he knew were probably verging on the dark grey and moved onto a headless corpse found in a rubbish bin at the Elephant and Castle underground station, which was altogether far less complicated.

★ ★ ★

The Macintosh computer was unveiled. Space Shuttle Mission Challenger 4 was launched. Torvill and Dean won the ice dancing gold medal at the Winter Olympics. In short, life went on.

On one of her nightly visits to the hospital, Pixie held Colin's hand, silently looking out of the window, watching the February rain fall.

And Colin opened his eyes.

It was a flicker at first, just a flutter of the eyelids and it had happened before. She looked at Colin, sighed heavily and returned to staring at the rain drops. Then, doing a double take, she looked back and saw that Colin's eyes were open.

'Colin, Colin my love. Are you back with us?' she said as she scrabbled for the emergency call button over the bed. Two nurses came dashing into the room to see Colin blinking slowly and trying to open his mouth.

'Could you please wait outside the room while we see what's going on here? Alan, it might be nothing. Please wait outside.'

'Yes, come on Dixie,' said the other nurse, using the schoolboy nickname Alan had suggested as he became more familiar with his lover's carers.

Mr Hill, the consultant Pixie had met many times since he had explained the extent of Colin's injuries when he was first admitted, walked rapidly down the corridor and burst in the room, leaving the door open.

'Bloody hell, I don't believe it!' he exclaimed as he bent over Colin and held his hand.

'Colin, can you hear me? If you can hear me and understand, please try and squeeze my hand.'

Everyone present held their breath.

'I felt it – he did it!'

'Colin, I need to check your responses, to see if you are

ready for us to stop giving you some of the drugs you've been on. We've got to reduce the relaxants to see how well you can move, OK?'

'That was another squeeze guys! Right, we need all the people here now. Sophie, can you get the team together? Then let's see about losing these tubes. He seems to be trying to open his mouth to talk which is a great sign.'

Pixie watched anxiously through the open door as Colin's head was raised slightly and the tube to his mouth was gently removed. He opened his eyes again and this time looked directly at Pixie while trying to smile and talk. His voice was very hoarse and all Pixie could hear was a quiet almost choking noise. The wonky smile was enough for Pixie though because he knew it came from Colin's heart. The smile reached his watery eyes and she reciprocated with a huge grin and for a change, tears of sheer joy.

'Should we call the wife now?' asked Sophie.

'I think it might be best to leave that until the morning nurse,' said George Hill, as he looked directly at Pixie.

'That OK Dixie?' he said, thinking once again how pleased his partner, Tim, would be to hear the news. They had spent many an evening discussing the devotion of the man who visited Colin every night and had been touched to receive the very fine malt Pixie had brought to the hospital on Christmas Day.

Pixie nodded, wondering if she'd ever be able to thank this busy man for the compassion he had shown.

* * *

Rummaging for change, Pixie dialled Telly's number, trying several times before being composed enough to find the correct digits. Finally, hearing Telly say hello she pushed a ten pence piece into the slot on the pay phone.

'Tel, it's Pixie.'

'This better be bloody important darlin'!' he growled, in his usual style which others would have taken as an insult but Pixie knew was concern.

'Telly, it's Colin, he's awake! He came round a few hours ago but I didn't want to leave him before now. The docs have just given him some drugs so he can rest. Can you believe it Tel? It's a bloody miracle!'

'Pix! Mother of God! I'm on my way already.'

'No, Telly, there's really no need. I'm going to stay with him tonight. Perhaps you can let Gavin know? The doctors are still working so there's not much more I can tell you but Mr Hill, the consultant, isn't going to let Rita know until the morning. I just wanted to tell someone and thought who better to tell than Tel!'

'Get back to him then love. Come straight over when you get back or give me a shout and I'll come and pick you up, you hear?'

* * *

Colin slept the night away. Pixie didn't. Rubbing her face in exhaustion she retrieved her jacket and coat, kissed Colin gently and went to see the nurse in charge.

'Look, um, I'd better make myself scarce. I know you have to make a few calls, let a few other people know. So, well, I'll come back this evening ... after ... Could you please tell Colin that I'll definitely be here tonight.'

The nurse watched Dixie leave the ward, feeling desperately sorry for him and Colin.

As she picked up the handset, the nurse wondered who she should call first: the police liaison officer, the wife, the daughters? Finally deciding on the wife and dialling the number, she thought about the cold hard immaculate woman who had never displayed a drop of emotion or a flicker of affection for her sick husband. The dial spun back around to zero and the ringing tone sounded.

* * *

Disbelief then anger hit Rita like a ton of bricks. Propped up on one elbow, she half sat, half lay in bed listening to the almost tangible excitement of the nurse. As she replaced the handset, she stared at the cream telephone as if it were an instrument of torture.

'How fucking dare he fucking wake up!' she screamed into her pillows, furious as she saw the riverside apartment and all her other plans crumble to dust.

Two hours later, calm and composed, a painted on and carefully practiced face attempting to show pleasure and affection at Colin's recovery, she sat by Colin's bed, watching him sleep. Inspector Grey and Sergeant Vickery raised eyebrows to one another and swapped a look of surprise.

They stood outside the room watching through the large window as a nurse performed various tasks, writing on Colin's notes as she did so. Vickery raised his hand and smiled at Rita who cracked her face just enough to cause the smallest of movements.

'Well, this is going to be a barrel of laughs guv,' Vickery said out of the corner of his mouth, his smile still in place.

As the nurse completed her observations and left the room, Grey asked her if it was OK if they tried to speak to Colin when he woke up. 'Well, for a short while should be fine. He can't really speak yet except in a whisper and we're not sure about brain damage or memory yet.'

Promising to tread softly, the two policemen entered the room.

'Isn't it amazing! You must be absolutely thrilled!' Vickery said to Rita, almost teasing her.

'Yes, it's wonderful,' she replied in a tone that said she thought it anything but.

Colin opened his mouth and licked his lips. He was propped up in bed, supported by pillows.

'Is he thirsty?' asked the DI.

'How am I meant to know? I'm not a bloody mind reader,' she snapped. Then, realizing her error, quickly added, 'It's been a bit of a strain. I'm going to get a coffee and have a break. I'll ask a nurse to come and see to him on my way to the canteen.'

Gathering her coat and bag, she left the room.

The policemen watched as Rita walked straight past the nurses' station and were staggered by her callousness.

'I'll get the nurse,' said Pat Vickery.

They stood back as she patiently wet Colin's lips and held a glass of water to his mouth. He had not fully recovered his motor skills and water dribbled down his chin which she wiped with tissues while gently giving words of encouragement. He smiled in recognition at his two colleagues.

When they were finally alone, Grey pulled a chair close to Colin's side.

'Well mate, right bloody song and dance we've been through while you've been sleeping! Great to see you awake at last though. We're going to need you to help us sort out the mess OK?'

Colin was trying to talk but only a raspy cough emerged so he raised his hand slightly and opened his palm. Grey understood and took the proffered hand.

'Col, I'm guessing you can understand me. A squeeze for yes?'

Colin gave a weak squeeze.

'Do you remember what happened mate?'

Another single squeeze.

Colin tried to speak again and this time Grey could hear the faintest whisper.

'Ree, Ree.'

'Col, mate, it ain't all good. I'll tell you what has been happening and you squeeze my hand when I ask you if you understand OK? Then I'll tell you what's been sorted.'

So, with Vickery one side of him and Grey on the other, Colin listened as the story unfolded. Ree's arrest and imprisonment, the baby, the impending trial, Jimmy's death. Grey stopped occasionally for Colin to drink and to ensure that he understood everything he was being told.

'I can't wait for you to tell us where you got the bloody shooter Col. Christ, what were you thinking? On second thoughts, I don't want to know. Look, I think we've got it covered, you might get a tap on the wrist but no one is broken-hearted over Jimmy. What we're going to need to know about is the girl. We need to know what happened. How and why did she end up with a gun in her hand and pulling the trigger? I know you can't talk now but can you let the nurse know when you are up to it? From what I can make out, the poor cow was just in the wrong place at the wrong time. If that's the case then I need your help to get her out of the slammer. I've got to go now and talk to the old man but soon as you are up to it, we'll be back, OK?'

With a single squeeze, Colin sighed in exhaustion and fell asleep as his colleagues left the room.

* * *

Rita did not reappear. Instead she left a message with the

nurses that her husband was talking to the policemen, his colleagues, so she would return tomorrow. The medics discussed Rita's attitude in disbelief.

* * *

Pixie rang the hospital before going to see Colin, anxious not to bump into anyone else who might be visiting his lover. Assuring him that Colin was alone, Pixie asked if there was anything he needed, then called Telly who drove to them both to the hospital.

Finally finding a parking space Telly pulled up the handbrake and unclipped his seatbelt.

'Oh Tel, I'm so scared he won't remember me, or us or what happened.'

'Pix, there's really no point in worrying about all that before you know what the score is. Come on, pull yourself together and let's go an' see the old guy. I'll just say a quick hello then go off and get a coffee. I have my book so you just take your time. I'll be waiting for you in the canteen. Stay as long as you like, it's fine. Now, come on, let's get in there and see how he's doing?'

The old friends walked into the hospital and up to the ward, full of anxiety and trepidation.

'Coast's clear Dixie!' said a now familiar nurse who sat filling in forms at the nurses' station.

Colin was awake and beamed at them both as they entered the room. Taking a chair beside him, Pixie held Colin's hand and kissed him lightly. Colin's croaky tiny voice managed a whispered hello.

She told him not to try to talk but Colin went on, smiling. 'Where's your frock? Never did fancy you as a fella!'

Overjoyed, Pixie knew that whatever happened, Colin was back.

George Hill came in excusing himself in front of his patient's visitors.

'Hello Mr Arnold. Just wanted to see how you are. I see that Dixie is with you so I'll try to drop back a bit later.'

'His name's not Dixie! It's Pixie and I love the bugger. He looks better in a frock but she probably didn't want to make the nurses jealous eh?'

George Hill grinned widely.

'Well, glad to see that you are on the mend. I'll pop by again,' he said already looking forward to passing on the latest news when he got home.

After welcoming Colin back and a few words about the family, Telly took himself off to the canteen.

Holding hands, Colin slowly explained to Pixie that Vickery and Grey had been to see him. Tomorrow he wanted them to come back so he could tell them in his own words exactly what had happened and most importantly, start the ball rolling to get Ree released as quickly as possible.

'Just leave it with me babe – I won't mess-up this time. I'm still a copper and I'll be talking to coppers not dealing with low-life.'

After fond goodnights, Pixie found Telly engrossed in his book in the waiting area outside the ward.

'Canteen shut and kicked me out – thought I was one of the customers in me caff! Maybe I should be kinder to the fuckers in future eh?' he smiled at Pixie.

As they drove home, Pixie took the opportunity to explain the situation to her friend.

'Hopefully they'll bring this all to an end. We talked briefly about Rita; he says he's not going back there. He's coming home with me. Would you believe that the old witch didn't even wait around today for him to wake up? He's going to need a lot of physio and TLC but I reckon I'm up to it with a bit of help from my friends of course. Now, let's go and find Gavin.'

* * *

Waiting at Pixie's, Gavin was beside himself with excitement but had been warned by Pixie and Telly that the doctors were taking things cautiously and were not sure yet if Colin had any recollection of events or had suffered brain damage of any kind. Trying to control his excitement and praying that Colin had the ability to set Ree free, all Gavin could do was wait. It was the slowest most agonizing passage of time he had ever experienced.

He was dozing off when he heard the key in the door; he immediately awoke and asked for news.

Sobbing with relief, Gavin collapsed back onto the sofa and wept into Pixie's arms when he realized that everything was going to work out.

Chapter Thirty-nine

Vickery and Grey were back at Colin's bedside the following morning.

'Great you can talk Col,' said the DI, 'but before we go on, let me tell you how I see it – my version might be helpful, if you know what I mean.'

Understanding, Colin agreed, knowing that he was being invited to give a statement that was entirely truthful or allowing one to be taken that would do the trick. Grey knew what he was doing and Vickery was about to learn a thing or two.

'Right Colin. I'll try to be brief and then, if you agree, we can type it all up and get you to sign a statement, get the ball rolling PDQ and everything will be put right. Ready?'

Colin nodded his assent.

'OK. You'd met with a grass who had information about a serious crime which was about to go down. It would involve the same gang who'd done the Goldhawk job. He gave you a gun which you were to mark, return to the grass and he would leave it at the scene so you could tell he was good for information and you'd sort a payment out to get the names of the gang. You were walking to your car. On your way you saw a girl you recognized and her boyfriend being mugged at gunpoint. You shouted out and aimed the gun you'd been given, thinking that would stop the crime. The gunman, instead of dropping his gun or running away, aimed the gun at you and fired. You were shot. As you went down, you instinctively squeezed the trigger of your gun, not knowing that it was loaded. It went off and the mugger fell to the ground. The girl, known as Renee Lovell, recognized you and ran to see if you were OK. As she leant over you she took the gun from your hand. Then the mugger shouted, she saw him aiming his gun directly at both of you so she fired the gun she now had in her hand. You tried to get up but collapsed, hitting your head on a metal drain as you hit the ground. After that you remember nothing. By the way, did I tell you that we've been working on a headless corpse found in a bin at Elephant? Looks like he might have been Jake Peters and was rubbed out because a gang found out he'd been passing information to the cops?'

Colin gave a knowing nod.

'So, you happy with that mate? Want to add anything? You saw a crime. Tried to stop it. Girl protected herself and you?'

'Yes mate, type it up and I'll sign. Thanks.'

'Was that just about what happened Colin? Really? You want to tell me and Pat anything off the record?'

'Yes, I'll tell you a bit more.' Colin sighed. 'What do you want to know? I'm not under caution am I?'

'No, Colin, you are not under caution. Where did you get the gun?'

'It doesn't matter where I got the gun. It really doesn't matter. You'll know that Alan Dixon has been visiting here. You'll know that he is known as Pixie, that he is a transvestite prostitute and that Ree lived in his house. That's where I recognized her from.'

'Yes, and you were more than a customer eh? Were you being blackmailed?'

'Yes and yes. I was trying to put a stop to it but Jimmy had managed to get some pictures.'

'Did he get the money?'

'Yes, but Pixie says she got it back. That's not important. The most important thing is that you get Ree out of prison. I love Pixie, have done for many years, but our love isn't worth the price of an innocent kid being locked up. She really did fire to defend herself and me.'

'Christ, you're a dark horse Colin but hell if I was married to your wife I think I'd prefer a bloke!'

'It's not like that – but thanks, I think.'

'We'll leave you to get some rest mate and come back later.'

The two policemen made their way out of the ward.

'Christ – what a story,' said Pat Vickery once they were back in the car. 'Do you think it was the truth? Who would have thought it? DI Arnold, a fucking pervert!'

'Enough Pat,' Grey snapped. 'He was a fucking fine copper and a fucking good friend. I wish I'd have known and I would have helped him sort Jimmy out. I don't want any of this shit getting out, you hear?'

'Hey, no problem boss. Live and let live. Take love where you can find it eh? Never would have guessed, but that Pixie has done more for Colin than his bitch of a wife has ever done. Do you reckon she knows? Christ, if she does then she's probably well pissed off that her husband isn't dead!'

Now all they had to do was prepare a statement and have Colin sign it. Returning to the hospital later that afternoon they found that Colin was asleep so they waited in the canteen, eating a meal and drinking coffee to kill time.

The nurse on the ward told them that Colin needed to eat first and have his observations done, then they could talk to him. Another long and boring forty minutes passed before Grey slid a tray raised on wheels in front of Colin.

'This is the statement, Col, you know the drill, are you up to reading this or shall I read it to you?'

Wearily, Colin asked Grey to read the statement then, with a little help, managed to sign a wonky signature which was additionally witnessed by a passing doctor.

'We'll do our best to get the girl and her kid out of nick as soon as possible. Shouldn't take long, speak to the top man at the nick, and get him to get a trot on. This will totally exonerate her, show that all she did was pick the gun up and shoot Jimmy before he had the chance to shoot either you or her. You concentrate on getting better. You've really fucked up your old woman's plans I reckon, she'd have preferred you to have died mate. Just as well I never got around to paying all your pension to her eh?'

'Rita, yes, still got to face her wrath, haven't I. I suppose she'll be in with the kids later, if she can be bothered. That's if she's not playing bridge or having her bloody hair done. Anyway, we'll see what the doc says and hopefully it won't be too long before I'm out of here, out of the country too, for good. We've talked about it, Pixie and me. Never thought that this was how it would happen but what the fuck. We'll move to Spain. No one seems to give a shit about anybody else there. Shack up with who you like. Best for everyone really. Anyway, see that my pension gets paid into *my* account – I'll need it if I'm to keep Alan in frocks!'

Grey and Vickery left Colin to rest. He would need all the strength he could muster to face the charming Rita.

* * *

Ree was told to prepare for departure and was anxious, thinking that she was about to be transferred to a dedicated mother and baby unit in Durham or some other godforsaken place. No one would give her any information because the whole procedure was highly irregular and the few who did know that her release was imminent, had no wish to tell her just in case something went wrong.

Gavin was like a dog on heat, couldn't eat, sleep or think until his family were home with him. If he had grown a tail then he would have chased it. The regulars at the café knew what was going on and the place was a hive of gossip and speculation, mostly harmless and all hoping to see Gavin, Ree and Daniel reunited.

DI Grey finally got the word and decided to tell Colin in person. He drove to the hospital feeling happy at the prospect of imparting some good news for a change. Usually he delivered what were laughingly called death-o-grams or just arrested people. Today he was actually going to make a whole load of people incredibly happy and one woman very unhappy indeed.

'A fax has been sent from the CPS, all the paperwork has now been delivered to the people who need to see it and the prison knows to release her tomorrow, end of. All charges are dropped and matter closed. That's it mate, over and done with. As for you, get better and get your passports sorted. Does Alan's picture show him as a man or a woman by the way? Only joking, only joking. I wish you all the best, I really do. Maybe see you in the Robin near the station before you go – have a bit of a send-off for you both?'

Colin laughed.

'Thanks, Bruce. You've been great. Not sure that Pix is ready to meet the guys but I really hope that you will stay in touch. I believe you'd like Alan and I would like to think of you becoming our friend. You'll always be welcome to sort your passport out with a picture of you dressed as a man or woman or even as the decent pig you are and come and visit us in the sun. 'I'd like that Colin. I'll hold you to it!'

He left with almost as big a smile on his face as Colin had when he lay back against his pillows and fell into a deep and satisfied sleep.

* * *

It wasn't long before he was woken by something – Rita's unmistakable heels clipping down the corridor prefaced only by his nurse announcing her arrival.

'What the fuck do you think you've been playing at, you bastard? I found the picture you know. I found the fucking thing and threw up – I stained the fucking carpet. How could you have been shagging that thing all the time? Was it better than shagging me? Tell me? 'Cos Christ knows you're crap at sex. Or do you take it up the arse Colin? Do you like that? So, you fuck with a man wearing a cheap wig and even cheaper dress then get yourself shot and now you think you're fucking Jesus, back from the dead! Are you just doing all this to piss me off? Because if you are, you're doing a bloody good job. So now what? What the hell are we going to do? How do we come out of this bloody mess with any pride intact? What will everyone think? Who knows already? Tell me. For fuck's sake, I'll be a laughing stock!'

Ranting and raving, waving her hands in the air, she continued getting ever more red in the face. Colin closed his eyes and waited for silence.

'Do you know Rita, I really couldn't give a flying fuck what you or your stuck-up poxy fucking so-called friends think of me, or of you, or of anything actually. I guess it's money that's your problem eh? Fine, we'll sort the money out – sell the house and keep all the money. I wouldn't be surprised if you haven't put it on the market already. I'm guessing that you've already rinsed the accounts so I won't worry about our savings. You are a cold hard bitch Rita. Always have been. Being married to you has been a hell on fucking earth and if that's all I had to look forward to then by Christ I'd kill myself right now. I never want to see you again. I love Pixie and I know that we will spend the rest of our lives together. Who will you have Rita? Oh, just yourself? Do you really have any friends? If you and the kids don't like it, then tough shit, I really, really don't care. Now fuck off and leave me alone.'

Rita spat in her husband's face.

'Rot in hell, cunt!' she said as she stormed out of the room, colliding with a well-dressed man walking the other way.

'Get out of my fucking way!' she screeched as she clipped her way to the exit and hit the doors to let her out.

'You have just met my delightful wife. Probably for the first and last time. Sorry she didn't stick around for formal introductions!' said Colin as Pixie walked into the room that still smelt of Rita's ire and expensive perfume.

Wiping the spittle from her lover's face she laughed.

'If ever I have her manners or decide to wear that perfume then you have my permission to kick me into touch. Everything is fine lover. Gavin's had a call – Ree is getting out. My Ree and her baby.'

Colin smiled.

'You knew didn't you, you sly old bugger, I rushed over here to tell you but you already knew! So, Telly is taking Gav over in the morning to collect them. The flat looks fabulous, all beautifully kitted out and ready. I've been shopping and filled the cupboards, bought Ree a load of new clothes as I expect she'll want to get rid of the stuff she's been wearing. I can't believe it's all happening Col. It's all finally normal, well as normal as we'll ever be I guess.'

A nurse arrived with a meal for Colin and Pixie left him to try to eat while she met with Mr Hill who spoke about the future.

'It's going to be a long, slow process. After a few more weeks in here Colin will go to a convalescent home, somewhere on the coast if you like, then after about three or four weeks he can go home. He'll need a lot of looking after but should be over the worst of it by then. Now, Pixie, I think the patient has probably finished eating and could do with some company.'

He watched the two men together and hoped that his relationship with Tim would prove to be as strong.

Chapter Forty

Gavin and Telly were about half an hour early. The chain of events, and the speed at which Ree's release had been arranged, was overwhelming. Laura was waiting back at the flat with Pixie, desperate to see her daughter and grandson. The minutes ticked by painfully slowly as Gavin swung the car door open and sat with his back to the prison, resting feet on the pavement, unable to bear watching the gates.

Hearing the sound of the heavy metal door he turned around saw it opening. Ree stood there with two other people, tiny specks against the imposing height of the steel gates they had just walked through. Scanning around, Ree spotted Gavin who seemed rooted to the spot. She waved and her boyfriend seemed to come to life and sprinted across the road before scooping Ree into his arms while Telly ambled across at a more sedate pace. Hugging and kissing her boyfriend, Ree laughed and cried. Daniel brought them back to reality.

'I think young Daniel here is hungry again! Now put each other down you two and take this baby home and never darken this door again.' Lizzie smiled as she passed the baby to his mother.

The prison officer offered to carry the suitcases but Ree told him to stop.

'Lizzie, I really don't want any of this stuff. The only

things that are special to me I have put in the changing bag. Take the rest of the stuff in there and give it to the girls. Some of them have nothing and, well, I have everything and everyone I need right here.'

Kissing her cheek and giving a final hug, Lizzie said her goodbyes and disappeared with the prison officer back inside the prison and its gruesome walls. Ree carried Daniel over to the car and eventually he was fastened in the back seat with his mother beside him.

Staring in wonder at everything around her, Ree could not wait to do all the things she had dreamt of and desperately longed for. She felt as if she had been away for years. The trees were bare and the cold was biting. The promised heat of the summer when she was incarcerated was long gone and forgotten, erased by a harsh winter, but the occupants of the car thought it was the greatest, most wonderful day they had ever known.

Chapter Forty-one

While Ree settled Daniel into the nursery, Mark and Gary helped Gavin move his stuff from the café.

'We'll miss your naked dash from the bathroom when you thought no one was looking – big man!' said Mark.

'But we won't miss the hair you always leave around the plughole!' laughed Gary.

Gavin hugged them both, glad that these young men were his friends.

'Enjoy your living room guys. I was going to leave my stash of porn mags behind but didn't think they'd be up your alley!'

Having taken a week off work instead of the two Telly tried to enforce, the new family settled down in their home. Laura, Pixie and their other friends kept their visits brief but welcome and Telly helped by sending Mark over with cooked food.

'Telly says that he wants the parents of his namesake to spend time together, hated thinking of Gavin having a busman's holiday and that he'll give you both a set of Greek worry-beads when Aristotle becomes a teenager!'

* * *

The days flew by, full of laughter and love.

Ree knocked quietly on Pixie's door. They had decided to spend Gavin's first day back at work with a brisk walk followed by tea and an all-day breakfast at the café.

'Hello, sweetheart,' said Pixie. 'I didn't know what to wear. What do you think? Reckon I'll turn a few heads?'

She was dressed in a bright pink jogging suit and had dusted down a curly strawberry-blonde wig.

'I didn't have the shoes, so these will have to do,' she said, slipping her feet into a pair of green sequinned stilettos.

As they strolled along the bank of the Thames, Pixie turned to Ree with a concerned look on her face.

'Ree, I've something to tell you. I hope you don't think I've been interfering or nothing but I've suggested to your mum that she should move out of the refuge and into your old flat in my house. It's a long trek for her to come and see you and she'd be on hand to look after this little treasure. What do you think babe? She said she'd only do it if you said it was OK.'

'Oh, Pix. I don't know what to say! I think it's the best idea ever!'

When they got to the café, Ree entered first, trying to cope with pushing the door open and steer the pram in front of her. She wondered why Pixie stood back and didn't raise a finger to help.

A roar of applause and shouts of congratulations hit her ears. The room was full of their friends and café regulars, including Meg from the market. She was overcome as Gavin dashed over.

'I think it's time I made an honest woman of you,' he shouted above the noise.

* * *

Pixie pushed the button on the intercom with the false-nailed index finger of her right hand.

'Hello love, it's Pixie.'

'Dixie?'

'No love, it's Pixie – I've come for Colin.'

The door lock buzzed and Pixie entered the ward.

Dressed in her leopard print blouse, blonde wig, red skirt and silver stilettos, she walked to the nurses' station carrying the distinctive bag that had once contained twenty thousand pounds but now held far more mundane things.

'Thought I'd show you girls what you've been missing all this time! Is he ready? Am I too early?'

'Pixie!' squealed Sophie, the nurse who had been there when Colin came out of his coma. 'I swapped shifts to be here because I wanted to say goodbye to you both.'

'And you, my dear, have been a treasure.' Pixie kissed her gently on the cheek.

'I've brought you and your team a little token; I'll never be able to thank you enough for your kindness. It made a difficult time more bearable and Colin and I will never forget it.'

She reached into her bag and dropped a clutch of small boxes onto the nurses' desk.

'There's one for each of you. Not much but I hope you will use them and think of us when you do.'

Sophie opened one of the boxes and pulled out a nurse's lapel watch. She turned it over and read the engraving: 'Love knows no bounds.'

'Dixie! Sorry, Pixie! I love it! Thank you – it's been a pleasure for us all and we are delighted that things have turned out so well. Come with me, Colin is waiting. Mr Hill is with him but I'm sure he won't mind you going straight through.'

They walked into Colin's room. He was in a wheelchair, dressed in jeans and a leather jacket which had been a gift from Pixie to celebrate his leaving the force. Pixie dashed over and kissed him squarely on the lips, leaving behind the faint stains of her crimson lipstick.

'I'll let you two get on,' said Mr Hill.

'I'm so glad you are here Mr Hill, I have something for you and was going to leave it with Sophie if you weren't around.'

Pixie reached into her bag and produced a bottle of malt.

'It's the same as I gave you at Christmas so I hope you enjoyed it!'

'Pixie, thank you! There really was no need you know.'

'Wait, there's more,' said Pixie, handing the consultant a rather large box.

'Where'd you get that bag from Pix?' said Colin, 'The same shop as Mary bleedin' Poppins?'

Opening the box, George Hill found a cut-glass decanter and two glasses. They had the same engraving as the watches Pixie had just given to the nurses: 'Love knows no bounds.'

'It's a small token of our appreciation,' said Pixie. 'I hope you will find someone to use the second glass – a friend or a lover and you will both drink a toast to us.'

'Pixie, I don't know what to say. I will give the second glass to Tim, my partner, and we will drink your health tonight!' Hill blushed, realizing that he had spoken in front of his staff nurse, Sophie.

'I heard nothing!' she said clamping her hands to her ears. 'I say nothing either!' She moved her hands to her mouth.

'But I do see something! Pixie you look great and Colin, you better look after her – she's one in a million. Now get out of here. You have an ambulance to catch!' She laughed and kissed them both before leaving the room.

As Pixie wheeled Colin out of the ward, George Hill's thoughts were of Tim and the toast they would raise that night. To be as bold as Pixie was beyond him right now but maybe he had made a start today and could, in the future, be as proud of his love. He hoped that it would be soon. He turned to Sophie, emboldened.

'Would you like to come to dinner with Tim and me tomorrow night?' he asked.

'Mr Hill, I would be delighted,' she replied. 'Shall I bring my own glass?'

⋆ ⋆ ⋆

Back at Pixie's flat, Colin continued to recover and the two of them made plans for the future, the first of which was to buy a set of tapes promising to teach them how to 'speak Spanish like a native' in only three months..

They had few visitors, preferring it that way, though Colin was delighted when Bruce Grey and Pat Vickery came over one night.

'We didn't think you'd ever agree to coming for a leaving bash at the Robin, mate. So decided to visit,' said Grey.

'Yeah, we had a bit of a whip-round and brought you these,' announced Pat as he handed over a large toy donkey, a completely over-the-top straw sunhat, two pairs of sunglasses and a bottle of cheap Spanish wine.

'They are to get you in the mood and this here is a slightly more traditional retirement gift,' his ex-colleague said, handing him a rather large and expensive diver's watch.

'We reckoned a gold one would be no good for when you go snorkelling!'

The other significant visitor was Louise, Colin's youngest daughter, who brought bits and pieces from the house.

'We don't know why you didn't leave Mum years ago Dad. At least we all escaped to college! Anyway, we all miss you of course and I can honestly say that Mum doesn't miss you at all … Of course all of us want an open invitation to come and visit you in Spain and promise that we won't all come at once!'

* * *

Ree became Mrs Gavin Cooper at a quiet ceremony held at the Southwark Registry Office in June. The reception was anything but quiet – a Greek-themed evening held in a function room on the river.

After much dancing to Duran Duran and Wham and the traditional plate smashing, the newly-weds decided to make a quiet exit with their sleeping child. Pixie and Colin stopped them at the door.

'Wait, before you go, I want to tell you something. It's important,' she said.

'You know that Colin and I really wish you all the best don't you and we are sorry that the wedding gift was only small but we are saving all our pennies for Spain.'

'Oh Pixie, you've given me so much ever since I came to London that just having you here and having you as one of the witnesses was all I ever could have dreamt of. Anyway, the bed linen is lovely though I'm not sure I'll be using it until Daniel understands how difficult pink satin is to get clean!'

'Darlin', that gift was meant to be a joke! I have decided to sell up totally rather than let the flats out but before you even think that you'll be back on the streets where you started I want you to know that I'm giving you both the flat you're in and I'm putting your mum's in trust for Daniel. Now, be on your way, the two of you, back to your flat, the flat that nobody can take away, ever.'

Gavin and Ree were speechless as they hugged Pixie and Colin in an effort to convey their feelings.

★ ★ ★

Laura walked over to the doorway and watched her daughter and son-in-law walk away beside the river holding hands and pushing her grandchild in his pram.

'Hey love, come back in and dance with me?' said Gerry putting his arms around her from behind.

Turning, Laura kissed his cheek.

They went inside and danced.

Acknowledgements

The research for this book took me into many dark and extremely desolate places but, everywhere I went I encountered amazing people who inspired hope and love. I thank God for those good people. Paul, you have always kept the faith and encouraged and enabled me. You will forever be a very shiny star in my world. Bev and Robert; I love you both so much. Thank you for all you do and all you give. My beautiful Louise and her lovely Derek; two of life's truly good people. Yvonne and Don, Woo and Gramps, Will, Denise and Karina – you have no idea how much I value your kindness, friendship and acceptance. Thank you so much to Ken, Ceri, Steve, Rachel and Jack for the jacket shot. Carol, a wise new friend whose attention to detail has saved my bacon! Steve; you always said I hope you dance; well yes, I do believe I do, but only with your help and love. And to you, I love you because you saw beneath the beautiful.

A donation from the sale of every copy of this book will be made to ChildLine because sadly it is so very necessary.

The Author

Dawn Annandale is best known for her memoir *Call Me Elizabeth* and the sequel *Call Me Madam*. She currently lives in Kent with her children and a very naughty dog. *A Kind of Life* is Dawn's first novel. Her second, *Ripples* will be published in spring 2014.